ON THE TRAIL OF A KILLER

"My name is Savannah Reid," she said, pulling her badge from inside her sweater where she kept it on a chain. "I'm the detective who's investigating the murder of Jonathan Winston. I was hoping I could ask you a few questions . . . about Jonathan . . . about the fashion industry."

Danielle's hazy smile faded and her eyes instantly became alert and guarded. "About where I was the morning in question?"

Savannah nodded. "I'll probably get around to that, too." Savannah pulled her notebook from her purse. "Can you think of anyone who had a grudge against Jonathan, who might have wanted to kill him?"

"Yeah, me. He ripped off some of my best designs and made a fortune from them. Other than me . . . it could have been Beverly. Being his wife and all, I'm sure she had plenty of motives. Or it could have been the guy Beverly's been seeing."

"Can you think of anyone else?"

"Could have been Fiona, his ex. I took him away from her years ago and she never got over it. She divorced her second husband last year and I heard she was after Jonathan again."

"Anyone else?"

"Nobody I can think of right away. He gambled a lot. Drank. Chased women. He did all kinds of things that might have gotten him shot."

* * *

Praise for G.A. McKevett and JUST DESSERTS:

" . . . a pleasant read . . . "

—*The Snooper*

"Look out for this 'steel magnolia' on the crime scene now!"
—*Mystery Lovers Bookshop News*

"Recommended."

—*Library Journal*

G. A. McKEVETT

JUST DESSERTS

KENSINGTON BOOKS
KENSINGTON PUBLISHING CORP.
http://www.kensingtonbooks.com

KENSINGTON BOOKS *are published by*

Kensington Publishing Corp.
850 Third Avenue
New York, NY 10022

First Kensington Hardcover Printing: May, 1995
First Kensington Paperback Printing: May, 1996
10 9 8 7 6 5 4

Printed in the United States of America

CHAPTER ONE

"There's just gotta be a better way to spend a Friday night." Setting the bottle of "Flaming Desire" red nail polish on her partner's dashboard, Savannah Reid spread her fingers and studied her manicure in the dim light of the yellow halogen streetlight. "Freezing my bee-hind off in an old Buick . . ." she drawled, ". . . waiting for a fugitive pervert to show his ugly face isn't exactly my idea of a good time."

Dirk Coulter slid lower in his seat and propped his forearms on the top of the steering wheel. "Well, I have to tell you, I'm hurt," he said. "I've done my best to entertain you for the last hour with my scintillating conversation, my dry but sophisticated wit, my—"

"Oh, can it, Coulter. Until five minutes ago, when I started doing my nails, you were snoring like a bulldog with a sinus infection."

"And I would have gotten a nice nap if you hadn't started that damned nail polish routine of yours. That shit stinks . . . reminds me of ether . . . of my operation . . . makes me wanna barf."

"Yeah, yeah, so I've heard, darlin'. The old war injury, right?" She paused to blow on each nail.

He rolled down his window several inches and waved his hands around to circulate the pungent acetone fumes. "When are you gonna find another way to occupy yourself on a stakeout? I'm telling you, breathing this stuff is killing me."

"I'll quit when you stop smoking."

He said nothing, but glowered at her.

She continued to puff on her nails. "I've never heard of anyone getting cancer from secondhand 'Flaming Desire' fumes. Have you?"

He rolled the window back up and opened a thermos of coffee. The aroma mingled with the residual polish fumes and the stale odor of cigarette smoke. "You can be a real bitch sometimes, Reid."

She chuckled. "Yeah, I know. But I've got great nails."

"And your priorities in order," he muttered.

Holding up her hands for his inspection, she sighed. "I can always tell how an investigation's going by my manicure. If it's going lousy, I've got perfect nails . . . too much time on surveillance."

"And when it's going well?"

"I usually break off two or three during a bust."

He gave her outspread hands a sideways glance and snorted as he took a sip of coffee. "Then I guess it's time we nailed this bastard."

"Yep, high time." She turned away from him to look out the window and hide her satisfied smile. In the past five years of working with Dirk, that was the closest thing to a compliment on her physical appearance she had received. Even though she had grown a tad overweight in the past couple of years—okay, thirty pounds, give or take—and turned forty, she was still pretty good-looking, in her own estimation. Receiving attention and flattery from the opposite sex was something she had always taken for granted.

But Dirk was definitely not the mushy type. Other than an occasional "Good bust, kid," he had kept his praise to himself. He was as thrifty with his compliments as with his cash.

Cheap, sarcastic, stingy and cynical, even by cop standards—Savannah loved him anyway. She didn't always *like* him, but he had grown on her when she wasn't looking. Spending several hundred nights together in tough areas like this one, watching, waiting, hoping for the best, trying not to fear the worst . . . it either drove two people apart or drew them closer. Thankfully, their long, sleepless nights in Dirk's old 1962 Buick Skylark had done the latter.

For the hundredth time in the past hour Savannah looked out the car window and studied their surroundings. To the far west, she could see that the nightly Southern California coastal fog had rolled in from the beach, drifting through the affluent waterfront areas of San Carmelita and up the equally exclusive hillsides. Finally it had worked its way into the valley on the east end of town where they sat, the not-so-affluent or exclusive section of the city, the area most of San Carmelita's upper-crust citizenry would like to forget. And usually did.

All was quiet in front of the apartment house in question. Down the block in front of the next building, a flock of teenaged boys in grungy T-shirts and baggy shorts zipped up and down the handicap ramp on skateboards. Across the street a couple were making out in an old Ford that was approximately the same vintage as the Skylark; half an hour ago they had disappeared below window level and hadn't come up for air since.

Otherwise, the street and sidewalks were empty. Unusually empty, Savannah thought, for a Friday night in the projects. That was fine with her. It had been a hard week, and she didn't mind collecting a little of the city's money, just sitting here, painting her nails and doing her best to irritate Dirk.

Dirk took a sip of coffee from his Winchell Donuts mug. "Do you think he'll show?"

"Sure he will." She picked up the polish bottle and began a second coat. "I don't know if it'll be tonight, but he's going to come see his old lady. A guy breaks out of prison after seven years . . . he's gotta be hornier than a twelve-peckered 'possum on a Saturday night."

Dirk shook his head. "Sometimes your Southern heritage just comes shining through, Reid."

"Like the top of your head when you don't get all of them itty-bitty hairs lined up right, darlin'?" She gave him a smirk that deepened the dimples on either side of her mouth. Ordinarily that particular smile worked its charm on him, but this time it did little to dilute the insult. His ever-increasing baldness was a sore spot these days. Dirk's wife, Polly, had just left him for a younger guy . . . one with shoulder-length blond hair who played bass in a rock band.

"Sorry," she said. "Low blow."

"Very low. I'll be singing soprano for a week."

Suddenly he sat up straight and prodded her with his elbow. "Hey, look!" he said, nodding to the building across the street.

For a second Savannah stared at the long streak of "Flaming

Desire" that now decorated the back of her hand. "Thanks," she mumbled.

But when she saw the object of his attention she forgot the mishap. A skinny blond woman hurried down the sidewalk toward them, wearing a halter top and a short denim skirt. Her feet were bare in spite of the cool night. Looking happy but anxious, she walked with a shaky be-bop to her step. Drugs had obviously taken a permanent toll on her nervous system. Savannah guessed she was probably around twenty—but closer to fifty in street years.

"It's her," she said. "The girlfriend."

"Looks like she's been shopping."

"Sure does." Savannah retrieved a pair of small binoculars from the floorboard and zeroed in on the bags the young woman was carrying. "Joe's Liquor . . . looks like a bottle of champagne, some flowers, and . . ." She stared harder at the small pink bag. ". . . And something from the Naughty Lady's Nook. Hmm-m-m. The in-laws must be dropping by."

"I don't think so," Dirk replied dryly. "But she *is* going to be having a visitor."

Savannah trained the binoculars on the woman's face. Skeletal, pale, and gaunt, only her eyes were alive. Even in the dim light of the street lamp, Savannah could see the excitement registered there. As the woman approached the front of the complex, she stared up at a corner window on the third floor. Savannah noted the look on her face . . . anticipation, mixed with apprehension.

Night after night, Savannah saw that expression in the eyes of abused women—women from the affluent waterfront, the exclusive hillsides, and here in the east valley. The look of love, fear, hate and dependence, all mixed into one.

"She's not expecting a visitor," Savannah said softly, lowering the glasses.

"What?"

"He got by us somehow. He's already up there. Come on; let's nab the son of a bitch."

"Those bleeding-heart liberals at City Hall spend all that money on these places, and for what?" Dirk puffed and turned a deeper shade of red as they climbed the second set of stairs. "It still looks and smells like a shit heap."

Savannah followed him through the door at the top of the stairwell and into a dim, narrow hallway. "It's better," she said, trying, as always, to counteract at least some of Dirk's negativity. The man absolutely radiated pessimism and, codependent that she was, Savannah couldn't resist trying to brighten his world. Whether he wanted it brightened or not. Nobody should be allowed to wallow in fatalism to that degree, she thought, even if they enjoyed it.

"Beverly Winston has done a good job on housing renewal," she said as they walked down the hall, which was now illuminated with intact lightbulbs and boasted walls that were very nearly graffiti-free, thanks to the controversial councilwoman's efforts. "The toilets and stoves work, and the playground has more grass than used hypodermic needles. I call that an improvement."

"You're easily impressed." Dirk referred to the scribblings in his little black notebook and pointed to the door bearing the numbers 347.

"Shall I do my usual?" Savannah asked with a tense smile. The fugitive inside definitely qualified as a bad guy. While serving a ten-year term for brutally raping a twelve-year-old girl, he had attacked a doctor in the prison infirmary and escaped. He wouldn't be thrilled about being picked up.

Dirk nodded. "Go for it . . . Betty."

"The guy's name is Jim, right?

He glanced again at the notebook. "Yep; James Robert Barnett."

Savannah pulled her Beretta from the shoulder holster under her tweed blazer and held it up before her, while Dirk drew his Smith and Wesson and positioned himself on the other side of the door.

Standing with her back against the wall, she leaned over and pounded on the door. "Hey, Marco! It's Betty. Open up, you jerk!" she yelled drunkenly.

Silence from inside.

She hammered again. "Damn it, I know you're in there, and I've gotta talk to you about the abortion. It's your kid. The least you could do is pay for it, you no-good bum!"

A door farther down the hall opened a crack, but nothing from 347.

Savannah kicked the door a couple of times. "If you don't come to the door this minute, I'm gonna call your old lady and tell her what you and me's been up to. I swear, Marco, I'm not gonna take this lyin' down! Open up!"

They heard soft footsteps approaching the door and both raised their weapons, pointing them toward the ceiling.

"There ain't no Marco in here," said a female voice. "Go away before I call the cops."

Savannah grinned at Dirk and lifted one eyebrow. "Good one," she whispered. Then she yelled, "You got a woman in there with you, Marco? Who is she? I'm gonna knock down this door and stomp a mud hole in her, I swear!"

She pounded again, until the sound echoed up and down the hallway. A couple of other doors opened. Everyone on the third floor appeared to be intrigued by the "Betty and Marco Affair."

Finally the door began to slowly creak open. The blond woman's nose and one eye appeared in the crack. "Look, bitch," she said. "I told you, there ain't no Marco in this apartment. Now, if you know what's good for you, you'll get the hell out of here . . . now!"

Savannah moved in front of the door and showed the woman her gun and badge. "Don't say a word," she whispered, slowly pushing the door open a bit wider. "Let me see your hands."

The young woman appeared stunned for a moment, then understanding dawned in her eyes. "No," she said, shaking her head. "Please . . . don't."

"Shh-h-h. . . . We want Jim, not you." Savannah beckoned her to come out. "Step into the hall. Hurry!"

The blonde hesitated as her fear seemed to fade into relief. Quickly she slipped through the door and entered the hall, her hands held high in surrender.

One look told Savannah she didn't need to frisk her. The woman was already wearing the costume from the Naughty Lady's Nook—a leopard teddy and thigh-high stockings with garters. The see-through fabric wasn't sufficient to conceal even her bare necessities, let alone a weapon.

"Who else is in there, besides Jim?" Dirk asked her, averting his eyes as he pulled her away from the door and down the hall a few feet.

"My daughter," she said, her teeth chattering. "She's on the couch. Jim's in the bedroom."

"Is he armed?" Savannah asked.

She nodded. "Yeah. He's got a shotgun."

A shotgun. Savannah cringed; she hated shotguns. A pistol, even a rifle, could leave a nice little hole, a fairly neat corpse under the right circumstances. But she had never gotten over the damage a shotgun could do to a person. In the course of her career she had seen half a dozen shotgun victims, and each one only served to remind her of how much liquid was contained inside a human body . . . until a shotgun blast splattered it all over a room or the inside of a vehicle.

Like any other cop, Savannah had entertained the thought that she might be killed in the line of duty. And no matter what, her mama and siblings in Georgia would insist on an open casket. It was just the Southern way. If she had to be shot, she prayed it wouldn't be with a twelve-gauge.

"You stay right out here," Savannah said. The door across the hall opened and an elderly lady peeked out. "We're going to send your daughter out to you," she continued, "and then I want the two of you to go into that apartment right there and wait until this is over. You got that?"

The blonde nodded; so did her neighbor.

"If you make any sound at all, or try anything funny, it could get your daughter or you killed. Understand?" Dirk said, shoving his face close to hers.

"But if everything goes all right, you're off the hook," Savannah added.

Tears of relief flooded the woman's eyes, and Savannah watched as several of the street years slipped away. Maybe there was hope for this one after all.

Savannah turned to Dirk and nodded toward the door. "Ready?"

"Ready." He resumed his position beside the door.

Savannah did the same, then slowly pushed the door open. Thankfully, it didn't creak. From her vantage point, she could see half of the small room; she knew Dirk could see the other half.

"The girl?" She mouthed the words to him.

He nodded. "Clear," he whispered.

Gun drawn, she entered first, keeping her eye on the two doors at the rear of the room. Familiar with the layout of the apartments, she knew the right one led to the bedroom, the other to a small broom closet.

Peripherally, she saw the girl, maybe four or five years old, huddled on a ragged sofa to Savannah's left. She wore faded pink *Beauty and the Beast* pajamas and a frightened look on her grubby little face.

This was the kind of situation Savannah hated most, one with kids. She despised the fact that she had to scare these children half out of their minds and, by invading their home and arresting their parents, prove everything they had been taught about cops being lowlife scum. With the perpetrators, she didn't mind being the villain; they could look at it any way they wanted to—whatever made them most comfortable with their rationalizations. But she hated being the bad guy to a kid.

"Come here, sweetie," she whispered, concealing her weapon behind her thigh and motioning to the girl. "It's okay. Just go on out there with your mommy."

With a sophisticated mistrust beyond her young years, the child studied Savannah with a wary eye.

"Go now," Savannah said sternly. "Hurry!"

As she had anticipated, the girl responded more quickly to harsh words than kind ones. She bounded off the sofa and ran through the door.

Savannah waited until she heard the door close across the

hall. Mother and child were safe for the moment; two less to worry about.

From beneath the bedroom door she could see a thin beam of light. Good . . . when the bad guys were dumb it only made their job easier. She turned out the one lamp in the room. By the dim hallway light, coming through the partly open front door, she watched Dirk move into place beside the bedroom door, gun ready.

She had no doubt that good ol' Jim Bob—child raper, prison escapee—was positioned, shotgun aimed, on the opposite side of the door.

Neither she nor Dirk were interested in committing suicide by bursting into the other room. And she didn't need her years of experience on the force to tell her that Jim wasn't going to come waltzing out for a breath of fresh air any time this century.

That meant one thing; it was show time, again.

Moving well back from the door and to the side, she dropped to one knee and braced her elbow on the other. Holding the Beretta in her right hand, she cradled the butt in her left palm, Weaver style, and sighted down the barrel.

She gave Dirk the look. Ready?

He nodded. Ready.

"Marco!" she shrieked. "I took care of your other bitch! Now you come out here right now and face me like a man!"

It wasn't difficult to sound tense and upset. The voice that rang in her ears was demented enough to convince even her. She'd definitely been on this job too long.

"Get out here, you bastard, or I'll call the cops on you for whacking me around the other night. And I still got the busted lip to prove it."

She waited another five seconds. Nothing.

Glancing around, she was relieved to spot a phone on the floor beside the sofa. It was plugged into the wall . . . a good sign.

"Okay, that's it," she said. "I'm callin' 'em right now. First you knock me up and don't do right by me. Then you shack up with that skinny blond bitch. I'm gonna—"

The door opened. Just a crack. A long vertical beam of light streamed through, unbroken.

Savannah could feel Dirk tense. She could feel the guy on the other side of the door. She could hear him breathing. Hard. Her own finger tightened on the trigger.

"Who the hell are you?" he asked, his voice strained and high.

"It's Betty," she barked. "Don't go actin' like you don't know it's me."

"Look, Betty, you better get out of here or I'm gonna blow your fuckin' head off," he said. The barrel of the shotgun appeared through the crack.

A split second later Dirk's foot hit the middle of the door with a crash and it flew open.

A scream of pain, then a low groan, signaled that his timing had been perfect. Contact had been established, up close and personal.

Jim Bob lay sprawled on his back, the shotgun on the floor beside him, bright red blood oozing from a dark split down the middle of his forehead.

Savannah ran into the bedroom, kicked the shotgun out of his reach, and stood, Beretta aimed at his head, grinning down at him.

Handcuffs pulled, Dirk hurried in, rolled him over, and cuffed him. As Dirk hauled him to his feet, the guy stared at

Savannah through the bloody, matted hair that hung down into his eyes.

"Are *you* Betty?" he asked, obviously disoriented and more than a little confused.

She chuckled and shook her head. "Jim Bob, you catch on quick, don'cha, darlin'?"

Several hours later, as they left the station, with James Robert Barnett safely returned to the custody of the State of California, Savannah giggled, remembering the look on James's face. "Is it my imagination," she said, "or are criminals getting stupider these days?"

Dirk draped his arm across her shoulders, and they headed across the rear parking lot toward the Buick. The sun was beginning to rise over the Spanish tiled roof of the station. The smell of pancakes and bacon from a nearby coffee shop scented the air. "Yep; it's your imagination. They've always been stupid. You and me are just gettin' better."

CHAPTER TWO

Sated by a breakfast of cheese blintzes with fresh strawberry compote and a dollop of sour cream, Savannah waved goodbye to Dirk and the Buick and dragged her tired body up the sidewalk to her house. In this neighborhood she had no view of the famous coral-and-turquoise sunsets over the Pacific. If she wanted to take a walk on the beach she had to get in her car and drive five or six miles, then hope for a parking space.

Her financial status placed her somewhere between the "haves" on the hillsides and the "have-nots" in the east valley. She supposed, here in midtown, she was classified with the have-a-little-but-never-enoughs.

But she loved her house. The quaint, Spanish style cottage sat back from the busy street, shaded by a giant magnolia—her pride and joy. The tree provided a little bit of southern comfort to a Georgia girl who was a long way from home.

The white stucco walls gleamed in the early morning light, providing a stark backdrop for the brilliant crimson bougainvillea that had taken over the front of the house. The bougainvillea had crawled up the small trellis she had provided for it several years ago and had continued up the roof, arching gracefully over the door. At first she had battled with the vines, cutting them back every few months. But in the end she had decided it would be much easier to just pretend she liked them. Eventually she didn't have to pretend.

"Hi, Bogey," she greeted the bougainvillea as she ducked through the colorful archway and unlocked the door. "How dare you look so bright and chipper when I haven't had any sleep for thirty-six hours! Tone it down a bit, huh?"

The moment she opened the door and stepped inside, two enormous black cats bounded toward her. The animals were sleek and silky, coats like polished ebony, and both wore black leather collars, studded with rhinestones. They studied her with thoughtful pale green eyes. Bending down to scoop up the mail from the floor, she scratched first one and then the other behind the ears. "Good morning, Diamante, Cleopatra."

They each responded with enthusiastic mews and began to rub against her legs.

"Are you two delighted to see me, or are you out of food?" she asked as she walked through the house to the kitchen. There, next to the stove, sat two empty bowls.

"Guess that answers my question." She filled both dishes with dry cat food, then, feeling guilty, took a can of tuna from the cupboard and gave each a healthy portion.

As she made herself a cup of hot cocoa, laced with a little Bailey's and topped with whipped cream and chocolate sprinkles, she could feel the past few hours catching up with her. Her muscles were beginning to set like cement on a hot, dry day. Her limbs felt about as heavy.

If she didn't crawl into a warm bath soon, she would be as stiff as Granny Reid, back in Georgia. But Gran had a good excuse: She was eighty-two. Savannah was less than half that.

"Maybe it's not the years, but the mileage," she mumbled as she sauntered to the bathroom.

Just the sight of the pretty room, with its old-fashioned rose print wallpaper, lace-edged towels, and pink geraniums blooming on the windowsill, made her feel better. The deep, claw foot Victorian tub beckoned her—as though she needed seducing. On the vanity, a white wicker basket awaited, filled with scented soaps, oils, gels, and moisturizers. Behind the door hung her favorite garment, her thick, snuggy terry-cloth robe.

Ah-h-h-h . . . she could hardly wait.

Pulling the shades, Savannah closed out the harsh white sunlight and replaced it with the golden glow of several pink votive candles.

With great ceremony she poured a generous portion of gardenia bath gel into the tub and turned on the water full blast.

But when she looked around for her cup of hot chocolate she realized she had left it in the kitchen. Oh, well . . . just one more short trek back into the real world before she could lose herself in the fantasy.

As she walked into the kitchen, the phone rang, startling her out of the dreamy reverie she was already conjuring.

"Go away," she told it. She glanced at the clock on the stove—five forty-five. "Whoever you are, go back to bed and leave me alone."

The answering machine picked up the call, and Savannah

heard her own message play. She cringed when she heard the grating nasal voice of her captain.

"Reid, it's Bloss. I know you're there. Pick up the phone."

She made a face at the machine and a mildly obscene suggestion, only allowing herself to express her thoughts in semaphore. She had an irrational paranoia that the person on the line just *might*, through some strange quirk of technology, hear her if she spoke.

Captain Bloss had only been her superior for three weeks and she had already managed to piss him off at least half a dozen times.

"Pick up, Reid. I just talked to Coulter and he said he dropped you at home ten minutes ago."

Damn you, Dirk, she thought, reaching for the phone. *Sell me out, why don't you?*

"Yes . . . hello, Captain," she said, panting into the phone. "I just got back from a run. Lucky I heard the machine."

"Yeah. Right."

He sniffed, a long liquid snort that made her shudder. Maybe she'd give him a giant box of tissues for Christmas . . . if he hadn't fired her by then.

"I've got a homicide downtown . . . one of the shops on Main Street. It was called in fifteen minutes ago by the janitor. We have a couple of patrolmen on the scene. I want you to handle it," he said.

"Now?" she asked, suddenly feeling much more tired and much older than Granny Reid.

"No, Detective Reid," he said in a caustic tone, "whenever you get good and ready. You know . . . after your facial and massage and before your tennis lesson."

She bit her lower lip and fought down her temper. This wasn't the time to "get her dander up," as Gran would say.

"Where is it?" she asked, grabbing the notepad and pen beside the phone.

He gave her the address. It was located in the renovated, historic part of town, near the old mission. Ten years ago downtown had been on its way to being classified a slum area. Now it was high-priced real estate, boasting exclusive boutiques, cappuccino bars, custom bikini shops, and jewelry stores selling handmade African beads.

"So, you've contacted Dirk about this?" she asked.

There was a slight pause on the other end. "Not about this particular case," he replied. "I want you to take care of it. I've got Dirk tied up on something else."

Savannah was taken aback. She and Dirk almost always worked together, especially on the homicides and more violent crimes. Not that she didn't welcome the opportunity to go solo for a change, but she couldn't help wondering why.

Something told her not to ask.

"I'll be there in ten minutes," she said. But Bloss had already hung up.

She ran up the stairs and into the bathroom. Turning off the faucets, she stared wistfully at the mountain of bubbles, glittering in the golden candlelight.

"Oh, well," she said as she blew out the votives, filling the room with the fragrance of carnation-scented smoke. So much for a few moments in fantasy land. Back to the real world—such as it was.

When Savannah arrived at the appointed address she wondered why Bloss hadn't filled her in on one small detail: The murder scene was none other than the most exclusive boutique in town, owned and operated by Jonathan Winston, Councilwoman Beverly Winston's husband.

Apparently, members of the media *hadn't* been running a bubble bath when they had been notified. They had beaten her there and had already set up lights, camera . . . action.

Savannah recognized several of the reporters from local television stations, the two newspapers, and even a crew from a Los Angeles network station.

She was relieved to see two of her favorite patrolmen standing guard at the front door, which was barricaded with yellow SCPD banner tape. The last thing she needed was a murder scene that had been compromised.

"Detective Reid!" shouted Rosemary Hulse, a reporter for the San Carmelita *Star*. She came running up to Savannah and produced a small tape recorder out of thin air. "Are you in charge of this investigation?"

"Yes, Rosemary. It seems I am." Savannah forged ahead, knowing better than to slow her pace. In the past she had hesitated and found herself swamped by waves of reporters.

"Do you know who killed him? Do you have any suspects at this time?" Rosemary pressed.

For a second or two Savannah considered being honest and admitting that she didn't even know who the "him" was yet; then she decided against it. There were plenty of opportunities in the course of any investigation to appear incompetent; she didn't need to get a running start at it.

"No comment at this time, Rosemary," she said. "I'm sure we'll be releasing a statement a little later, if you guys can just hang tight."

She reached the door and the patrolmen, who looked relieved to see her. Jake McMurtry and Mike Farnon had been boyhood buddies and were now cops on the same beat. Both were fairly new to the force, and from the rather chalky color of their complexions she surmised this was their first murder scene.

"Hi, Jake, Mike," she said. "Is the victim inside?"

Jake nodded. "In the office in the back. He's behind the desk."

Savannah stepped over the tape, and the two men followed her into the building, closing the door securely behind them. The spectators continued to gawk through the bronze-tinted floor-to-ceiling windows.

"Who is it?" she asked, now that they were out of earshot.

Jake gave Mike a quick look, which Savannah interpreted as ominous at best.

"Uh . . . we're not sure," he said. "It's . . . uh . . . sorta hard to tell."

She felt even more pessimistic. "Is that because you weren't well-acquainted with Jonathan Winston and his staff, or because it's . . . messy."

"Messy," Mike said without hesitation. "Very messy."

"Oh, goody." She could almost feel her cheese blintzes do a polka.

"The janitor found him about an hour ago," Mike said, waving a big, beefy hand toward the hall that led away from the showroom. "He called it in at five-thirty. We were just down the street, so we came over to check it out."

"Where is the janitor now?"

"He's sitting out in our unit," Jake said. "He begged us to let him leave the building. He's a little spooked."

"Okay; I'll talk to him later." She scanned the elaborate entry of pink marble, bronzed mirrors, and accents of brass that gleamed like gold everywhere. "Anybody but the two of you and the janitor been inside?"

"Nope. We made sure nobody touched nothin'," Jake said proudly.

"Good work," Savannah said. "I'll be sure to mention that in my report." She stopped in the middle of the showroom and studied every detail. An antique armoire nearly covered one wall and was filled with exquisite gowns, the likes of which Savannah had never even seen before, let alone worn. An elegant mural graced the opposite wall—a delicately scrolled *J.W.*, the trademark of the highly successful designer.

The room appeared pristine, certainly not the scene of any violence. Flower arrangements were undisturbed, as were the photo albums on the low cocktail table in front of the white leather sofa. The pale gray carpet showed no signs of traffic, other than a few footprints leading to and through the center of the room.

"Did you guys walk through here before?" she asked.

"Yeah . . . to get to the front door," Mike admitted.

"It's okay; just asking." She looked down at their feet. Damn, they were wearing shoes with heavy tread.

"Let me see the bottoms of your shoes," she said, squatting down.

They looked at each other, puzzled. "What?" Jake asked.

"Hold up your feet. I want to check your soles." She grinned. "One foot at a time is fine."

They did as she asked. Other than a bit of gum and assorted street debris, they were clean.

"I know you guys need traction on your beat," she said, "but when you walk into a murder scene with carpeting, it's better if you have slick leather soles. Those tractor treads of yours can pick up all kinds of good stuff and walk out the door with it. One guy I know took off with a casing, the only one on the scene. He found it later that night, but by then it was thoroughly mangled."

"Um-m-m . . . sorry, Detective," Mike muttered, looking embarrassed.

"Hey, no problem. Now you know. Just check your shoes before you leave."

She took one more quick look around the room, absorbing everything she could, then headed down the hall toward the rear of the building.

"Back here?" she asked.

"Yeah, and to your left," Jake said.

She noticed they weren't following her closely as she approached the room in question. She couldn't blame them: It wasn't easy, your first time. Hell, it wasn't easy the hundredth time. She had never been able to fully understand what one person could do to another. More than once she had wanted to change her species affiliation after seeing the mayhem of which human beings were capable.

Even before she reached the door to the room, Savannah could smell it—the unmistakable, unforgettable stench of death. The coppery odor of the blood, combined with the stink of feces and urine. And, of course, there was always that universal element that could be detected on a much more primitive level than smell: residual terror. It seeped through your skin and into your bloodstream and nervous system until you could taste it, bitter in your mouth. A very small taste of what the victim had suffered in those last few moments.

The office door was standing wide open. A vacuum cleaner lay sprawled across the threshold.

"The janitor said he opened the door, saw the body, and dropped his vacuum," Mike explained.

"I'm not surprised," Savannah said softly as she stepped over the cleaner and into the office.

The victim lay on his back behind the black lacquer, brass-trimmed desk. One glance told Savannah the cause of death: at least three shotgun blasts.

The most she had ever seen before was one per corpse at a double homicide.

"They certainly wanted to kill him good," Mike said, hanging back in the doorway.

Savannah didn't reply. She knelt a couple of feet away from the body and flipped her mental switch to automatic pilot. Emotions disengaged—until later. Intellect was running in high gear.

If she thought of this corpse as a human being, she wouldn't be able to function. Anger would supplant reason.

The man himself was gone. The only thing she could do now to help him was to bring his killer to justice by studying the clues his remains provided.

One of the blasts had been directly to the face, destroying any hope of an easy identification. His features had been reduced to little more than a gory red mist of tissue particles that had sprayed across the white wall directly behind him, like a macabre Rorschach test. The level indicated that he was probably standing when shot.

Another blast had hit and removed the better part of his right arm. The remnants of torn flesh and shattered bone lay on the carpet behind him. Apparently he had been lying on the floor when that one had hit.

The third shot had ripped away the outer half of his right

thigh. As with the arm, those tissues and fluids had oozed into the carpeting.

"I'd say he got it in the face first," she said. "At least for his sake I hope so."

"Yeah," Mike replied, taking a step closer. "He wouldn't have felt a thing."

"He was looking down the barrel of a shotgun for . . . we don't know how long." Savannah shook her head. "I'm sure he felt a rather sick, sinking feeling that he was about to die."

Without touching the corpse or moving anything, she walked around the body, viewing it from each side, making mental notes. He was well-dressed, in a cream silk shirt with tan linen pants. Not a particularly tall man, he could be considered well-built in an amateur weight-lifting sort of way. Judging from his jewelry—a heavy gold chain around his neck, a Rolex watch, and a distinctive diamond-and-ruby ring in the shape of a horseshoe—he was a man of means.

Not a robbery, she thought, *or they would have cut off his finger, if necessary, to get that ring.*

The small amount of hair that remained on the victim's mutilated head—the part that wasn't drenched with blood—appeared to be steel gray.

Instinctively, Savannah had known who he was from the moment she entered the office. But she had been shoving down the thought in her mind, hoping she was wrong, reminding herself not to jump to conclusions.

"Do you think it's Jonathan Winston?" she asked quietly.

"I've only seen him once or twice," Jake said, "but the hair looks like his. I remember him being about that size."

"Did the janitor ID him?" she asked.

"Naw. He was so scared, he wouldn't have recognized his own mother. When he saw all the blood he just ran like hell."

"I don't blame him," she replied. Turning to Mike, she said, "How about you? Do you think it's Winston?"

"Hard to be sure without the face." Mike cleared his throat and glanced away, suddenly interested in the tips of his shoes. "But I'd say it could be him. I figure it probably is."

"Yeah, me, too. Why do you suppose a classy guy like Jonathan Winston would get himself blown away?" she said, thinking aloud. "A sour business deal? Personal problems . . . ?"

"Maybe somebody didn't like what his wife's been doing at City Hall," Jake suggested.

Savannah felt a deep pang of sadness when she thought of Beverly Winston. Although she had only spoken to the councilwoman briefly a couple of times, she really liked her. For the past few years Savannah had watched approvingly as Beverly worked her way up the political ladder. She had spearheaded many humane programs to benefit the city's neglected children and battered women, as well as the homeless and destitute, a constituency that had been overlooked by her predecessors. Word was, she intended to run for State Assembly next fall.

In the course of her own career Savannah had told far too many people that their loved ones had died or been gravely wounded. It was the hardest thing she had to do in the line of duty. But it was always so much harder if she knew the person.

God . . . she didn't want to tell a great lady like Beverly Winston that someone had blown apart her husband's body with a shotgun in his own office.

"Let's get the deputy coroner down here," she said, "and a criminologist to collect samples and take the pictures."

She stood, pulled a journal out of her purse, and began to

make notes and brief sketches of everything she could see that might be important.

Mike walked toward the desk and reached for the phone.

"Not that one," she said, grabbing his arm. "We've gotta check for prints and the redial; see who he phoned last."

"Oh, yeah . . . sorry," Mike said. "I'll call from the unit. I need to check on the janitor anyway."

"I'll want to talk to him, too. But not just this minute. Make sure we know where to find him later today."

Savannah followed Mike out the front door and past the mob of reporters. She had to get her homicide kit from her trunk. The lab technicians would dust for prints, vacuum the carpet and furniture for any trace evidence, and take all the scrapings, samples, and photographs that were necessary, then get back to her with the results.

But Savannah liked to take her own pictures. Sometimes she saw something in them later that she hadn't noticed in the official photos.

Through the window of the squad car she could see Jake talking to an elderly man, who appeared to be scared to death. He hadn't committed the murder; one look at him told her that. She would need to talk to him, though, to see if he could tell her anything, no matter how small, that might help. But it could wait until later. If the corpse inside was who she thought he was, getting a positive identification was the primary consideration.

"Savannah!" Rosemary Hulse called as she ran across the street to intercept Savannah before she could reach her car. "What's happened?"

"A homicide," she replied, opening her trunk and taking out the oversized briefcase that contained the tools of her trade: camera, surgical gloves, sample jars and a putty knife for scraping, banner tape, and plastic zipper bags. Savannah believed in being prepared.

"I already knew that. Who's dead?" Rosemary asked bluntly. Reporters were always blunt—maybe even more so than cops.

Savannah paused for a moment, case in hand, before she slammed the trunk closed. In her mind's eye she could see the amputated arm, the mutilated thigh, the shattered face.

"We don't know for sure," she said softly. "And I'm afraid it's going to be a while before we do."

Savannah stood at the edge of Sunset Park and marveled that one square city block could contain at least half of the town's citizenry at once. On the second Sunday of each month, San Carmelita held an arts-and-crafts show in this picturesque park near the beach. Assigned their eight-by-ten space of grass, the artisans had erected colorful booths to display their wares: pottery, tole-painted woodwork, paintings, and air-brushed T-shirts.

On top of a hastily assembled plywood stage a country band wailed the dilemma of a cowboy in love with four women. A brightly costumed juggler and a G-rated belly dancer had each assembled a small audience of their own.

A cold, wet nose pushed its way into Savannah's palm and she looked down to see Fiero, her favorite K-9 cop. The handsome German Shepherd had brought along his partner, Officer Carl Browning, and the two of them were entertaining a group of children with Fiero's tricks.

"Fiero, up!" Carl said, holding his arms straight out in front of him, his palms up.

The dog jumped, twisted in the air, and landed on his back in Carl's arms. Delighted, the kids laughed and applauded. One offered the dog a raspberry snow cone, which he downed with two gulps.

Savannah plunged into the throng, weaving her way through the food booths operated by charitable organizations. The smells of smoked teriyaki beef kabobs and freshly baked cinnamon rolls filled the air. Ordinarily, Savannah would have stopped to indulge, but at the moment she had no appetite—thanks to what she had seen that morning and what she would have to do now.

Beverly Winston's housekeeper had said that she was helping out today at a booth sponsored by Hope Haven, a shelter for battered women. Savannah could see their distinctive red banner flying at the other end of the midway.

As she drew closer, Savannah spotted Beverly in the booth, handing out brochures and soliciting donations. She wasn't a pretty woman—at least, not by the ultrafeminine Southern standards with which Savannah had grown up. The councilwoman wore no makeup, and her graying ash-blond hair hung in a straight, no-nonsense style to her collar. Her casual look consisted of a stiffly tailored navy pantsuit, a white shirt, and a red silk scarf. Savannah smiled wryly, noting that Winston's colors were as politically correct as the smile she wore while she answered questions and shook hands.

Savannah browsed around a neighboring needlework booth and watched Beverly carefully for several minutes. When she had seen the councilwoman before she had always appeared calm, confident, at ease with herself and the world around her. But today her smile seemed strained, her posture unusually stiff, her movements jerky.

Could she have been told already?

It was certainly possible, but Savannah didn't think so. She couldn't imagine a woman continuing to work a street fair booth after learning that her husband might have been murdered.

Savannah noticed that her attention seemed diverted every few seconds from the people she was addressing. Her eyes searched the crowd momentarily, as though she were expecting some sort of confrontation or attack.

An uneasy feeling began to stir in the pit of Savannah's stomach. She didn't want to contemplate the possible implications right now. There would be plenty of time to do that at leisure. Unfortunately, she had an unpleasant job to do, and she might as well get on with it.

Just as she had left the piles of embroidered pillows and crocheted afghans to walk over to the councilwoman's booth, Savannah saw a familiar figure approaching the display from her left. She moved quickly to intercept him.

Gary Anderson was a smug, obnoxious reporter who worked with Rosemary Hulse. But he lacked any of Rosemary's tact or discretion. More than once Savannah had stopped him from shoving his camera and tape recorder in the face of a grief-stricken family member.

"Anderson," she said. He continued on, blatantly ignoring her.

She quickened her pace and grabbed his upper arm, whirling him around.

What a wimp, she thought. Her own biceps were better developed than the one she was squeezing hard enough to get his undivided attention.

"Detective, what a pleasant surprise," he said with a sarcastic grin that didn't conceal the fact that he was wincing.

She dug her nails in a bit deeper and glanced over at Beverly

Winston. The woman was watching them from the corner of her eye, a look of concern on her face.

"Are you enjoying the street fair, Gary?" Savannah asked in a pseudocasual tone.

"Oh yes, very much," he said. "I come down every month to check out the pottery."

Her blue eyes locked with his and she gave him her best visual zap. He winced again without being squeezed.

"Don't do it, Anderson," she said softly.

"Don't do what?" He gave her the wide-eyed, innocent look, and a smirk that made her want to smack him.

"Don't be a jerk. She hasn't been informed yet."

He snapped to attention, reminding her of a beagle. "So it is him."

"We don't know; it may be. But either way you're not going to jump her bones right now. You're not. Got it?"

Her hand tightened again, and the look on her face defied him to resist.

"Like I said . . ." He yanked his arm out of her grasp and shrugged. ". . . I was just coming down to check out the pottery."

She waited until he had walked to the other side of the park before she approached the booth. Beverly was watching her every move, and the somewhat concerned look on her face had progressed to definitely worried.

"Detective Reid," she said when Savannah reached her. "How nice to see you."

For the second time in three minutes Savannah had been told that someone was glad to run into her. For the second time she didn't believe a word of it.

"When was it we last talked . . . ?" Beverly extended her hand and shook Savannah's with the perfect degree of firmness and strength. ". . . that meeting at the Women's Center on self-defense, right?"

"Yes, I think so," Savannah said, not returning her smile. She glanced around. There were far too many people nearby. This wasn't the time or place.

"Mrs. Winston . . ." Savannah leaned across the table covered with brochures and placed her hand on the woman's forearm. "I need to talk to you. It's very important."

"Now?" she asked, nodding toward the line of people waiting to speak with her.

"Yes. I'm sorry. If you could just come with me for a few minutes . . ."

Beverly turned to an elderly woman, who was sitting in a folding chair beneath the display's awning. "Marge, could you watch the booth for me? I have to take care of something."

"Sure." Marge pulled herself to her feet and slid into the space Beverly had vacated. "Take your time."

"Thank you." Beverly retrieved her purse from beneath the table, slung the heavy leather strap over her shoulder, and followed Savannah away from the crowd.

"Would you mind?" Savannah asked, waving a hand toward her red Camaro, which was parked on the street. "We could sit in my car and talk."

"Of course. That would be fine."

As Savannah unlocked the passenger door and ushered Beverly inside, it occurred to her that the councilwoman didn't seem surprised. She hadn't demanded to know what news Savannah might have. Usually the first thing people asked was, "What is it? What's wrong?"

Maybe Councilwoman Winston was just a very cool, collected individual.

Savannah slid into the driver's seat, took a deep breath, and switched into intellect mode, as she had at the crime scene. If she allowed herself to feel the pain of giving someone such terrible news, she wouldn't be able to carefully judge the person's reaction. And she would have only one brief moment to do it.

"Mrs. Winston, have you—"

"Please, call me Beverly," she said without meeting her eyes. "Everyone does."

Savannah studied her curiously. It was as though she was postponing the moment of truth, a very unusual reaction.

"Thank you, Beverly." Turning, as best she could in her bucket seat, Savannah faced the other woman directly. "Have you spoken to anyone from your husband's showroom or your home since you left this morning?"

"No, I haven't."

Again, she hadn't asked the inevitable questions.

"Then I'm sorry to have to tell you that there has been a shooting at Mr. Winston's business on Main Street. Apparently it happened early this morning. I'm afraid the wounds were fatal."

"Shooting? Someone was shot?"

Savannah watched Beverly carefully, every nuance of her expression, her voice. But all she saw was stunned amazement.

"Yes, I'm sorry."

"But . . . how can that . . . ? Someone was killed . . . at Jonathan's showroom?"

"That's right. In his office," Savannah added gently, hoping to lead her slowly to the grim truth.

Beverly Winston shook her head and stared straight ahead, watching a group of children, bearing snow cones and balloons, pass in front of the car. "Who? Who would do a thing like that?"

For a moment Savannah didn't reply as she pondered the significance of the fact that Beverly had asked about the identity of the perpetrator rather than the victim.

"We don't know. Not yet. But we're working on it."

"So terrible," Beverly whispered. "There . . . in his office."

"I need to ask you a favor, Beverly," Savannah said. "Would you please come down to the morgue and see if you can identify the body for me?"

Beverly seemed to snap out of her trance as she turned to Savannah and nodded. "Oh, yes . . . of course. I should be the one to identify him. Jonathan would want it that way."

The two women sat quietly for a moment. Savannah's mental gears were spinning. This wasn't at all the way she had anticipated this conversation would progress. Beverly Winston wasn't a stupid woman—not by a long shot. If she had murdered her husband, surely she would have been more clever than to suggest that he was the victim before being informed.

"Beverly, we haven't formally identified the body. We don't really know who he is yet."

"Oh, it's Jonathan, all right." She paused to wipe her hand over her eyes, as though suddenly very tired.

"How can you be so sure?"

Beverly chuckled, but it sounded more like a stifled sob. "You didn't know my husband, did you?"

"No, not personally. Do you have any idea who might have wanted to harm him?"

She laughed again, a sarcastic, bitter sound. "Oh . . . several ideas," she said. "Jonathan didn't exactly bring out the best in people. It could have been any of us who knew and loved him. I'm afraid, Detective Reid, you have your work cut out for you."

CHAPTER THREE

The San Carmelita County Morgue was one of Savannah's least favorite spots on earth. Her prejudice went beyond the depressing, industrial-gray walls, the grungy old fart at the front desk who always tried to hit on her, or the acrid smell of chemicals—and that was on a good day when they weren't autopsying a ripe one. On those occasions the atmosphere could definitely be classified as Harmful to Sensitive Persons, or any human being who wore a nose on his or her face.

The main reason Savannah hated the morgue was far more of an emotional issue than a visual or nasal one. She had lived a multitude of unpleasant, sometimes heart-wrenching experiences here, and when she walked through those spotless, glass-and-chrome front doors, the feelings inevitably came flooding back. Unfortunately they brought back with them accompanying memories of times when she had brought other people here to view their mangled loved ones, and when she, herself, had been asked to identify one of her fellow officers, killed during a drug bust gone bad.

But, despite Savannah's distaste for the place, this was an important element of the investigation. Not that they depended upon a positive ID from Mrs. Winston—there were half a dozen other ways to ascertain the identity of the victim. Mostly, Savannah had brought Beverly Winston here so that she could watch and evaluate the woman's response when she saw her dead husband.

That fact made Savannah feel a bit like a ghoul, but, hey . . . it was all in a day's work.

"Well, hi there, good lookin'," the front-desk clerk said in a voice so cheerful that it seemed incongruent with the dismal surroundings.

Loud, invasive, cocky, and aggressive, Officer Kenny Bates seemed to possess a much higher opinion of himself than was held by those who knew him. On the first day she had met him, five years earlier, Savannah had decided that someday, when she had an extra five minutes to blow, she would contemplate and evaluate all the convoluted trailways and byways of Ken Bates's psyche. Perhaps then she would unlock the secret: Was he really an insecure, tortured man trying to overcompensate, or was he just a pompous jerk?

So far, she hadn't found the time.

"This is Councilwoman Beverly Winston," Savannah said, trying to convey the gravity of the situation in her tone.

Bates was oblivious.

"Hi! Nice to meet you," he said, flashing a toothsome smile that was only somewhat sullied by the hard-boiled egg yoke stuck between an incisor and its neighbor. He leaned both elbows on the waist-high counter and tilted his head to one side while perusing the councilwoman's features. Fortunately he confined his curiosity to her face, rather than giving her his usual elevator sweep, head to toe and back again, pausing at each floor to savor the view.

Maybe the recent departmental workshops about sexual harassment had enlightened him. Or maybe Beverly Winston was just a little too mature and sedate for his tastes.

"We've come to make an identification," Savannah said as she fixed him with her sternest smarten-up-asshole look. Again, Officer Kenny didn't have a clue.

"Could I please have the log?" Savannah asked, leaning across the counter and grabbing the clipboard out of his hand. She pulled a pen from her purse and jotted down her name, Beverly's, and the time.

"So, when are you and me goin' out?" he said, lowering his voice to what he probably considered a deep, husky, sexy whisper. But "sexy" wasn't what came to Savannah's mind. His tone reminded her of a few obscene phone calls she had received at three o'clock in the morning . . . and was just about as stimulating.

With considerably more force than was required, she shoved the clipboard across the counter to Bates. The hard, sharp edge caught him in the diaphragm, momentarily knocking the wind out of his sails.

"If you would, please, come with me." Savannah turned to Beverly and gently took her elbow. "Down this way. It won't take long, I promise, and then it'll be over."

Feeling the woman stiffen at her touch, Savannah instantly released her. "I'm all right, Detective Reid," she said, lifting her chin. "Let's get on with it."

Savannah wondered, not for the first time, if a prominent

jawline truly was indicative of strong character. In Councilwoman Winston's case, it appeared to be so.

With a wave of her hand Savannah gestured toward the corridor to their right. "This way," she said, matching Winston's curt tone. If the councilwoman wanted businesslike rather than maternal treatment, no problem.

Savannah's leather-soled, sensible flats made no sound to accompany the staccato clicking of Beverly's Gucci pumps as they walked briskly down the hall. The gray linoleum floor glistened, reflecting white circles of light from the institutional fixtures overhead.

Glancing at Beverly, Savannah was somewhat surprised by her cool, collected demeanor. Of all the times she had walked people down this far-too-long corridor to view the remains of their loved ones, Savannah had never seen such a subdued reaction.

Even if the person being conducted down the hall later turned out to have been the killer, he or she usually showed more emotion than this.

"How long have you and Mr. Winston been married?" she asked. She supposed it was a bit tactless to bring up the subject at a time like this, but it would have been more awkward to continue on in silence or to try to make small talk about the weather or the last Lakers' game.

"Twenty-three years," Beverly replied in a flat monotone. "We married very young. The first two years were good."

"And the rest?" Savannah asked, pressing gently.

"The rest were convenient."

Unaccustomed to such candor, Savannah gave Beverly a quick sideways glance, which she intercepted. The woman stopped abruptly in the middle of the hall and took a deep breath.

"Detective Reid," she said, "I'm not going to insult your intelligence by lying to you. By the time you're finished with your investigation you'll know that my marriage was . . . rocky, at best."

Savannah returned her steady gaze. "I appreciate that, Beverly. A bit of honesty goes a long way in trying to uncover the truth."

"The truth is . . . if that body in there is Jonathan, I won't be surprised. I've been expecting something like this. My husband has been committed to a self-destructive path for years. It was only a matter of time."

"You seem pretty certain it *is* him."

She shrugged, and her expression became even more bitter. "Call it a hunch," she said.

A door to their left opened and an attractive, petite Asian woman stepped into the hall. She wore a white smock and a gentle smile that radiated an unearthly serenity.

Savannah beckoned her. "Dr. Liu, this is Councilwoman Beverly Winston," she said. "She's here to see if she can identify this morning's homicide victim."

"Yes, of course. He's here in the examining room," she said, indicating a set of double doors farther down the hall. "Give me a moment, please, and then you can come on in."

Savannah knew the coroner would be draping the body, preparing it to be viewed with the least amount of emotional trauma to the parties involved. One look at Beverly told her that she, too, had understood the purpose of the delay.

Gone was the congenial politician who had shaken her hand only half an hour ago. She appeared exhausted, pale and drawn, with the practiced facade lowered. Beverly Winston seemed to have aged ten years in the past thirty minutes.

For a moment the woman closed her eyes and pressed her

fingertips to her temples. Savannah could only imagine how badly her head must be aching.

Once again the heavy silence between them grew thicker by the second. Thankfully, Dr. Liu appeared at the door. "Thank you for waiting," she said. "You may come in now."

She held open the door to the examining room, and Savannah motioned Beverly inside.

If the morgue was Savannah's least favorite place, this room was her least favorite single spot on earth. Within these sparkling white walls, decorated with *Gray's Anatomy* maps, she had seen more than one sight that had made her old before her time. The first time she had viewed a mangled child on that stainless-steel table in the middle of the room she had felt like she was thirtysomething going on eighty-five.

Dr. Liu had carefully covered the body with a white cloth, and she stood aside, quietly allowing Savannah to proceed.

Turning to Beverly, Savannah saw that the coldness, the almost nonchalant attitude she had observed before was slipping away. The woman's eyes were fixed on the white sheet, her face nearly as pale.

"This won't take long, Beverly," she said. "I'd just like you to take a look at . . . his left hand and see if you can make the identification for us."

"His hand?" Beverly's eyes met hers, and Savannah saw the beginnings of these raw emotions she usually witnessed in this room. "Why his hand? I want to see his face."

Savannah studied her for a moment, feeling a wave of sympathy that took more out of her than a ten-minute, full-out foot chase. "No, you don't," she said softly. "Really . . . the hand will be enough."

Beverly shook her head. "But I do. Why can't I . . . ?"

"Mrs. Winston, I don't believe you could make a positive identification from the facial features. Is there some other part of the body you would prefer to view?"

Understanding dawned on Beverly's face. "Oh, he was shot in . . . I see." She paused and shuddered slightly before continuing. "The hand will be fine. Actually, the forearm. My husband has a distinctive tattoo on his upper forearm. A black panther . . . from his wilder days."

Savannah glanced questioningly at Dr. Liu, who nodded slightly. At the crime scene she hadn't seen his forearms, but the doctor would have, once the body had arrived and had been stripped.

Carefully, Savannah reached down and pulled the sheet back just a little, enough to bare the corpse's left forearm. There, faded over the years but unmistakable, was the crude tattoo of a panther, crawling up the arm, his claws raking long red "scratches" on the flesh.

Beverly Winston closed her eyes and swayed forward. Savannah reached for her, thinking she was going to faint. But she recovered herself and pushed Savannah's hand away.

She stepped closer to the table, where she stood for a long time, staring down at the gray-white arm with its exotic ornamentation.

Carefully, Savannah studied her face, watching for any telltale signs of guilt, remorse, anger . . . anything that might give a clue to the woman's feelings. All she saw was shock and sorrow. Either Beverly Winston was deeply hurt by what she saw or she was a damned good actress. Savannah hoped it was the former, but she reserved the possibility that it could be the latter. Earlier in her career Savannah had been deceived. Giving people the benefit of the doubt might work well in intimate relationships, but in the world of crime it could be deadly.

"Am I to assume . . ." Savannah said quietly, ". . . that this is Jonathan Winston?"

Beverly said nothing but gave a curt nod, still staring down at the tattoo. She took one step closer to the table and touched the arm lightly with one fingertip. Then she lifted the hand, bent over, and placed a kiss on the knuckles.

"Oh, Jonny," she whispered, "you've done it now, haven't you?"

She made a small sound that was very like a stifled sob, replaced the hand, and patted it once. Turning to Savannah, she said curtly, "Yes, Detective Reid, this is . . . *was* my husband, Jonathan Winston. You have your positive identification. Is there anything else I can do for you?"

Savannah didn't reply for a moment, nonplussed by the woman's contradictory behavior. She didn't know what to make of her.

"I'd like to ask you some questions, but I can take you home first if you—"

"Home? Oh, no, I can't go home at this hour of the day," she said adamantly, shaking her head. "I have so much to do at the office. Could you drop me by City Hall? We could talk there."

"Are you sure?" Savannah searched the woman's eyes, but her soul was shuttered. "I'm certain that the good citizens of San Carmelita could do without you for a day or so, considering . . ."

"Yes, I suppose they could," Beverly said as she headed toward the double doors, high heels clicking as briskly as before. "But today, of all days, I need them."

Looking back at Dr. Liu, who was still standing by quietly,

wearing a look that was as confused as Savannah felt, she said, "Thank you, Doctor. I'll be in touch."

As the coroner watched Beverly's hasty exit, she shook her head and mouthed the words, "Good luck."

"Thanks," Savannah said, then added silently, *I have a feeling I'm going to need it.*

Although Savannah had expected a flock of reporters to have descended on City Hall, she was surprised at the size of the crowd. She counted seven news vans—four from Los Angeles—and more than a dozen teams with videocams, microphones, and other complicated-looking equipment she didn't recognize.

Reconsidering, Savannah decided that it wasn't strange at all for the press to be here in such impressive numbers. Beverly's family, the Harringtons, had been pillars of the San Carmelita community for four generations. One of the major boulevards through town had been named after the original Harrington, one of the city's settlers.

The peaks of the family Tudor mansion could be seen rising above all others at the top of the hill. For nearly a century the sight had served to remind San Carmelita's citizens that the Harringtons were, indeed, an extraordinary clan.

The last surviving branch of the familial tree walked beside Savannah, chin high, back straight, a somber but dignified, politically correct expression painted across her pallid face.

As the reporters descended on them, Savannah saw Beverly falter for only a moment, then recover and meet them head on at the bottom of the marble stairs.

"There have been reports that your husband, Jonathan Winston, has been murdered. Is that true?" asked a broad-shouldered male reporter whom Savannah recognized by his profusion of perfect silver hair. He was one of the primary field reporters for a major network station in Los Angeles.

Despite his size and intimidating manner, Savannah wedged herself between him and Mrs. Winston. Holding up her hand in traffic-cop fashion, she brought him to an abrupt halt. His cameraman nearly ran into him from behind.

"We have no comment at this time," she told him sternly. "The police department will be releasing a statement later today. But *this* is *not* the time."

Several others tried to elicit a response as well, only to be met with the same firm resistance. Savannah had no problem being tough with the press. While many of them conducted their business with dignity and compassion, she found others to be insensitive, obnoxious, and overbearing. More than once she had wanted to feed a reporter his camera, or maybe use it on him as a suppository.

Beverly seemed to appreciate having someone run interference for her. Savannah figured that she was the kind of woman who took care of others more often than others cared for her. With her hand on the councilwoman's elbow, Savannah deftly guided her through the crowd, up the marble stairs, and through the heavy wooden doors of the old Spanish-style building.

In the entry a sentinel motioned them through a metal detector and nodded a greeting to both. "I'll keep them outside as long as I can," he said with a crooked but sympathetic smile.

"Thank you, Jerry," Beverly said as they hurried past. Savannah could see the guard's affection for the councilwoman all over his face. A lot of people loved this lady—a fact that made Savannah all the more uncomfortable with the questions she would soon be asking her.

Before they reached her office they were intercepted by an

apparently harried and concerned chief of police, Norman Hillquist. One of the qualities Savannah had always admired about the chief was his ability to remain unruffled no matter what the circumstances. She had seen him face mobs of disgruntled constituents, the occasional desperate criminal, and ruthless political opponents without breaking a sweat on his wide brow.

But this morning . . . he definitely looked ruffled. He was even sweating, in spite of the lightweight white golf shirt he wore. Apparently he had received the call while on the green. She couldn't remember a time when the chief had forsaken his game for anything as mundane as a homicide. His career was his life, but golf was his obsession.

"Detective Reid," he said, hurrying to her side, "I'd like to have a word with you."

He nodded briefly to Beverly Winston before ushering Savannah through the nearest door and into a supply closet. He shut the door behind them, and Savannah was momentarily confused by the darkness. Then he threw the light switch, and she experienced a pang of claustrophobia as the towers of photocopy paper, stick-on notepads, and adhesive tape seemed to close around her.

Or, perhaps, it wasn't the office materials intimidating her after all. Maybe the source of her discomfort was the almost palpable agitation radiating from the chief as he leaned closer to her, his breath warm on her cheek. She could smell the faint odor of beer and spices and guessed that he had enjoyed his usual Bloody Mary on the course.

"Was it him?" he asked. "Did she identify Winston?"

"Yes, I'm afraid so," Savannah replied.

"Damn." The look of concern deepened on Hillquist's tanned face and he shook his head. "Okay, so what have you got?"

She stared at him for a moment, puzzled, then glanced down at her watch. "I've been on the investigation for an hour and a half, give or take ten minutes. I don't have a hell of a lot yet." He didn't appear amused, so she continued. "Shotgun, three wounds—face, arm, leg. The janitor found him in his studio office on Main Street. No signs of forced entry or a struggle. Nothing obvious lying around at the scene."

"Have you questioned Mrs. Winston yet?"

"Only briefly. That was my next step."

"Are you intending to do that now?"

Somehow she got the feeling he wasn't going to like her answer. "Well, yes . . . I mean, she is the next of kin, and—"

"Have you interrogated the janitor?"

"Ah, no, but I got the idea from the patrolmen on the scene that his statement would be rather predictable."

He raised one carefully trimmed eyebrow. "Oh, really? Are you forgetting, Detective, that the person who calls in the homicide is often the perpetrator?"

"No, Chief," she replied, trying not to sound or look miffed. "I haven't forgotten. I was simply proceeding with my investigation in the manner which I felt was most appropriate under the circumstances."

"The circumstances, Detective Reid, are these: Jonathan Winston has been murdered and his wife is the most influential force on this city's council—and, may I add, she has been a steadfast supporter of the police department in all of her decisions. This is a small town, Savannah, full of individuals with big mouths. Councilwoman Winston could be destroyed within twenty-four hours, and a lot of people's dreams with her."

"I realize the gravity of the situation, Chief," she said, trying to appear more patient than she felt. Although she seldom experienced symptoms of claustrophobia, the closet walls appeared to be closing in around her, and the atmosphere suddenly seemed stale and suffocating. "I'll proceed carefully; don't worry."

She reached for the doorknob, but he blocked her, his hand closing around her wrist with a grip that was slightly too tight.

"I think you should interview that janitor first," he said. "I definitely believe that would be the smart thing to do, under the circumstances."

Savannah's temper flared. He had no right to interfere with her investigation like this. Questioning the next of kin at her own discretion was *her* call. Or at least it should have been. Since when did the chief of police take over one of his detective's cases?

On the other hand, she wasn't in any position to argue the fine points of departmental protocol, having become accustomed to some of the simpler pleasures of life, such as receiving a bi-monthly paycheck, eating, and having a roof over her head and clothing to wear.

"Yes, sir, I'll do that right away," she said, too sweetly. "Thank you for your input, sir."

Dirk didn't always catch the subtle nuances of her insults, but Norman Hillquist wasn't police chief for no reason. His eyes narrowed and he moved a step closer to her. "You're welcome, Detective," he said with equal sarcasm. "I'm sure I'll have more suggestions as the case progresses."

"I'll be looking forward to that, sir," she replied as she yanked open the door and strode into the hallway.

Yeah, sure, she was looking forward to their next rendezvous and the words of wisdom he would so generously bestow upon her . . . just like she was looking forward to senility, arthritis, denture breath, and wearing bladder control lingerie.

Yep . . . boy howdy! She could hardly wait.

CHAPTER FOUR

"I told you . . . you can't talk to Hank right now! He's got a bad heart and he ain't feelin' good."

Savannah stood on the back porch of the ramshackle old house—no one had answered the front door—and studied the janitor's wife through the rusted screen. Today was definitely going to be one of those days when everyone and their uncle's dog's cousin was out to give her a hard time. The woman was huge, nearly filling the doorway with her bulk, which appeared to be as much muscle as fat. Deciding that she really wasn't up for another tussle within twenty-four hours of the last one, Savannah donned an extremely patient look.

"I understand, Mrs. Downing. I'm sure he is very upset after what he saw this morning. But this is a homicide investigation and I *must* talk to him . . . now, not later. I'll take it slow and easy with him, I promise. My dad has a heart condition, and I know how to treat Mr. Downing. You don't have to worry."

Savannah could feel her tongue turning black, even as she uttered the blatant lie. Never having known her father, she had no idea whether he had a heart condition or not. But it sounded good, and she justified the falsehood the same way she had all the others she had uttered in the line of duty.

Granny Reid was right, though: It would all catch up with her someday. When she least expected it her tongue would turn black, shrivel up, and fall out of her head, just as predicted. God always got you in the end.

"Well . . . all right," Mrs. Downing said, relenting a bit. She pushed open the screen door a crack and crooked one finger. "Come in here and sit yourself down at the kitchen table."

"Thank you, Mrs. Downing," she said gratefully, deciding that perhaps sin was such a popular pastime because it often worked so well. "Thank you very much."

While the old woman shuffled away to summon her husband, Savannah pulled out one of the aluminum-framed chairs and sat on the cracked leatherette with its red pearlescent design. She smiled, remembering Gran's dinette set, which had been so similar. Gran had bought it when Savannah had been ten, and she had thought it the most beautiful dining-room furniture in the world.

Her memory was also twanged by the pungent, familiar odor that emanated from the bowl in the center of the table. In typical Old South tradition, the colorful bowl contained slices of cucumber and onion, pinches of fresh dill and parsley, swimming in a solution of vinegar, water, and a tiny dab of sugar. Her mouth watered, and it was all she could do not to reach over and nab a slice.

But if she did, they would surely smell the vinegar on her breath. A peace officer had to watch that sort of thing.

Caught in her nostalgic reverie, Savannah looked around the room, half expecting to see her grandmother's cat clock on the wall, with its pendulum tail and rhinestone-studded eyes that shifted from left to right and back with each tick. But the dining set and the marinade had been where the similarities stopped. Gran's kitchen was always spotless, dishes done and put away, appliances sparkling, and an immaculate white towel spread on top of the dryer below a basket of fresh fruit and miscellaneous sweet treats.

The only food in evidence in Mrs. Downing's kitchen was the dried red pasty material on the dirty dishes that were stacked on the counters and in the sink. But Savannah didn't pause mentally to make a judgment; she had seen worse than this. Much worse.

"Here he is," Mrs. Downing said, shoving her husband in front of her as she returned to the kitchen. "Now go easy on 'im. He's had a rough day."

"We all have," Savannah muttered as she stood and offered her hand to Hank Downing.

His handshake was weak, and she could feel a tremor run through him as she squeezed his fingers. One look at his gray pallor told her that Mrs. Downing hadn't been exaggerating. He *did* have health problems, and his experience this morning had obviously taken years off his life.

"Please sit down, Mr. Downing," she said, pulling out a chair for him. "This will only take a few minutes, really."

"I done told them two officers everything I know, missy," he said as he sank onto the chair, propped his elbows on the table, and covered his face with his hands. Savannah knew the gesture well, having both seen it and used it herself countless times. But she knew from experience that the action didn't work. You could still see it all, there in your mind's eye, every lurid detail, indelibly recorded.

"I don't know what else you people want from me," he said wearily.

"I'm the detective who's investigating the homicide." She ignored the surprised look he gave her, relieved that he didn't make an issue of her gender. A tiresome subject.

"Was it him?" Mrs. Downing asked, She had been hovering near the stove, trying to pretend that she was doing something besides eavesdropping. "Was the guy who got kilt Mr. Winston?"

"Yes, I'm afraid so," Savannah said, watching Hank's reaction to the news. Mixed emotions. Grief, maybe a little relief. "Did you know Jonathan Winston well?" she asked him.

He shook his head. "Naw. He was the boss. I was the hired help. That's all there was to us."

"Can you tell me what happened this morning?" she said gently.

Drawing a deep breath, he asked, "How much do you want to know?"

"Everything."

"Okay. . . ." He glanced at his wife, and she nodded her support. ". . . I got to work a little after five this morning. I'm supposed to have the place all spic and span before anybody gets there. Mr. Winston is . . . was . . . really picky about that. He always wanted everything to look perfect when his friends came in."

"Did he have a lot of friends?"

"To hear him tell it, everybody was his friend—least ways,

anybody important. I wasn't his friend," he added softly. "I just worked for 'im. Guess that didn't make me important enough."

Savannah pulled out her notebook and began to scribble. "I understand, Mr. Downing," she said. "Please, go on. You arrived and . . . ?"

"First thing I noticed when I drove up was that the place was all dark. Mr. Winston was usually the last one to leave, and he'd always make sure there was some lights left on, you know, for security."

"But the property was completely dark?"

"I thought so, till I walked down the hall. Then I saw there was a light on in Mr. Winston's office."

"Just a second. Did you come in through the front door or the back?"

"The back. And that was the second thing. It was unlocked. Mr. Winston's always real careful about that. He carries a big wad of bills on him, and he's afraid somebody's gonna stick him up. Do you think that's what happened?"

Savannah thought back to the devastation the shotgun had wrought on the body. Anyone interested in robbing the corpse would have taken more care not to damage the goods—like the roll of cash in his pockets. And he was still wearing his jewelry. No, not likely.

"We don't know yet, Mr. Downing. We're considering all possibilities at this time. You say there was a light on in Mr. Winston's office. Was his door open?"

"No, but I could see it shinin' underneath. That's why I didn't worry no more. I just figured Mr. Winston had nodded off to sleep there in his office—he did that sometimes—and forgot to turn on the outside lights and lock the doors."

"Did he sleep at the office often?"

Hank lowered his voice and leaned closer to her, a conspiratorial gleam in his faded blue eyes. "Passed out is more like it, I reckon," he said. "Mr. W liked to take a nip of that expensive Scotch from time to time."

"Oh, Hank," Mrs. Downing interjected, "if you're gonna tell her, tell her the truth. He was soused half the time, and the other half he was drunker than a skunk."

Savannah gave Hank a questioning look, and he nodded sheepishly. "I just don't think it's right, speakin' ill of the dead and all."

"I understand. But I need to know all you can tell me about Mr. Winston's life, so that I can find out why he died. That's all any of us can do for him now." She waited for the guilty look to leave Hank's face as her words sank in. Then she continued. "So, tell me . . . what happened next?"

"I started cleaning, just like I do every morning. I vacuumed the showroom and the hall and did all the dusting."

Savannah groaned inwardly. No wonder the place had been so pristine. Unwittingly, he would have vacuumed or dusted away any evidence the perpetrator might have left behind. She made a note on the pad to remind the lab techs to pay special attention to the contents of the vacuum's bag.

"About how long do you think you spent cleaning the front of the building?" she asked. "That is, before you discovered Mr. Winston's body?"

He thought for a moment; she could see he was trying to be as accurate as possible, the mark of an honest witness.

"Probably about twenty minutes, give or take."

"Okay, now please think back carefully, Mr. Downing. As you were cleaning, did you notice any sign that someone had been there since you had cleaned before? Fingerprints, smudges, tracks on the carpet, anything?"

Understanding and distress clouded the old man's eyes. "Uh, oh, I guess I fouled that one up. I shouldn't have cleaned everything so good, huh?"

"It's all right, Mr. Downing. You didn't know." She gave him what she hoped was a not-too-bitter, consoling smile. "Do you recall anything out of the ordinary?"

"Not really, but then, I wasn't especially lookin' for nothing, neither."

The old man shrugged, and Savannah noticed again how frail he seemed. How could he have fulfilled his duties as a janitor with a bad heart and hardly any flesh on his bones?

Then she reconsidered. This was hardly the home of a wealthy man, or even a man who had made plans for a comfortable retirement. He worked—not for personal fulfillment but to survive. As Gran used to say, "A body can do most anything . . . when he has to."

"I don't remember nothin' unusual . . . until . . ." He gulped, and his face turned a shade more gray. "I knocked on Mr. Winston's door, and when he didn't answer I opened it a bit to peep inside. That's when I saw his foot stickin' out from behind the desk . . . and the blood . . . all that blood and stuff all over the wall."

Savannah waited patiently for him to collect himself. She wasn't surprised at how the grisly sight had affected him. She didn't suppose she would be particularly interested in eating anything with a tomato-based sauce either for the next few weeks.

Mrs. Downing walked over to her husband and placed her large beefy hands on his shoulders. Looking up at her, Savannah watched the hard lines of her face soften as she stroked his hair.

"I didn't want to walk around that desk," he continued in a choked voice. "But I knew I had to, just in case there was something I could do for him. But the minute I saw him, layin' there all blowed up like that, I knew there weren't nothin' I could do. I was in the war, you know, and I'd seen guys blowed up that way. There's nothin' nobody can do 'cept offer up a prayer that he's with his Maker."

"And is that what you did, Mr. Downing?"

A twinge of guilt crossed his face. "Nope, I can't say that I did. To be honest, I beat the feet to get out of there just as quick as I could. I ran down to that little drugstore on the corner, the one that's open all night, and I told them I had to use their phone for an emergency. I didn't say that prayer until I was back here at home and in my own bed."

He looked at Savannah with red-rimmed eyes that reflected the grief and horror the experience had caused him. There were always so many more victims of a crime like this than was obvious at first glance. So much pain and suffering. Nightmares. Depression and health problems. So many people's lives damaged.

"We're very grateful to you for what you did, Mr. Downing. If you hadn't found him when you did, it might have been hours before he would have been discovered. And every minute counts at a time like this."

She rose and shoved her notebook and pen into her purse. "And speaking of time counting . . . I'd better get going. Is there anything else you'd like to tell me before I leave?"

He squinted, concentrating for a moment, then shook his head. "Nope, nothin' I can think of."

"Here, take my card," she said, pressing it into his palm, "and if you remember anything at all, no matter how small and unimportant it may seem to you, be sure to call me. Will you do that?"

"Sure. I will. I want to help any way I can." He stood, pushing himself up from the table with an effort. "Mr. W wasn't exactly the nicest fella I ever met in my life, but he didn't deserve what he got. Not even an old hound dog with a bad case of the rabies would deserve to get shot up like that."

"I agree, Mr. Downing. Thanks again."

As Savannah backed the Camaro out of the driveway, she waved to the old couple in the doorway. Mrs. Downing looked a lot less imposing now as she slid her arm around her husband's shoulders.

Hank Downing looked like a broken man. Something had snapped inside him this morning when he had walked around that desk and seen the same carnage he had hoped to leave behind him on the battlefield.

Damn the bastard who had pulled that trigger. How many lives had he destroyed within a matter of seconds?

She was going to get him. If not for Jonathan or Beverly Winston, for Hank Downing.

By the time Savannah returned to the morgue day shift personnel had left and the obnoxious clerk had been replaced by an eager, bright-eyed rookie who was thrilled spitless to be a part of the SCPD. The simple act of offering her the clipboard to sign in seemed to make him unnaturally happy. Ah, yes . . . she remembered those days when she had been deliriously in love with the idea of being a real, honest-to-god cop. Great days.

Both of them.

Disillusionment had come swiftly.

Savannah glanced at the log. No, Dr. Liu hadn't signed out yet. Good.

She left the rookie, guarding his post like a pit bull with a ham bone, and walked down the hall toward the examination room.

The door stood open a crack, so she knocked twice, then stuck her head inside.

"Jennifer?"

The deputy coroner sat on a high stool at one of the stainless-steel tables, her head cocked sideways as she peered into a microscope. "Savannah . . . did you bring me a hamburger and a chocolate shake?"

"Didn't know you wanted one."

Jennifer looked up and sighed, running her hand along the back of her neck. "The hamburger was just a whim," she said, "but the chocolate shake is mandatory. You know, a PMS thing."

Savannah laughed, enjoying a rare moment of female camaraderie. PMS wasn't a subject that was open for discussion with the male sector of the department. Those members of the masculine persuasion were far too quick to blame any female opinion they didn't support on Premenstrual Syndrome. More than once Savannah had told them that the initials stood for "Putting up with Men's Shit."

"Hey, I know what you mean," she said as she slid onto a stool beside the doctor. "During that last week if it wasn't for naps and double Dutch chocolate ice cream, life wouldn't be worth living."

Reaching into her purse, Savannah pulled out an enormous Snickers bar and handed it to Dr. Liu. Three seconds later the candy had been unwrapped and the first section devoured.

"Thanks," she said, closing her eyes in ecstasy as she chewed. "You saved my life."

Savannah shrugged. "Ah . . . you'd do it for me."

"Don't be so sure." The doctor laughed. "Chocolate cravings

and water retention don't exactly bring out the best in my character."

Nodding toward the corpse, which still lay on the metal table, covered with a sheet, Savannah said, "So, what have you got for me so far?"

"He got popped in the morning . . . probably around fourish. Other than that, I don't have much yet. Don't rush me. I'm a lady who takes her time and does it right." Jennifer lifted one delicate eyebrow suggestively. If anyone else had said the same thing with that gleam in her eye, Savannah would have thought she was attempting to be risque. But Dr. Liu seemed so . . . intelligent . . . so elegant . . . so unsullied by anything so mundane as a roll in the hay.

Pointing to a plastic tray at the end of the long table, the doctor said, "I'm finishing up with the clothing and personal effects now. You can fondle those, if you want."

Savannah gave her a curious sideways glance. Yep, no doubt about it: Dr. Liu was being feisty. Hmm-m-m . . . she'd have to think about what that might mean . . . later.

"Pretty tattered stuff," Savannah said as she walked to the tray and studied its blood- and flesh-stained contents: Winston's clothing, gaudy jewelry, snakeskin wallet, and grossly overburdened money clip. The motive had definitely not been robbery.

"Hey, this could be helpful," she said when she saw the credit card–sized personal organizer. A device like this often contained a wealth of information about its owner, including telephone numbers, addresses, important dates and appointments.

Jennifer, who had returned her attention to the microscope, glanced up and shook her head. "I don't think so. I'm afraid it bit the dust along with Mr. Winston."

"Damn." Savannah punched the *On* button with the predicted lack of response. "New-fangled gadgets . . . they're a bite in the ass. There's not even a broken clock face that can show us the exact moment it was shot."

She picked up the diamond-studded Rolex from the tray. In keeping with every other irritating element of her day, it was ticking away happily, efficient as ever. Only the spattering of blood suggested that it had been present during the crime. In all the years she had worked homicide, only once had Savannah found a stopped watch on a victim, damaged at the moment of the attack. This "blessing" had thrown the entire case into confusion. Mickey Mouse's white-gloved hands had indicated that the murder had happened nine hours before the coroner's estimation. Savannah had spent two weeks trudging through the mire of contradictory information only to find out that the victim had worn the watch only for sentimental reasons. Mickey hadn't worked for years.

Moving on to the snakeskin wallet, Savannah examined its contents. They were depressingly predictable. Gold cards, driver's license, several business cards bearing telephone numbers that had been written in various feminine styles.

Savannah scribbled down each name and number, noting that none of them appeared to be male. Interesting. Any man with nearly a dozen women's cards in his wallet would inevitably have some problems in his marriage, which might explain Beverly's somewhat cool acceptance of his death.

"When you get finished there take a look at this," Jennifer said, still peering through the microscope.

"Interesting?" Savannah asked, her curiosity aroused by the barely subdued enthusiasm in Jennifer's voice.

Jennifer grinned, stood, and vacated her stool, making room for Savannah. "Oh . . . I think you'll think so."

Climbing onto the stool, Savannah studied the strange specimen that lay on the slide. It appeared to be a soggy, blood-soaked mass of something that had, perhaps, once been pink. "What is it? Or should I ask, 'What *was* it?' "

"A piece of paper. I found it in the right pocket of his slacks."

"Right leg?" Savannah asked, wincing as she remembered the mangled thigh.

"Yeah, that's why there's so much damage to the document, but if you look closely, you can see what it was."

Document? It seemed a strange choice of words for her to make. *Probably another list of women's phone numbers, maybe rated with stars*, she thought as she leaned over the scope and tried to look through it.

She wasn't big on microscopes. In fact, she had maintained a major grudge against them since ninth-grade biology class, when Mr. Reeves had insisted that they look with *both* eyes, cocking their heads to one side. She had never gotten the hang of it and had, therefore, received a D in the class.

But Mr. Reeves had kicked the proverbial bucket years ago and was peacefully interred in a Georgia cemetery . . . God rest his dear soul. So, with a delicious surge of defiance, she closed her left eye tightly and stared down the scope with her right.

At first she wasn't sure what she was seeing. It appeared to be an even intermeshing of fibers, with black splotches. Then she reminded herself that the substance was being magnified many times over.

The dark spots were letters.

Slowly, as she stared, they began to form into some semblance of order. "R . . ." she said. "Is that an R?"

"Good girl," Jennifer said, sounding a bit like Mr. Reeves had on one of his better days.

"And an E . . . S . . . TR . . . A . . . restaurant? Is that it? No, wait a minute . . ." The rest came into focus clearly. She lifted her head and stared at Jennifer, who looked both pleased and intrigued. "It's a restraining order," she said.

"That's right. I've been able to figure out enough of the rest to know that it was granted *to* him, not *against* him."

"A *man* getting a restraining order?" Savannah shook her head thoughtfully. "I don't mean to sound sexist, but most restraining orders are issued to women to keep men away from them. And they're usually only granted if the plaintiff believes her life is in danger." She looked through the scope again. "Can you tell who it was issued against?"

"Sorry. The shotgun blast obliterated that small piece of information when it took off most of his leg."

"I wonder," Savannah said, contemplating this new bit of information that just might help her wind up this case quickly. "I wonder . . . who was Jonathan Winston so afraid of?"

CHAPTER FIVE

Savannah scowled at the computer monitor, daring it to give her any more nonsense in the form of inaccessible files, disappearing cursors, or garbled rows of colorful and exotic symbols that only made sense to someone whose first language was computerese. "Don't you be temperamental with me, you ornery, no-good, cantankerous piece of—"

"Now, now," scolded a deep voice over her shoulder. "Don't let the captain hear you criticizing his new toy." Dirk glanced up and down the row of desks, but there was no one close enough to be within earshot. "Honestly, between you and me I think he's having an unnatural relationship with this machine."

Savannah grinned, glad to see him. Even though she complained about Dirk constantly, she genuinely missed him and his caustic sense of humor when he wasn't around. "Oh, really? I didn't know such things were possible between a man and his computer."

"Haven't you ever heard of virtual reality?"

"Of course I have. Where do you think I've been, under a rock? Everyone's heard about virtual reality."

Actually, she had only seen one short news segment about a weird computerized machine that could replace sexual intimacy for the human race . . . some sort of outfit you could slide into that would basically feel you up, or some such nonsense. But she didn't dare share the fact that her knowledge of the subject was so limited. Undoubtedly Dirk would feel it was his life's mission to inform her of every sordid detail.

Pulling his desk chair over to hers, he plopped down and leaned toward her, his elbows on his spread knees. "Well, rumor has it that the captain's got this funky black rubber suit hanging in his office closet. It's got wires and plugs sticking out all over—especially in the groin area. And sometimes when he tells Mary Lou to hold all his calls he pulls the blinds on his office door, takes out the suit, and . . ."

She waited patiently for him to continue, refusing to ask for what was coming next. He would tell her whether she asked or not; he always did, after making her wait, her curiosity whetted. But the anticipation was never worth the meager payoff.

"And I understand that he . . . shall we say . . . partakes of some rather steamy, better-than-life erotic experiences that bring new meaning to the term 'interactive.' "

Savannah fixed him with a baleful eye. "I don't want to hear this. I've had the day from hell so far, and I don't want to make it any worse by conjuring up lurid images of the captain and his . . . interactive wet suit."

"They say someday he'll short the whole thing out and fry the old mountain oysters . . . if you know what I mean."

"I was raised in the South, Dirk. Of course I know what you mean. But I'd rather not think about the captain's mountain oysters, if you don't mind."

"Hey, don't knock it. The day is coming when we'll all have virtual reality computers right at home. Just think: no more singles' bars, no escort services or blind dates. We won't have to worry about knocking somebody up or having them hassle us about the 'commitment thing.' "

Savannah stared blankly at him, only half hearing what he was saying.

"Just think, Savannah; you could program me into your system, summon me up any time you want, and make me your love slave."

She lifted one eyebrow and gave him a hey-why-are-you-playing-in-that-mud-puddle-you-stupid-boy? look.

"If I desire the company of a gentleman," she said in her most sultry Georgia drawl, "I don't need to employ the artificial affections of an interactive computer, thank you. Personally I think it's pathetic that anyone would try to substitute a machine for what only a flesh-and-blood, living being can do for you."

A brief vision flashed through her mind—the black-and-chrome "personal massager" with full ensemble of attachments stashed under her bed. But her mind expertly skirted the issue. A blinding moment of self-realization could sure knock the hell out of a good argument.

"Would you mind terribly if we changed the subject?" She returned her attention to the computer monitor and again her fingers flew over the keyboard.

"Sure, no problem." Dirk leaned back in his chair and lit up a cigarette. Savannah could have told him to put it out; the city had passed a no-smoking ordinance a year earlier, banning smoking in public places. The rule was seldom followed inside the police station. In general, cops smoked more than anyone she knew . . . except firemen.

But she decided not to chastise Dirk this time. Something told her that the two of them were going to be having a bit of a tiff in a few minutes anyway; no point in starting early.

"So . . . whatcha working on?" he asked, leaning over her shoulder and peering at the screen. "Restraining orders? Why are you going through those files?"

Here goes nothin', she thought. Dirk steadfastly held the opinion that successfully solved homicide cases boosted one up the rickety ladder of departmental politics. And Dirk intended to retire in a few years as high on those rungs as possible. He wasn't going to gracefully accept the fact that she had been assigned to a homicide case—an *important* homicide—without him.

"I'm checking out a lead on a case," she said with pseudo-nonchalance. "No big deal."

"Restraining order? On that guy we busted this morning? The girlfriend didn't act like she had a restraining order against him."

Savannah cleared her throat, her eyes trained on the screen. "She didn't . . . at least I don't think she did. It's for the Winston case."

"Winston? Jonathan Winston's murder?"

"Yeah. That's the one. Bloss stuck me on it this morning. I think it's going to be a real pain."

She continued to stare at the monitor, aware of the rapid acceleration of his breathing beside her. The silence thickened around them, the only sound being the click of her fingertips on the keyboard as she filtered through the information in the court records.

"Bloss gave *you* the Winston case? You alone?"

She could hear the bitterness and envy in his voice, and her temper began to rise along with his. Who did he think he was, anyway? So she had been given a priority case. So what? He didn't seem to mind when *he* was given opportunities that she wasn't invited to share.

"I asked Bloss to include you in this," she said, trying not to sound as though she wanted to throttle him for his silly, adolescent jealousy. "But he said you were busy with something else."

"Oh, yes, I've been busting my balls on something really big, all right. I've been filling out all those goddamned forms and writing the reports for that two-bit bust we did this morning. I thought you were home, resting, taking it easy. I thought I was doing you a favor."

"You were," she said, fighting the urge to snatch the remaining hairs off his head. "And I really appreciate it."

"Sure. You show it by hogging this case—probably the biggest homicide investigation of the year—all to yourself. I'm covering the bases for you, and you're cutting me out?"

Savannah slammed down her palm on her desk, upsetting the mug that held her pens and pencils. Whirling around to face him squarely, she said, "Damn it, Dirk, grow up. I didn't cut you out of anything and you know it. I didn't ask for this case, I don't want this case, I wish I could give you this case and you could file it in the general vicinity of those damned hemorrhoids that you keep griping about. But I can't. That's the way it is. Live with it."

He glared at her silently for several seconds. She could see he was searching for an appropriate retort. But one of Dirk's most endearing qualities was his inability to be articulate when he was steamed about something. Winning an argument with him was almost too easy to be satisfying.

After opening and closing his mouth several times like a landed carp he stood so abruptly that his chair rolled back against his desk with a thud. "You're a real bitch, Reid. You know that?"

"Ah . . . yes, I believe you told me that earlier this evening."

"But I didn't mean it then."

His face was flushed a shade of red that he usually needed a couple of belts of Jack Daniel's to achieve. She watched as he stomped to the door, lower lip protruding, and she was reminded of her little nephews when they had been told they couldn't have seconds of Rocky Road ice cream.

"Hey, Dirk," she called after him.

He paused at the door and turned around. "Yeah?" he said gruffly.

She screwed up her face in an equally childish expression and stuck out her tongue at him. "Nanny, nanny, boo, boo. . . ."

"Fuck you, Reid."

The glass in the door and the windows rattled as he slammed the door behind him.

"Hmm-mm-mmm, a three point seven, I'd say," she mused, then returned to the computer. "Let's see now . . . where was I?"

Ah, yes. There it was—the list of restraining orders granted since the beginning of the year. She ran a quick check for "Winston" and found it almost immediately. Opening the file, she perused the particulars.

Jonathan Winston
1553 Prescott Way, Apt. #23

An apartment down on the beach? The old Harrington mansion was at the top of the foothills, overlooking the city. Apparently Beverly hadn't been kidding when she'd said the marriage wasn't going that well.

Threatened with bodily harm . . .

"Yeah, no shit," Savannah said, thinking about the grisly condition of the corpse. She glanced at the date and felt a small tingle of satisfaction. Ten days ago.

Hereby requests and is granted
the court's protection from one . . .

"My God," Savannah whispered, staring at the name on the screen before her. She flipped off the monitor but continued to sit there as she mulled over the significance of what she had just seen.

Slowly, woodenly, she rose and picked up her purse and jacket. "Damn," she said as she headed for the door. Of all the names she could have found on that screen the last one she had wanted to see was Councilwoman Beverly Winston's.

Normally if Savannah drove down El Camino Boulevard toward the harborfront area at sunset, she took a moment to appreciate the beauty of the drive. The picture most often used on San Carmelita postcards, the scene had never lost its power to make Savannah grateful she lived in Southern California. These sunsets were almost worth giving up the seasons in Georgia. Almost.

Uniform rows of giant palms lined the street, black silhouettes against the turquoise-and-coral marbled skies. The boulevard wound downward to the pier, which stretched even farther into the sea . . . as far as you could walk into the Pacific without getting your feet—and a lot more—wet.

Once the city pier had been much longer, but a sizable tropical storm had rolled onto the shore several years earlier, flooding the first three blocks of seaside properties and ripping away the end of the pier. The structure looked as if it had been ravaged by an enormous shark.

For several long years the remaining portion of the pier had been closed to the public, who didn't seem to mind its unstable condition. Dedicated fishermen insisted it was their right to fall off the jagged end if they damn well pleased. The pier had always been the best place in the county to catch a fresh seafood dinner.

Last year Beverly Winston had led a campaign to get enough money to repair what had remained of the pier, so that it once again would be accessible to the public. As Savannah drove along the waterfront, she saw families staked out along its length, reeling in their catches, enjoying a bit of the sea's bounty, and, more importantly, each other's company.

"Jonathan Winston was afraid his wife was going to kill him," Judge Wyckoff had told Savannah when she had called him to ask about the restraining order. "Winston told the court he had uncovered some 'indiscretions' on his wife's part and she had threatened to murder him if he exposed her."

"How did Beverly Winston respond to the charges?" she had asked him.

"She didn't admit or deny them, but she agreed to stay away from him. They were already legally separated, and he had moved out of the mansion and into an apartment."

As Savannah pulled into the parking lot of the exclusive apartment complex, she tried to reconcile the image of the Councilwoman Beverly Winston who had cared passionately whether the city's kids were able to fish on the pier with their parents with the woman who could have threatened to murder her husband. A concerned, dignified humanitarian—a raging, vindictive wife. The two just didn't mesh.

But the contrasting images did have one thing in common, Savannah thought as she left her car and headed for the apartment foyer with its rockery atrium complete with a pool of koi.

Whatever role she played the one trait Beverly Winston always displayed was passion. And, being one herself, Savannah had always had a soft spot for passionate women. It was going to be tough, bringing a woman like that down. In more ways than one.

The more ritzy the apartment, the more difficult the management, Savannah thought as she slid the borrowed key into Jonathan Winston's front door. The supers in places like this always took their jobs oh so seriously, to the point of being pains in the ass.

After examining Savannah's badge for what seemed like ten minutes, the man had called 911 to verify its authenticity. When he had finally connected with the desk sergeant he had demanded a full physical description of Savannah and argued with the sergeant as to whether Savannah's eyes were green or blue. Yes . . . a definite pain.

Key finally secured and door opened, Savannah was ready to search the recently departed's apartment. On one arm she carried an enormous canvas tote, used to collect any materials she thought might aid in her investigation: address books, photos, letters, bills, etc.

In a rare moment of cooperation the super had verified that

Jonathan lived alone. Nevertheless, Savannah entered the dimly lit apartment with caution.

As her eyes adjusted to the subdued orange sunlight that filtered through the vertical blinds, she took in the contemporary furnishings: the gray leather sofa, the chrome-and-glass cocktail table, the marble fireplace and black lacquer dining set. Red and blue cushions thrown on the sofa, chairs, and around the hearth added a bit of color, as did the Oriental rug.

Not bad . . . for a bachelor's pad, she thought as she stepped into the room and closed the door behind her. Apparently Mr. J. Winston was doing okay financially on his own, or the missus was forking over some pretty hefty alimony.

She walked over to the sliding glass doors and pulled the blinds open to a breathtaking view. Below, only a few yards away, the waves rolled up onto the beach, leaving lacy rows of foam to fizzle into the sand. The town of San Carmelita curved to the right, a graceful inlet, a quiet harbor. The entire city was visible: the copper dome on the county courthouse, the tiled roofs, the old adobe mission. Everywhere white stucco gleamed golden in the light of the setting sun.

Leaving the canvas tote on the floor, Savannah turned back to the room and perused its contents in the additional light. Jonathan Winston had kept his apartment as pristine as his showroom. Every bit of glass sparkled, free of dust or fingerprints. Every cushion was carefully placed at just the right angle, as were the magazines on the cocktail table. The dove gray Berber carpeting showed no soil, no signs of traffic. Even Granny Reid—whose kitchen floors were rumored to be so immaculate you could eat off them—would have been impressed, Savannah decided.

Not one item in the room was out of place, nothing . . . except . . .

The videotapes.

In the ebony-and-chrome entertainment center everything was perfect, compact discs neatly filed, audiotapes arranged alphabetically. But in direct contrast to the usual exacting placement the videotapes were a mess. Some lay on their sides, some on the wrong end. Some protruded from the front of the display; others were shoved to the back.

While Savannah employed much the same "system" at home, she didn't think the misarrangement was in keeping with what she had seen of Jonathan Winston's preferences. And he seemed to have been a man who indulged any and all of his preferences.

As she moved toward the entertainment center to rummage through the videos, she heard a small, almost inaudible shuffling sound behind her. Less than a second later she had whirled around, the Beretta in her hand.

"San Carmelita Police Department," she declared in a voice that projected more courage and authority than she ever felt at times like this. "Walk out here. Hands on top of your head. Now!"

They never did it; they never froze, halted, dropped it, or came to you just because you told them to. But there was always a chance.

Ready for anything, expecting nothing, she waited. Again she heard the soft shuffling sound—probably sneakers on carpet. Louder. Heading away from her toward the back of the apartment.

Taking cover behind each doorway and wall along the way, she followed the footsteps. "Freeze, damn it!" she said, "or I swear, I'll shoot you!"

Her threat was an empty one, considering that she hadn't even seen the subject in question. Rather than pausing, the footsteps picked up the pace as her quarry headed for the kitchen and the back door of the apartment.

Savannah stuck her head around the kitchen doorframe. The room was empty. No sign of the "visitor," other than a door that stood wide open to a service hallway and stairwell.

Hurrying through the door, Savannah peered up and down the stairwell but saw no one, nothing. Whoever had been there had gotten away.

"Shit!" she said, staring down the empty staircase that zigzagged back and forth from floor to floor. Savannah had a personal rule: She hated running, felt it was an unnecessary drain of energy. If they made her run, she took them in. It was a matter of honor . . . maybe of vengeance. Either way, it was a standard she lived by.

"I saw you, you bastard, and I'll get you, sooner or later," she shouted down the stairs. Her voice reverberated from wall to wall with a resonance usually associated with Hollywood-created deities.

She hurried back into the apartment and over to the window, hoping to see the intruder if he passed through the parking lot. But after a couple of minutes she decided he had been intelligent enough to take another route.

As she returned to the kitchen to secure the back door against any future visitations, her foot collided with an object, sending it skidding across the floor. She bent over to see what it was . . . a videotape. Reaching for it, she reconsidered and pulled a pair of surgical gloves from her jacket pocket. After putting them on she picked up the tape, taking care not to smudge any prints.

The box was a generic black container, used to hold personal videotapes. Nothing had been written on the white label affixed to the spine. Gently, she opened the box and found an equally unmarked tape. She recognized the style, a special type of videotape that was used in a camcorder, then modified to be viewed in a VCR.

Was this what the intruder had been after? Had she interrupted him rifling through the tapes in the living room? That would explain the lack of neatness and order in the entertainment center.

How convenient, she thought as she dropped the tape into the canvas tote. *How nice to have evidence just dropped into your lap*.

She decided not to get too excited about it. Instead she would continue as she had intended when she had arrived. She would gather the photos and documents that might give her an insight into Jonathan Winston's life.

The tape was interesting; she looked forward to viewing it. But Savannah had learned long ago never to trust anything in this business that came too easily.

CHAPTER SIX

Savannah sat in her well-worn, well-loved easy chair, an over-stuffed, wingbacked affair, covered with a soft mauve chintz. Propped up by rose-printed, satin-fringed pillows, Savannah was surrounded by her favorite things: her terry-cloth robe, her new silk pajamas from Victoria's Secret, Diamante, Cleopatra, and a dish of sumptuous dessert. But she was still in a lousy frame of mind.

Seldom did she experience any mood so heavy that it couldn't be lifted by a hefty slice of chocolate cheesecake, drizzled with Chambord. The addition of the delicate raspberry liqueur had been her latest hedonistic discovery. A culinary triumph of this magnitude could usually keep her in high spirits for at least a week. But it had been a week and a half, and she decided it was time to resume her never-ending quest for what she fondly called,

"The Consummate Consumption." Cheesecake just wasn't cutting it anymore.

"Sorry, ladies," she told the cats, who were intertwining themselves between her arms and legs, rubbing, purring, begging for a bite. "This is *definitely* people food. I didn't ask for any of your salmon liver pâté . . . or whatever that foul-smelling stuff was. Go away."

To her surprise they obeyed—a rare occurrence.

No sooner had they disappeared into the kitchen than she found she missed their company. Apparently this was one of those nights when it didn't feel so good to be alone, free, independent, and unencumbered by anything so stifling as a significant relationship.

She had to admit that sometimes after a day like today it would be nice to have someone to come home to. Someone to snuggle with, make love with, hell . . . even fight with. Just someone.

As she took the last bite of cheesecake and licked every molecule from the fork, she resigned herself to the fact that she was going to have to view the videotape that lay on her coffee table. Usually she would have been eager to run through the door, shove the tape into the VCR, and see what she had. But tonight she had postponed the moment with dinner, the bubble bath she had missed earlier, and dessert.

It's time, kid, she told herself as she rose from her chair, slipped on a surgical glove, and picked up the tape. *Let's watch a little home movie. Probably something boring—vacation shots, a baby crawling or with food running down its face.* One could always hope.

Was she really hoping that was all it was? Even the thought confused her. Savannah had always been proud of her high level of ambition and tenacity when it came to her job. Since when did she find herself hoping she wouldn't find a lead? Maybe she was getting soft in her old age.

Having popped in the tape, she returned to her chair and picked up the remote from the pie-crust end table beside her.

"Let 'er rip," she whispered as she punched the button and leaned back in the chair, ready for Disneyland footage, proud parent memorabilia, maybe marriage vows or . . .

As she had expected, it was the *or*. Home video, shot through the windshield of a car. On the long black hood of the automobile sat a graceful, feline ornament. Jaguar.

"Guess whose car," she said sarcastically. "Guess whose tape."

The date in the lower right corner showed that it had been taped about three weeks earlier. *Mmm-m-m, recent stuff*, she thought.

The videographer was scanning what appeared to be a parking lot in a fairly rural area. Although the site looked familiar, she couldn't quite place it.

His camera movements were jerky, disconcerting, sweeping from side to side too quickly. Martin Scorcese he wasn't, she decided.

But he did know how to use a zoom lens. Pointing the camera at a large sign at the edge of the lot, he pulled in the image, close enough for every detail to be perfectly clear. Now Savannah remembered. Of course . . . the Blue Moon Motel, one of the classier no-tell motels on the edge of town.

How predictable, she thought. *And, gee, I wonder . . . who do you suppose he's hoping to catch on film?*

Like a prompt, unwelcome answer to her rhetorical question, the photographer zoomed in on room 136. The blue door with its white crescent moon and assorted stars opened, and a couple emerged.

At first Savannah didn't recognize them. The woman wore jeans, sneakers, and an oversized sweatshirt, her hair pulled back into a ponytail. Her escort's attire was equally casual. Their moods seemed to match their clothing as they walked along, arm in arm, a distinctive bounce to their step. They talked animatedly, the man bending his head to listen to the woman, then laughing heartily at what she had said.

They were in love.

Savannah watched, her heart thudding against her ribs, her palms damp, as the man ushered her to a car and handed her gently inside. He gave her a leisurely kiss on the lips, then a quick peck on the forehead.

She had never seen these people like this . . . at ease, rested, happy, looking at least ten years younger. Love could do that for you when it was the real thing.

The woman drove away; he did the same, the camera recording both departures. Then the screen turned to snow.

Mechanically, Savannah clicked the remote to stop, then rewound the tape. She wouldn't watch it again. Having seen it once, she felt as though she had invaded the privacy of two special people. Two special people with a very special relationship.

As Savannah carefully returned the valuable piece of evidence to its black case, she put her emotions and her respect for the individuals aside for the moment. So . . . Beverly Winston had found happiness and love in the arms of a man other than her husband. And after ten years of being a widower, grieving for the wife he had loved and lost, Police Chief Norman Hillquist had found a companion to fill that empty place in his heart. No wonder he had been so adamant that she not question Beverly until he had talked to her first. No wonder he had been so protective of her.

Savannah had no intention of judging their actions.

But she *did* have to consider what this tape meant in terms of her investigation. No matter how she looked at it, Savannah could come to only one conclusion: with every passing moment it appeared more and more likely that Beverly Winston might have murdered her own husband.

And things weren't looking so good for Police Chief Norman Hillquist, either.

"Are you sure, Jennifer?" Savannah asked as she leaned over the coroner's shoulder and stared at the black case and videotape as though seeing it for the first time.

"That's right," Dr. Liu said as she flipped off the lighted magnifying glass and sat back on her stool. "There's only one set of prints on the whole thing. And we have a definite match with Beverly Winston's DMV thumb print."

"Only one set . . . on the case or the tape?" Savannah asked.

"The case. There, near the spine." She pointed to the white powder dust in that vicinity.

"Isn't that a little weird? I mean, what are the chances there would be no prints at all on the tape and only one person's on the case?"

The doctor shrugged and tucked a strand of her black hair into the brightly colored scarf that held it away from her face. "Almost nil, I would think. Someone had to stick the tape into the case. Someone would have had to touch it."

"Or wipe it clean and then use gloves or a cloth," Savannah added.

"I have to tell you, there aren't many times when I see an

object with only one person's prints on it either. Most things go through several people's hands in the course of their existence. Or, if something is handled by one person, they usually touch it more than just once."

Savannah sighed; she was tired already, and it was only nine o'clock in the morning. The cream-filled, chocolate-dipped Napoleon she had eaten for breakfast must have worn off. Time for another.

"Anything new on the body?" she asked, nodding toward the corpse, which was now in a drawer that was pulled halfway out of the cold storage.

"Blood tests are in," Jennifer replied, consulting her clipboard. "High alcohol content, well above the legal limit for driving. No drugs."

"So, Mr. Winston wasn't high, but he was definitely soused when he got it?"

"To put it indelicately . . . yes. He was positively pickled."

"Good," Savannah said thoughtfully. "Maybe the booze took the edge off. Anything else?"

"Just the stuff I told you on the phone last night. Time of death, around four in the morning. Cause, the one shot to the head. He was dead before he hit the ground."

"And the other two?"

"Just for effect, I guess."

"Yeah, quite effective." Savannah studied the sheath of stapled reports in her hand, a compilation of the lab tech's findings.

Or lack of them.

Unfortunately, most of Mr. Downing's cleaning had done away with everything outside of Jonathan's office. Even the contents of the vacuum bag were of little use; they could have been a month old. Many people could have come and gone through the showroom in the course of a month; far too many to consider every one of them a serious suspect.

Inside Jonathan's office they had found a number of fingerprints, and they were in the process of identifying as many as possible. So far they had collected prints that matched Jonathan's, Beverly's, Mr. Downing's, a pizza delivery man who had brought Jonathan dinner at about nine the previous evening, and a few others they hadn't yet paired with their owners.

Having read that there were no discernible prints on the doorknobs of the building, Savannah wasn't hopeful that the fingerprint route would lead them anywhere. If the murderer was smart enough not to leave prints on the door, he probably wasn't so stupid as to lay down a nice, clear set on a black lacquer desktop.

No signs of forced entry. Savannah supposed that Jonathan could have let in the killer but she didn't think so. A shotgun wasn't easy to just slip under your T-shirt and smuggle inside. Somehow she figured the murderer had sneaked in uninvited. Either Jonathan had forgotten and had left the door unlocked or he'd had a key.

As with all shotgun blasts, there was no single bullet to run through the ballistic tests.

"You know, Jennifer," Savannah said, frowning down at the report, "I don't think I'm going to have a lot of physical evidence to help me along here."

"Oh, well . . ." Jennifer shrugged and gave her a crooked smile. ". . . when did you ever see a case solved with a smoking gun or a perfect set of fingerprints?"

"Only in the movies, my dear Dr. Jennifer," Savannah replied dryly. "Only in the movies."

As Savannah guided the slightly past its prime, red Camaro along the curving foothill road, the altitude increased with every switchback, and so did the price of the real estate. She had moved from the young upwardly mobile types past the professional doctors, lawyers and Indian chiefs areas, into the I-don't-know-what-these-people-do-but-they-must-make-a-helluva-lot-of-money-doing-it neighborhood.

Her poor car was beginning to cough and sputter, as it often did when asked to do more than coast blithely downhill. Besides, she could feel its embarrassment. The Volvo, BMW, and Mercedes areas had been tough enough, but in this neighborhood there wasn't an automobile in sight. She supposed it was considered vulgar and common to leave one's vehicle out of the garage.

Long before she reached the top of the hill Savannah could see the graceful slate roof of the old Harrington mansion, rising above the pines that surrounded the place. When she had first seen the Tudor mansion ten years earlier she had thought it the most elegant, gracious house she had ever seen.

Today, as she rounded the final curve and looked up at the mansion, towering over her with its sloping lawns, herringbone brick walls covered with ivy, and mullioned windows, she felt a pang of sadness.

The master of the house, the lord of the manor, was dead. Worse still, murdered. Did the house know? Did it care? She supposed in its more than one hundred and fifty years it had seen its share of births and deaths as the generations came and went. The natural scheme of things.

But there was nothing natural about murder.

Savannah was sure that the act of robbing another of life badly upset the cosmic balance. While she wasn't sure about all the ins and outs of theology, divine retribution, or karma, she had seen firsthand how much sorrow that particular sin brought into the world. And she knew she would never want to be responsible for any act that caused that much pain.

Finding the ornate, wrought-iron entrance gates open, she guided the Camaro down the brick driveway to the circular area in front of the house.

"Now, please," she whispered to the car as she cut the key, "be on your best behavior. Don't drip oil . . . *please* don't drip *any* of your bodily fluids on this driveway. No transmission fluid, brake fluid, antifreeze, or rusty water."

As though in defiance, the car backfired, snorted, and bellowed black smoke out its rear end before the engine finally died.

"Thanks for not embarrassing me," she said sarcastically as she slammed the door.

After thumping on the heavy, carved teak doorway with the enormous brass lion knocker she was ushered inside by a pretty young woman wearing a traditional black-and-white maid's uniform.

"I'll tell Mrs. Beverly that you're here, ma'am," she said, leaving Savannah standing in the marble-tiled foyer.

As she waited, Savannah studied the grandfather clock, which must have been eight feet tall, the antique carousel horse mounted on a brass pole, and the waist-high Oriental vases that, even to her untrained eye, suggested an exorbitant price tag. Class. Good taste. Money, money, money.

Must be nice, she thought, feeling a small jab of envy. Beverly Winston had been given all of this. She had been born and raised in this grand house and probably took it all for granted.

Then Savannah reminded herself why she was here, and she decided that, all things considered, she was happy to be living her own life, rather than Beverly Winston's. Money didn't cushion one from the harsher realities of life. In matters of death and dying, the privileged and underprivileged suffered alike.

"Mrs. Beverly will see you now," the maid said as she scurried back into the foyer. "She's in the library. This way, please."

The library . . . Oh yes . . . didn't everyone have a library? Savannah had one and a half. Of course, they were also called bathrooms, johns . . . poop decks. The library bit was just a joke, fostered by an overabundance of reading materials piled on shelves and in baskets around the toilet.

But this was a *real* library with real shelves and real books, and a blazing fireplace and fresh day lilies in another expensive vase. And, of course, the lady of the house, looking every bit the part.

Beverly Winston reclined gracefully on a chaise lounge of maroon watered silk. In her hand she held a delicate porcelain cup, the matching saucer in the other hand. She wore a smoke-pink satin robe, which was the picture of elegance, but the color didn't flatter her this morning.

Although it was nearly ten-thirty, she looked as though she had just risen from bed. Her face was puffy, her eyes red and swollen, her skin an unhealthy combination of sallow and gray.

"Good morning, Savannah," she said, starting to rise.

Savannah held up one hand. "No, please. Don't get up for me. I'll just take a seat right . . . ?"

"Anywhere you like," she replied, waving a graceful hand to indicate several possibilities.

Savannah chose the end of the Victorian diamond-tucked sofa that was nearest Beverly and sat down.

"Would you like some tea?" Beverly asked. "It's jasmine. I bought it in San Francisco the last time I was there."

Usually Savannah refused food or drink when visiting a

home on business, but the delicate flower aroma of the tea beckoned to her.

"I'd love some, thank you."

Beverly smiled, pleased at her acceptance. "Leah, would you please get a cup of tea for our guest?" she asked the maid, who promptly disappeared.

Savannah postponed speaking of anything significant until Leah had returned with the tea and left again, sliding the dark wooden doors closed behind her.

"How are you doing, Beverly?" she asked, genuine concern in her voice.

"Who wants to know?" the councilwoman replied with a half smile. "The police detective or—"

"Just another woman who figures you must be going through hell and back," Savannah interjected.

For a long moment Beverly searched Savannah's eyes. Apparently finding the sincerity she was seeking, she replied, "How am I doing? Terrible. I didn't get any sleep at all last night just thinking about Jonathan . . . what he must have gone through . . . what we'll all have to go through because of him. It's such a sad waste."

"I'm so sorry," Savannah said, setting her tea on the side table next to the sofa. "I've lost loved ones myself, and I know there's nothing anyone can say or do to make it better."

"Is that why you came to see me this morning, Savannah?" Beverly asked, a wry smile on her tired face. She picked up the fringed end of her sash and ran the silk threads through her fingers. "Are you here to offer your condolences, Detective Reid?"

Savannah sighed. "Well, since you put it that way, I'm afraid not. I have to ask you a few questions."

"I'm sure you have quite a few," she muttered, taking another sip of her tea. "What took you so long?"

"I . . . uh . . ."

"Oh, yes, Norman interfered, didn't he? I told him not to, tried to convince him it was pointless, but he thought he was helping me. You know how men are."

Savannah couldn't help being taken aback by her candor in mentioning the chief. She had intended to work up to the subject gradually, after winning a bit of her confidence. But Beverly was acting as though their relationship was a given.

"My, my," the councilwoman said with a self-satisfied smile. "I do believe I've shocked you, Detective Reid." With a small, tired sigh, she leaned her head back on the chaise and closed her eyes for a moment. When she opened them she looked directly at Savannah, and again Savannah was unnerved by her straightforward, open manner. Most people in Beverly Winston's position were extremely guarded and defensive.

Either she was an exceptionally honest person or she was exceedingly cunning.

"Savannah, I'm not going to bullshit you," she said, her voice gravelly with fatigue. "I have nothing to gain by lying to you or holding anything back. You're a good detective and a smart woman; I can see that. Before you're finished you're going to know my life, inside and out; the things I'm proud of, the things I'm not. So ask me whatever you want. If I give you an answer, it will be the truth. If I don't want to tell you, I'll just say it's none of your business."

"Fair enough." Savannah lined up her mental list of questions and started with the most obvious. "Did you kill your husband?"

"No."

Well, that was short and to the point. Savannah wondered if all her answers would be so abbreviated.

"Did you pay someone to do it?"

"No."

"Did you ask, beg, persuade, bribe, or threaten anyone to do it?"

"No." She paused, then added, "I must admit the thought crossed my mind more than once. Jonathan could be an extremely irritating man."

"In what way?"

"He fooled around on me, he gambled more than he could afford, he drank like a fish, he was lazy and irresponsible, insensitive, and selfish. Other than that, he was a gem."

"You sound bitter," Savannah said softly.

"Yes, but that's only because I loved him so much. Some people think that hatred is the opposite of love. Of course it isn't; indifference is. As long as you have the capacity to love someone, you can hate them, too. Strong emotion is the same, no matter which way the river flows."

"If he was that worthless, why did you love him? Why did you marry him?"

In answer to the question Beverly rose from the chaise and walked over to the mantel, which displayed an array of photos in silver and inlaid hardwood frames. Picking up two of the pictures, she brought them to Savannah and placed the first one in her hand.

"These people were my parents. They've both passed on now."

Savannah studied the photo, which was faded and yellow with age. She wasn't sure what she had expected the Harringtons to look like, but she hadn't anticipated the stern, hard expressions, the extremely stiff postures, or the lack of contact between the man, the woman, and the small girl, whom Savannah assumed was Beverly.

The child in the picture looked miserably unhappy, lonely, alienated. Quickly Savannah readjusted her previous fantasy about how fairy-tale wonderful it must have been to be raised in a mansion like this.

"My father was a citrus rancher," Beverly said. "This house, the family fortune, was built on the backs of migrant workers who were terribly misused. Peter Harrington was a powerful man in his day. He was greatly feared, but he wasn't loved. Victoria Harrington was his idea of a perfect wife: beautiful, elegant, silent, and totally submissive."

"What kind of mother was she?" Savannah asked.

"Distant."

Beverly withdrew the first photograph and held out the other. Savannah saw a young couple in their late teens or early twenties: Beverly and Jonathan in better days. Their arms were draped over each other's shoulders, and they wore goofy, mischievous grins on their faces. Especially Jonathan, whose eyes sparkled with devilment.

"Looks like he was a bit of a pistol," Savannah commented, feeling again the pang of regret that a living, breathing person had been robbed of his life.

"A *bit?*" Beverly laughed. "Jonathan convinced me to toilet paper my first house—a former high school teacher who really deserved it. Jonathan and I climbed up on the freeway overpass at three in the morning to spray paint our initials. God, how times change. I've passed city ordinances that put kids in jail for stuff like that." Beverly pulled the photo back and looked down at it, her face softening. "Jonathan was my first lover," she said. "My only lover for years and years. He knew how to play, and he taught me that it was good to feel joy and passion. Emotions were *good* things, not frivolous and dangerous, as my parents had taught me. I'll always be grateful to him for that."

She replaced the photographs on the mantel, then returned to her chaise. "Does that answer your question, Detective Reid?" she asked tiredly.

"Yes, very well. Thank you." Savannah looked down at her notebook, which she had flipped open on her lap. "Mrs. Winston, could you tell me where you were early yesterday morning? About four."

"Four." She winced a little. "Was that when it happened?"

"We think so. Around that time."

"I was in bed, asleep. I'm a bit of a night owl, so I sleep in sometimes." Savannah heard the underlying sarcasm in her voice and thought how difficult it must be to lose a mate, then be suspected of committing the murder. She supposed Beverly Winston was entitled to a little bitterness.

"Excuse me, but . . ." Savannah cleared her throat. ". . . but do you have anyone who can vouch for the fact that you were here?"

"No," she replied evenly. "No one. I was sleeping alone, if that's what you want to know."

"Yes, thank you." Savannah scribbled in the notebook, not trusting anything to memory. "And how about yesterday evening around sundown? Say about eight-thirty?"

She quirked one eyebrow. "Do I need an alibi for then, too?"

"It's just a routine question."

"I was here, sitting in this chair, reading as I always do in the evenings. And before you ask, no one was with me. I read alone, too."

"How about Leah? Can she vouch for you?"

Beverly shook her head. "No. She and her husband—he's my gardener and handyman—only work for me from eighty-thirty a.m. to four-thirty in the afternoon. They live in the apartment above the old carriage house. I value my privacy too much to have help living with me twenty-four hours a day."

"How about the phone? Did you take any calls yesterday evening here at home?"

"No. I always turn off the phone after dinner and let the answering machine take messages for me. It's a policy I've had to adopt in order to preserve my sanity."

"I understand. That's unfortunate, because . . ." Her voice trailed away as Savannah watched the woman carefully. She was puzzled by her seeming nonchalance. Beverly was the prime suspect in a murder investigation; surely she knew that. She must also comprehend the importance of having an alibi under these circumstances.

"I'm sorry I have no alibi, Detective," she said, as though reading Savannah's mind. "Believe me, I would love to say I was giving a speech at City Hall before two or three hundred people at the moment my husband was being killed, but I wasn't. If I had known I'd need an alibi, I would have arranged to have a good one for you, but . . ." She shrugged her broad shoulders.

"Mrs. Winston," Savannah said, assuming a cooler, more detached tone, "are you aware of a home videotape taken of you and Norman Hillquist coming out of the Blue Moon Motel?"

"Yes," she said, her face freezing over, her voice tight. "I've heard of it. I haven't seen it."

"How did you hear about it?"

"Jonathan told me . . . in great detail. He was quite pleased with his results. Better than he had hoped for, I think."

"Do you recognize this?" Savannah reached into her tote and pulled out the large, Ziplocked plastic bag that contained the videotape in its black rectangular box.

"I can't be sure," she replied, eyeing it carefully, "but it looks like the kind of cases I buy on sale at the local department store. I tape some of the programs aired on public television when I'm away in the evening. I file them in boxes like that."

"Have you noticed if any of your boxes are missing?"

"No, but I wouldn't. I don't keep that close a track of them. What's the significance of that one box? I'm sure there are hundreds of them sold every day."

"This one," Savannah said slowly, "is special because it contains the video footage of you and Chief Hillquist at the Blue Moon."

Savannah could swear that the cool and incredibly calm Beverly Winston turned a shade more pale.

"And," she continued, "it has only one person's fingerprints on it. Yours."

Yes, definitely, Savannah decided. *Maybe even two shades*.

CHAPTER SEVEN

When Savannah entered Captain Bloss's office, as ordered, at three that afternoon, she was only mildly surprised to see Chief Hillquist sitting there, too. Usually he stood when she walked into a room—a quaint but rather endearing custom that she didn't expect but appreciated.

Today he just sat there, elbows propped on the arms of the more comfortable of the three chairs in the office, his fingers interlaced and his forefingers steepled against his lips. She waited only briefly for his customary smile and nod before realizing she would probably never see it again, at least not directed at her. Whatever rapport they had shared was a thing of the past, thanks to this damned case. A smile? Hell, she'd be lucky if she had a job after this.

"Park it, Reid," Bloss said, pointing to the remaining chair, a rusty folding type that was strategically placed in the corner.

As she sat on it, feeling the cold metal through the thin linen of her skirt, Savannah couldn't help being a little miffed. Not that they would stick her in the corner, like a naughty little girl, but that they didn't realize that she was well acquainted with the ploy. She used it herself, for heaven's sake. Shove the subject into a corner while you're interrogating him, boost his stress level, make him feel even more vulnerable, if possible. It worked. Once in a while.

But then, there was the other possibility. Maybe they realized that she knew the ploy . . . and they just didn't give a damn.

"So . . ." she began, eager to beat Bloss to the first punch, ". . . why have I been called on the carpet?" She glanced down at the gouged and scraped gray linoleum. "So to speak," she added sarcastically. The ugly flooring was a major sore spot with the captain. One factor in his negotiations when being shuffled between precincts was that his office would be given new carpeting. He was still waiting.

His color rose and the corners of his mouth dropped. At least he was bright enough to realize that he had been insulted. Savannah had a long-standing policy not to insult anyone who was too dense to get it.

"You aren't exactly on the carpet, Savannah," Hillquist said with forced friendliness. "We just want to hear how the investigation's going, what you've got so far."

"I don't have much more than I had the last time the two of you asked—less than twelve hours ago. I did go home and sleep for about four hours. The other eight haven't been all that productive, I'm sorry to say."

"Now isn't a good time to get smart, Reid," the captain said, leaning back in his squeaky, black wanna-be-leather chair.

Savannah gave him a benign smile that didn't extend to her

eyes. "What would you like to know . . . specifically?" she asked sweetly.

"*Specifically*," Hillquist interjected, "everything you've uncovered to this point."

"Everything?" She gave him a covert, questioning look.

He glanced at Bloss, paused, then said, "Yes, Detective, everything."

Reaching into her tote, she pulled out the notebook and flipped it open. Reading in a monotone, she said, "Time of death approximately four A.M. No substantial trace evidence found at the scene, at least not yet. No signs of forced entry. Three shotgun blasts. First one to the head, fatal. Other two, lower right arm and thigh. Cash roll, jewelry still on body. Blood alcohol level .14. No narcotics, prescription or otherwise."

"Get on with it," Bloss said, interrupting her. "We can read that stuff ourselves on the reports. You know what we wanna hear. Now what have you got?"

Her temper flared, and she snapped the notebook closed. "Yes, Captain, sir," she said, "I know what you want to hear." She turned to Hillquist and fixed him with blue lasers. "Yes, Chief, I know that the Winstons' marriage was down the crapper. I know that you and she were having an affair. I know that Jonathan knew. I know that he videotaped the two of you coming out of a motel and threatened to expose you both. I've seen the tape and I've run it through the lab. The only prints were Beverly's."

Hesitating, she waited for that to sink in; then she continued, "Beverly threatened Jonathan's life. It appears he believed her. He got a restraining order against her. I also know that the reason you wouldn't let me question her yesterday was because you wanted the opportunity to talk it over with her first." She paused and drew a deep breath. "How am I doing so far?"

Hillquist said nothing, but his fingers were no longer steepled in that irritating, condescending manner. His arms were crossed tightly over his broad chest and his face was frighteningly blank.

Realizing the gravity of what she had just said, Savannah felt her anger, and some of her courage, melting away. Dear Lord, when would she learn to think before she shot off her mouth?

Finally Bloss broke the silence. "Well, you've been quite the busy little beaver," he said in a castor-oil tone that made her nauseous.

Any other time she might have made a comment about sexual innuendos being inappropriate, but she decided to let it slide. She was in enough shit as it was; no point in digging the septic tank deeper.

"Is there anything else, Chief?" she asked, forcing a note of humility into her voice.

His face remained blank, enigmatic. Savannah could feel a drop of cold sweat trickle down the back of her neck and into her collar. Yes, she had definitely screwed herself this time.

"Do you have the tape?" he asked, so quietly that she wasn't sure if she had heard him correctly.

"I beg your pardon?"

"I said, do you have the videotape with you right now?"

Savannah glanced down into her tote at the most valuable piece of evidence she had collected so far in this investigation. "Ah . . . yes, as a matter of fact, I do."

His poker face disappeared and he gave her a look that went through her like a cold, sharp jolt of whiplash pain. In that moment the thought occurred to Savannah that Chief Hillquist could be a dangerous man under the wrong conditions. And she had a sinking feeling that she had just fulfilled some of those conditions.

He held out his hand. "I'll take the tape," he said quietly. "I have some tests of my own I'd like to run."

Every alarm on Savannah's mental professional switchboard went off: flashing lights, sirens, loudspeakers.

At this moment the chief himself could be considered a suspect. He certainly wouldn't be the first boyfriend who had smoked the husband of the woman he was seeing. To hand over to him a crucial, incriminating piece of evidence was unthinkable.

"Sir, I—"

"Detective Reid," he said, much louder than before. She could hear the veneer of his civility wearing thinner. "That isn't a request; it's a direct order. Hand me the tape."

She glanced over to Bloss. Why she would expect any assistance or support from him, she couldn't imagine. He gave her a smug I-eat-shit-for-a-nickel grin. She resisted the urge to smack him silly: maybe later.

With a feeling of defeat she reached into the tote, pulled out the plastic bag containing the tape, and placed it on Hillquist's open palm.

"Thank you, Detective," he said with no trace of gratitude in the words. "And there's one more thing. . . ."

"Yes?" She had a sneaking suspicion she wasn't going to like this one either.

"For the moment I insist that you keep the details of your investigation right here in this room. You are to discuss it with no one other than Captain Bloss or myself. Is that clear?"

She nodded.

He wanted more. "I said, is that clear?"

"Yes," she said, swallowing the bitter taste that was rising from her stomach into the back of her throat. "Yes, sir. Quite clear."

Too clear, she thought as she left the room, her recently lightened tote under her arm. The situation was all too apparent. Willing or not, she had just become part of a major coverup.

"Whoever said that police work was exciting?" Savannah muttered as she sat in the middle of her living-room floor, practically buried beneath an avalanche. Letters, phone bills, credit-card purchase reports, address books and journals . . . all documented the life and times of the deceased Jonathan Winston.

"Paperwork. That's all there is to being a cop. Someday they're going to find me dead, cold as a frog on a mountain, crushed by a ton and a half of paperwork," she told Cleopatra.

A hummingbird came to take a sip from Bogey outside, and the cat bounded to the window, tail switching, mouth quivering with anticipation.

"And you'll miss me!" Savannah called after her. "Damn it, you *will!*"

On the coffee table beside her was a legal pad and a pen. After carting this stuff home from the station—she had suddenly had a hankering to be as far away from there as possible—and sorting through it for two hours she had a sizable list of leads to be checked.

The search had been tedious, to be sure, but she knew a lot more about Jonathan Winston now than before.

Overall, his life appeared to have been running rather smoothly, for the first time in years. Other than the facts that his marriage was dissolving and he was murdered, Jonathan seemed to have had things under control.

After some financially difficult, first few years, the business was showing a profit. An impressive profit. His bills were paid, his savings account fat, liquid assets flowing nicely.

The only red flag was the fact that he had withdrawn several six-figure sums from his savings over the past few months, and Savannah couldn't find any record of where the money might have gone. Definitely a detail worth noting and pursuing.

A list of test results from his yearly examination showed that he was in top physical shape, exceptional for a man his age. Even his cholesterol level and weight were down. Savannah recalled her own physical last month and felt a passing hatred for J.W.

Oh, well, he probably didn't enjoy eating, and what was a little extra weight? She wasn't fat or even chubby. She was voluptuous, bodacious, and curvaceous. Couldn't ask for better than that.

At the thought of food, Savannah realized that it was nearly time for dinner. Having already changed into pajamas for the evening, she decided to send out for Chinese.

Just as she was about to abandon the U.S.S. *Winston* and call it a day, a tidy little bundle of letters caught her eye. The delicate blue paper with its lacy edge was definitely not from his stockbroker. Yesterday, while talking with Beverly in her library, Savannah had seen her stationery on the small rolltop desk. It had been a sedate dove gray, with a watermark of the mansion in the center. Far more formal than this.

A dozen or so letters were bound together with a thick rubber band. Not as romantic as satin ribbons, she thought, but . . .

Studying the first letter, she saw that it had been postmarked recently, only a couple of weeks earlier. The return address had no name but was from the neighboring town, Oak Creek. The handwriting was small, sedate, and definitely feminine.

Again, feeling as though she was invading someone's most

private affairs, she began to read the letters. Beverly wasn't the only one in that marriage committing adultery. The letters, from a woman named Fiona, were filled with flowery expressions of undying love and gratitude. Apparently the sex had been pretty good.

In the middle of the fifth letter Savannah realized that Jonathan and Fiona had once been married. It was equally obvious that Fiona wanted a reconciliation and expected it to happen soon. Either Jonathan had been contemplating leaving Beverly even before he had found out about her affair with the chief or he had been lying through his teeth to Fiona.

Either scenario was certainly possible, Savannah decided, based on her knowledge of men and their "wicked, wily ways," as Gran put it.

Savannah was just finishing the last letter when a knock on her front door startled her so badly, she almost dropped the page.

"Dang it . . . scare a body half to death," she grumbled as she rose stiffly from the floor—she had been sitting there a long time—and stumbled to the door on numb legs.

Glancing through the peephole, she saw a hideous, completely nauseating sight. Something pink, wet, maybe slimy, right there and magnified for her appreciation.

A tongue.

Dirk's tongue.

"Very funny," she said as she yanked open the door. "You know, Dirk, the most important thing about a good gag is knowing when to turn it out to pasture. You've worn that one thin."

"I'm glad you told me," he said. "Next time I'll be sure to hack a big green loogey first, just for variety."

"Why are you here?" she asked, not bothering to sugarcoat her tone. "Why didn't you call first, and what do you want?"

He thought for a moment, then said, "To make up—I didn't have a dime—and to share this with you."

From behind his back he produced a pink bakery box, which she knew contained her favorite food in the world: a Black Forest cake from the German bakery on the corner. It was . . . very simply . . . to die for.

It was also very expensive. Immediately her suspicions rose. Since when did old Dirk the Tightwad fork over thirty big ones for a cake? His idea of splurging was to buy Savannah her own thirty-nine-cent package of powdered minidonuts, rather than making her split a pack of six with him.

"I'm not going to let you into my knickers," she said, "if that's what you're thinking. Not even for Black Forest."

"Ah, hell, Van . . . I gave up on that years ago. Open the goddamned door before this fuckin' thing melts."

"That's what I've always loved and admired about you, Dirk," she said, standing back and ushering him inside. "You have such a wonderful, lyrical way with words."

"Must be the Irish in me."

"Yeah, must be."

The closest Dirk ever came to being Irish was wearing a green T-shirt on St. Paddy's Day and downing some green Guinness.

"What's all this?" he asked as he stepped over the piles of papers on his way to the kitchen.

"Winston's stuff," she replied, not really wanting to open that subject again.

"Anything yet?"

"Nothing good."

He set the cake box on her counter, opened the cupboard, and took out two large plates. "Have you had dinner yet?"

"No, I was just going to order out."

"Then you'll want a double-sized piece," he said, readjusting the angle of the knife to accommodate her appetite.

"Exactly. One for dinner, one for dessert."

No matter how rough the waters became between them, they always weathered the storm because they shared one common harbor: food.

Like her, Dirk was a hedonist who made no apologies about his constant search for fleshly pleasures. Only his strong sense of thrift kept him from destroying himself in an orgy of self-indulgence.

She gratefully accepted the overburdened plate and led him back into the living room. They assumed their usual seating arrangements on evenings like this: Savannah in her easy chair, Dirk on the sofa. He frequently dropped over, unannounced, to watch a movie or game or to share a pizza—if she was buying. At one time Savannah had thought his visits were mostly due to the fact that her big color television was more fun to watch than his postage-stamp-sized black-and-white.

But over the years she had slowly come to realize that, whether he would admit it or not, Dirk was lonely and enjoyed her company. If she was being honest, she would have to confess that she enjoyed his, too.

"So, what's the occasion?" she asked as she savored the flavors of chocolate, cherry, brandy, and cream, beautifully wedded into an orgasmically decadent culinary experience.

"What do you mean?" he asked, not meeting her eyes. Dirk could lie his butt off when he was on the streets, but he was lousy at it in his private life.

"I mean . . . the last time you bought me a Black Forest was for my fortieth birthday. And even then you got a bunch of the guys to chip in."

"Are you saying I'm cheap?" He looked only mildly offended.

"You're cheap. *Very* cheap."

"How can you say that when I—?"

"For heaven's sake, Dirk, you hang paper towels up to dry so that you can use them again."

"What's your point?"

"You're the only man I've ever known who actually darns socks. I've seen you walk into a nice restaurant with a sack lunch under your arm, order a cup of coffee, and sit there and eat your peanut-butter-and-jelly sandwich at their table."

"So? You get a lot more for your buck buying peanut butter than those expensive cold cuts, like bologna."

"Never mind," she said, suddenly feeling tired. "Why did you drop by tonight . . . really?"

"I told you: I wanted to make up."

"It wasn't that big a fight, Dirk. Neither of us bled."

"All right, all right; you sure are a suspicious old broad. I heard that you got hauled into Bloss's office. They said the chief was in there, too, and when you came out you looked pretty upset." He paused and put on his sensitive-man face, which usually made her want to barf. "I came over tonight because I thought you might need someone to talk to. I—"

"Bullshit. You're nosy, and you want to know what happened. You thought you'd come over here and ply me with Black Forest until you had gained my confidence. Then, once I lowered my defenses, you'd exploit my vulnerability, manipulate my basic human need for compassion and understanding from my fellow man. Is that it?"

He stared at her for a moment, nonplussed. Then he said

flatly, "Naw . . . I was just gonna butter you up with the cake and get you to spill your guts. That's all."

"Then you just flushed thirty bucks, *compadre*," she said, licking her fork. "Because I've been instructed in no uncertain terms not to discuss the case with anyone."

"You're kidding."

"Nope. Thoroughly gagged. I can notta say nada."

"Not even to another cop? I'm your partner, for God's sake."

"Sorry. My lips are sealed."

"Not too tight to eat my cake," he muttered under his breath.

"What did you say?"

"Nothin'."

Savannah watched his lower lip protrude slightly, as it always did when he pouted. Dirk was a big guy and a forceful personality; he was accustomed to getting his own way in the world. He instantly regressed to adolescence when he didn't.

"Seriously, Dirk, I wish I could tell you about it. I'm pissed, I'm confused, and, to be honest, I'm a little scared of this whole thing. I have the feeling I'm disarming a bomb and don't know which wire to snip first, the red or the blue. And I have this sinking feeling that no matter which one I choose I'm gonna blow it . . . in more ways than one."

The petulant look dissolved from his face, to be replaced by one of genuine concern. "It's that bad?"

"Yeah. It's that bad."

"Are you gonna be all right, Van?"

She nodded. "Sure I will. I mean, what could happen . . . really?"

"God, Savannah! Don't say that! Nobody should ever say that, especially a cop."

He was right, of course. Gran would say she was borrowing trouble, just uttering those words. She had opened the door for all those pesky little demon guys out there to come right in and plague her life.

"I'll be okay, Dirk," she said gently, touched by his obvious concern. "Really, I will. Don't worry."

But as the words left her mouth Savannah realized that she was saying them as much to comfort and convince herself as Dirk.

She was going to be all right in the end. Wasn't she?

Dirk didn't leave until just before midnight. Savannah was grateful that he had stayed until she was tired enough to go to bed and right to sleep. She had a feeling that had been his intention.

As she saw him to the door, he paused, his hand on the knob.

"If there's anything I can do, kid, anything at all to help, let me know. Okay?"

"Yeah, sure."

"I mean it."

"I know you do. I may take you up on your offer."

For what felt like a long time he stood, looking down at her. Every now and then Savannah felt something radiating from him, an affection, an attraction, something that wouldn't have been there had they not been different sexes.

They hadn't pursued it. Common sense dictated that they remain partners first, friends second, and lovers—not at all. In an office setting it might be foolish to mess around with your coworkers, but on the police force, it could be deadly.

However, their decision didn't mean that they didn't feel it from time to time, like now.

Dirk might be losing some of his hair, he might have gained a few pounds since she had first met him, and he would never be called pretty or cute. But he was still a handsome man, in a virile, street-rough sort of way. More than once Savannah had fantasized about what it might be like to hit the sheets with him.

As she stood in the doorway with him, so close that she could feel his body heat, a few of those choice fantasies decided to surface. She shoved them back down. Not now.

"There's something I want to tell you, Van," he said. The tone in his voice made her pulse rate increase substantially. "Something important."

"What is it?" she asked, feeling a bit breathless.

"Always remember . . ."

"Yes?"

"The blue one."

She stared at him, totally dumbfounded. "What?"

"The blue one. When you're disarming a bomb always cut the blue wire first."

"Really? Always?"

"Always. Hey, it's a good bet. I'm tellin' you, go with the blue. You'll have a fifty-fifty chance every time."

CHAPTER EIGHT

At approximately three-thirty in the morning Savannah woke to a shrill ringing in her ears. As she tried to reorient herself from the pleasantly erotic dream she was having to the less romantic reality, she ran through a quick mental list of what the horrendous buzzing might be. Fire extinguisher? No, fire extinguishers didn't ring. Fire *alarms* and smoke detectors rang. No, not that. The alarm. She punched a couple of buttons on the clock, even knocked it to the floor, but the infernal noise continued, jarring the teeth half out of her head.

The phone, she thought as the handsome lover in the sexy cowboy outfit faded into the dreamland horizon, lost to her forever. *Whoever it is, I'm gonna jerk a knothole in his butt. And what's more, I'm going to enjoy it.*

She turned on the bedside lamp and looked down at the clock on the floor. *Well, what do you know; it does happen some-*

times, she observed when she saw the clock had been broken in the fall and had frozen at exactly 3:32.

"Who . . . ? What . . . ?" she mumbled sleepily into the receiver.

She heard sniffling, then a voice with a Southern drawl even thicker than her own said, "Savannah, it's me . . . Atlanta. I didn't want to wake you up, but I'm really, really, really upset, and I have to talk to somebody. Please don't be mad."

Groaning, Savannah flopped back onto her pillow and shoved the phone between her ear and shoulder. It wasn't easy being the oldest of nine kids. Especially when—other than going to a lot of effort naming them all after Georgian cities—their mother had decided that she had done her duty to her brood and pretty much allowed them to fend for themselves. Stepdad Number Three didn't object. He drove a truck fifty-one weeks out of the year, so he wasn't exactly around to arbitrate, discipline, or nurture. As a result, most of the responsibility had fallen on Savannah's shoulders.

She hadn't minded back then; now it was getting a little old.

"Atlanta, you know I love you, sweetie, but you and I have seven other siblings, all of whom live within spitting distance of you. Why don't you call one of them for a change when you're really, really, really upset?"

" 'Cause you're the oldest," she sobbed. "You're my big sister, and you're the only one who understands. Macon's cranky since he lost his job at the service station, Marietta's miserable 'cause she's pregnant, Vidalia's fighting with Butch again and I think she's going to leave him, and Waycross is still in jail for stealing those hubcaps . . . they were off Judge Patterson's Cadillac, you know."

"Okay, okay." Savannah sighed and ran her fingers through

her hair, resisting the urge to pull out a hunk. If she were the only one who understood her sixteen-year-old sister, the kid was in trouble—because she didn't see what was so horrible in the girl's life that would cause such agony.

"So, what's up?" she asked, steeling herself for the soliloquy that was inevitable. Atlanta's sob stories could make Hamlet's "To be or not to be" speech sound like a pep rally led by Norman Vincent Peale.

"It's Mom again."

"Gee, what a surprise."

"She told me I can't see J.D. anymore. Ever! She said if she caught me talking to him, even on the phone, she'd take a razor strap to me."

"Mom won't take a razor strap to you. Trust me. It's just a quaint Southern figure of speech. Mom wouldn't know a razor strap if one came up and bit her on the ass." She paused, then added, "And if you tell her I said that, *I'll* take one to you the next time I see you."

"When is that going to be? I miss you. I want you to come home."

"Atlanta, I can't."

"Yes, you could."

"All right, I could, but I don't want to. I have my own life here now, and I like it."

"Sure you do. Who wouldn't?" She sounded awfully bitter for only sixteen. "You live in California. I'm stuck here in stupid old Georgia, and you've got it all. Sunshine. Palm trees. Beaches and—"

"Earthquakes, brushfires, floods, mud slides . . ."

"I've never even *seen* a beach!"

"You've also never been in a 6.2 earthquake or had to wet

down your roof so that it wouldn't burn. You've got it pretty good, kid. Don't bitch."

"Mom says you cuss too much."

"Mom's right. Do whatever she says. If she tells you not to see R.J.—"

"J.D.!"

"Whatever. If she says no, she's got a good reason. He's probably a punk."

"That's what *she* said. She thinks just because he wears black, heavy metal T-shirts and rides a Harley, that he's a—"

"He listens to heavy metal and rides a Harley! She's right; he's a jerk. He'll just get you drunk and knock you up. Don't you ever talk to him again."

"You're my sister, not my mother. Don't tell me what to do." The sobbing began again, this time in earnest. "Now that you're getting old, you're just like Mom. You used to be so cool, Savannah. But now you're getting all fucked up, too, and—"

"You watch your mouth, Atlanta Reid. A young lady does *not* use the 'F' word, and you know it! Mom *should* take a strap to you."

"You don't understand!" The sobbing crossed the line into hysteria. "Now you've let me down, too. No-o-o-oo-body understands!"

"Oh, come on, 'Lanta. Things can't be that bad. Maybe you're overreacting just a little."

Click.

Her sister had hung up on her.

Savannah couldn't believe it. First, she woke her up in the middle of the night and dumped on her. Then, just because she didn't play the poor-dear-poor-dear game the way she wanted her to, she hung up on her.

"You little shit," Savannah said as she replaced the receiver and turned off the lamp. "Fuck you, too."

No sooner had she begun to drift back into a nice dream—there was no cowboy in sight, but the Tarzan-type guy in a nearby tree certainly had possibilities—than the phone rang again.

"Damn it, Atlanta," she shouted into the receiver, "I understand that you're having a crisis of monumental proportions, and I don't want to be the one to violate your basic trust in humanity by turning you away . . . but do you suppose it could possibly wait until morning?"

There was a long, heavy silence on the other end. All Savannah could hear was her own labored breathing.

Then a soft, female voice said, "Excuse me?"

Savannah didn't need to hear more to know that it wasn't Atlanta on the line. Atlanta's drawl, plus that special whining quality, made her voice unmistakable.

This woman was older and had an Eastern accent.

"I'm sorry," Savannah said. "I thought you were someone else. Who is this?"

Again, a long pause. "My name doesn't matter, but I'd like to help you."

Savannah sat up, fully awake. "I would appreciate that," she said slowly, carefully. "How can you help me?"

She heard the woman on the other end take a deep breath, as though collecting herself. "Tomorrow night, at the Stardust Pavilion, there's going to be a charity fashion show."

"Yes? And . . . ?"

"And you should go."

Savannah began to scribble frantically on the pad beside the phone. "The Stardust . . . okay. Why should I go?"

"Because I have good reason to believe that the person who killed Jonathan Winston is going to be there. I just thought you should know."

Her tone sounded as though she was about to sign off.

"Wait a minute!" Savannah said. "If you really want to help me, tell me who it is."

"I can't. This is all I can do right now. You'll have to take it from there."

"Will *you* be there tomorrow night?" she asked.

But she could already hear the dial tone on the other end. She had been hung up on, twice in one night.

After staring at what she had written on the pad for a few moments Savannah turned out the lamp and settled into bed again, her mind churning.

Any chance of sleep was out of the question now. The king of the jungle had gone the way of the cowboy. When she closed her eyes the only man Savannah could see was a murdered Jonathan Winston. And the image was anything but romantic or sleep-inducing.

The moment Savannah stepped into the glittering gold-and-white ballroom of the Stardust Pavilion she knew she had committed a major fashion faux pas. So much for the theory that a simple black dress and a string of pearls were appropriate for all occasions. As far as the eye could see across the ocean of beautiful people, hers was the only black dress in sight. And pearls didn't appear to be the rage this season either.

How was she supposed to know that classic formal was out and colorful weird was in?

As she meandered around the perimeter of the gathering, Savannah attracted a discomfiting number of curious and contemptuous looks from the female sector. On the other hand, the males appeared less fashion-conscious, and their attention seemed riveted more on her ample cleavage and nicely turned calves than on her dress.

When she had called this morning to inquire about the event she had been told that there would be a little cocktail get-to-know-everybody party before the actual show. Apparently this was it.

Savannah felt as out of place as her funereal dress. High society held little attraction for her. She would have preferred to be down at Mike's Bar and Grill, swigging a beer and munching an order of Mike's famous onion rings.

But then, she was here to do a job, not party. Her presence was mandatory, her participation optional.

She took the better part of a half an hour to locate Beverly Winston, and when she did Savannah was shocked at the change. The councilwoman had gone through a metamorphosis. Her no-nonsense, totally business look had disappeared. Instead, she was a vision floating gracefully about the room in pale peach and ivory layers of the sheerest, most delicate fabric Savannah had ever seen.

Amazing what a trip to the beauty parlor, some face goop, and a haute-couture evening gown could do, Savannah thought, still not quite believing the transformation. And the diamonds dripping off her ears and fingers didn't hurt either.

At her side stood a tall, strikingly handsome man—not the chief, Savannah noted. Blond, probably in his late forties, he looked deliciously urbane in his gray, loose-fitting designer suit. His hair had a meticulously mussed look, one of those "casual" styles that required constant attention. Savannah liked to call it "carefully cultivated chaos."

He leaned close to Beverly when he spoke to her, too close to be a casual friend but not quite within a lover's proximity.

For a moment he glanced in Savannah's direction and saw her watching them. She looked away quickly, but she knew in the two seconds in which their eyes had met that he had realized that her interest was more than casual.

In her peripheral vision Savannah watched him bend his head to say something to Beverly, who immediately looked her way. The councilwoman appeared distressed for only a split second; then her professional mask slid effectively into place. She nodded a greeting to Savannah, who nodded back.

After saying something else to her escort Beverly slipped her arm through his and led him over to the edge of the room where Savannah stood.

"Detective . . ." she said as she offered her hand to Savannah. ". . . how nice to see you here tonight. I had no idea you were interested in the fashion industry."

"It's a recent fascination," Savannah replied smoothly, noticing that Beverly's hand was cool but damp.

"I'd like you to meet someone who is extremely influential in the business, designer and manufacturer Paul Connors. Paul has been a friend of the family for years. I'm sure you've heard of his line, Elite, etc."

"Oh, yes, of course," Savannah replied enthusiastically. "I have at least a dozen of your wonderful creations hanging in my closet, even as we speak."

Paul gave her a quick once-over, from the simple strand of fake pearls to her $19.99 pumps. "Really?" he said with a half grin, accepting her sarcasm with more grace than she had expected.

"No," she replied. "Not really. Most of us police types just buy right off the rack. Sad but true."

His eyes softened and he chuckled. "We've all bought off the rack at one time or another, Detective," he said. "There are some very nice choices available to the . . . shall we say . . . common man in department stores. I should know; I designed some of them. Under a different name and label, of course."

"Of course." Savannah decided to revise her initial opinion of Paul Connors. He was a snob, but he was a pleasant one, as ready to make fun of himself as anyone else.

"Paul is being modest," Beverly said, looking at her escort with obvious admiration. "Every year he puts this event together and donates all of the proceeds to a local charity. It's a tremendous amount of work, but he pulls it off beautifully."

Savannah looked around the room with its quietly elegant decorations and had to agree. From the exquisite ice sculpture of a school of dolphin to the snowy white linens and soft touches of gold in the floral arrangements, everything spoke of understated grace and refinement. Savannah filed away the information in a mental drawer marked SHOWERS AND BIRTHDAY PARTIES—DECORATING IDEAS.

Paul shrugged and looked a bit embarrassed. "No big deal," he said. "I'm not that altruistic. I do it because I enjoy it. When I don't enjoy it anymore I'll let someone else take over. But enough about me." He turned his full attention to Savannah. "Beverly says you're investigating Jonathan's death."

"That's right," she said.

He shook his head and placed a comforting hand on Beverly's shoulder. "I hope you catch whoever did it soon," he said. "Do you have any suspects yet?"

Savannah opened her mouth to reply but hesitated. Beverly filled in the gap for her. "Paul, this is a bit awkward," she said.

"I'm afraid that at the moment Detective Reid's primary suspect is me."

His smile vanished as he turned on Savannah. "What? That isn't true, is it?"

"We haven't drawn any conclusions yet, Mr. Connors," Savannah replied as diplomatically as possible. "At this point we're considering all possibilities."

"Well, Beverly is *not* a possibility. I've known this lady for years and she would never hurt another person, let alone murder someone in cold blood."

"Thank you, Mr. Connors," Savannah said, trying to calm him. Several persons nearby had paused to eavesdrop at the sound of his raised voice. "I'll take your opinion of Mrs. Winston into account."

That didn't seem to satisfy him. What did he expect, for heaven's sake? For her to give him her word that she would no longer suspect Beverly Winston, based upon his personal recommendation of her character?

"Seriously," he continued. "That's ridiculous. If you want to find Jonathan's killer, start investigating some of his enemies. God knows, he had enough of them."

"Like who?" Savannah asked. She could feel Beverly tense, but Savannah refused to even look in her direction.

"Like his ex-wife, Fiona O'Neal, the redhead in blue there by the stage. For years she had been threatening to blow his brains out—sorry, Bev—if he didn't come back to her."

Savannah's antennae began to beep furiously. Fiona O'Neal? The love-besot ex-wife with the frilly stationery?

"Or Danielle Lamont over there," he continued, pointing to a garishly attired woman who looked as though she had just stepped out of a sultan's harem. "She was in the process of suing him over some patterns she says he stole, and—"

"Paul, please stop." Beverly laid a restraining hand on his arm. "I appreciate what you're trying to do, but you know as well as I do that neither Fiona nor Danielle killed Jonathan. They simply aren't capable of doing something like that."

"Well, neither are you."

Beverly turned to Savannah. "Then I have complete faith that Detective Reid will figure everything out on her own. She strikes me as a person who's fair and thorough. I'm sure it's just a matter of time until she reaches her own conclusions."

"Well, I certainly hope so. Just keep in mind, Detective Reid, that a few false words can destroy even an innocent person in the political arena. Beverly is doing some very important work, and she has a lot more to do before she's finished."

"You don't need to worry about what I say to anyone," Savannah replied. "I take pride in the fact that I run a discreet investigation."

He studied her for a moment, as though he didn't quite believe her. Then his expression relaxed a bit. "I'm sorry," he said. "I didn't mean to imply that you don't know your business, Detective. I'm just worried about Beverly. She's been through so much already."

"Paul . . ." Beverly squeezed his arm and smiled up at him. " . . . why don't you leave us alone for a minute or two of girl talk? I could really use a gin and tonic."

Reluctantly, he left and headed across the ballroom toward the bar.

"I apologize for Paul's behavior," Beverly said as they watched him go. "He and Jonathan were close. He isn't taking what happened very well."

"You seem to be doing all right," Savannah said, trying to sound casual and concerned rather than judgmental.

"Of course I seem to be all right." Beverly gave her a bright smile, but Savannah could have sworn she saw unshed tears shining in her eyes. "Seeming like I'm doing all right is my job. And, like you, Detective, I do it damned well."

"I understand you got to rub elbows with the beautiful people last night." Captain Bloss sat, feet propped on his desk, fingers laced behind his head. Savannah supposed he was attempting to look superior. But he didn't impress her. As far as she was concerned, all he was showing was that his particular brand of antiperspirant wasn't up to the task.

"Not enough to get rug burn," she replied dryly.

"Why were you there?"

"I received an anonymous phone tip in the middle of the night that my murderer would be attending the charity ball. I thought it might be a good idea to go and check out the guest list."

"And did you . . . check out all the guests, that is?"

She had a feeling where this was going. "As many as I could."

"Did you talk to everyone?"

"There were over two hundred people there. I didn't have time to chat with them all."

Bloss paused to study a smear of chewing gum on the sole of his loafer. "Exactly how many potential suspects did you question there last night?"

She was starting to get that claustrophobic feeling, like he was backing her into a corner. "I don't recall . . . exactly."

"Let me put it this way . . ." He pulled a pack of cigarettes from his front shirt pocket and lit up. "Did you question anyone there other than Beverly Winston?"

"I didn't *question* Mrs. Winston. She and her friend came over to talk to me. *They* initiated the conversation." Savannah felt her face growing hotter by the minute. Who did he think he was, anyway, giving her the third degree when she hadn't done anything out of line? "I don't understand your concern, Captain. Don't you know that I have enough sense not to interrogate a suspect at a high-society ball?"

"To be honest, Reid," he said, sucking a long draw from the cigarette, "I'm not sure exactly how much sense you do or don't have. I thought the chief made it pretty clear yesterday that you were to leave Mrs. Winston alone."

"Was that before or after he confiscated my only consequential piece of evidence?"

His smug grin slid off his face, and he jabbed the half-smoked cigarette into an overloaded ashtray. "You're skating on thin ice here, Reid. You'd better think twice before you go insinuating that the chief of police did something improper by taking that tape. He told you; he's running tests on it."

"What tests? I already had it checked for prints. The contents are clearly visible if you stick it into any VCR. This whole thing is bullshit; there aren't any tests. That tape belongs with me or in an evidence locker. A first-year rookie knows that."

His face flushed an unattractive shade of greenish purple, and it occurred to Savannah that Captain Bloss was an ugly man, especially when he was livid.

"I don't like your tone, Detective Reid," he said. "You're running very close to insubordination."

Savannah's thin thread of patience snapped. "Well, *I* don't appreciate being entrusted with a case and then being told when, where, and how I can blow my nose while I'm on it. If you didn't think I would conduct this investigation properly, why the hell did you give it to me?"

"I'm beginning to ask myself the same question," Bloss replied, lighting up another cigarette and blowing the smoke out his nose. "I was under the false impression that, of all my choices, you were the most . . . cooperative."

" 'Cooperative'? I'm working alone on this case; you saw to that. Who am I supposed to be cooperating with?"

"I thought you were more flexible, more respectful of authority. I'm sorry to see that I was wrong in giving you this opportunity."

Respectful of authority?

Oh, okay, she thought, as the pieces began to fall into place with a loud ka-thunk. *Now I get it.*

"You gave me this case because you thought I was a pushover, a wimp who would kiss ass and do anything you and the chief told me to do. Right?"

He gave her an ugly grin that made her want to grab him by his stupid tie with its insipid pink palm trees and hang him from the nearest light fixture.

"Let's just say, I thought you were more flexible."

"Malleable is more like it."

The somewhat blank look on his face told her that he wasn't familiar with the word. She didn't find it particularly fulfilling, arguing with someone with a limited vocabulary.

Standing, she reached for her purse, jacket, and tote. "Captain, I don't mind telling you, I think this whole thing sucks. The chief is in love with a woman, has an affair with her, and her husband is murdered only days after he finds out about them. This does *not* look good for the chief . . . or the lady involved. If he were

John Q. Public instead of chief of police, he and his lady friend would have already been dragged in here and put through the wringer."

"The chief of police is *not* John Q. Public." Bloss punctuated his statement by bringing his fist down hard on his desk, sending the clutter sliding and bouncing across its dusty surface. "He deserves special treatment, dammit, and—"

"Yes, of course he does. But not if he killed someone, or is protecting somebody who did. We aren't talking about a parking violation here. This is first-degree homicide. And even a chief of police doesn't get away with murder."

Neither of them said anything—or even breathed—as her words hung in the air between them. Savannah couldn't believe that she had spoken them. She hadn't intended to be that blunt, but her temper had gotten the best of her . . . again.

Did she really believe that Police Chief Norman Hillquist killed Jonathan Winston?

No, she didn't.

Did she think he had something to do with it or knew who had done it?

Quite possibly. Why else would he be willing to break the law by interfering with her investigation?

Why else would Bloss be supporting him?

The answer to that one was simple: Bloss would support the devil in a party dress if he thought it would help his career. She wasn't naive enough to believe for one minute that he was doing this out of loyalty to a fellow cop.

"Detective, I think this conversation is over," Bloss said.

Savannah didn't like the cool monotone of his voice or the blank look in his eyes. At least when he was purple or green she knew where she stood.

She had seen friendlier expressions on the faces of defendants in the courtroom, glaring up at her as she had sworn their freedom away.

Instinctively she felt as though something had just changed between them . . . and not for the better.

"Like I said, this conversation is over," Bloss repeated. "Please leave."

Relieved at the thought of escape, she headed for the door. But just as she was almost free and clear she heard him call her name.

"Yes?" she said, standing just outside the door, looking at him over her shoulder.

"Come back in . . . say about three this afternoon."

"Okay," she said carefully. "Do you want to tell me why?"

He smiled, and she was reminded of the moment when Jaws had chomped off the back half of the fishing boat.

"Nope," he said. "It'll keep."

Savannah closed the door and headed down the hall, but her getaway lacked that certain sweetness.

She couldn't believe she had said those things.

Oh, well, the damage had been done. She had stuck her foot in the cow pie now. Actually, she had jumped in with *both* feet and done a little jig. Now she'd just have to wait to find out how heavy the penalty would be.

CHAPTER NINE

When Savannah stepped into Danielle Lamont's boutique she felt as though she had just been transported to some faraway exotic land. Not the Orient. Not some tropical paradise. But the quintessential Southern California, New Age, New Wave, Mystical, Magical Experience. She wasn't sure who was going to pop out first, a belly dancer or a fortune-teller.

A strange nonmelodic music was playing, something that had a weird undercurrent of sounds that reminded Savannah of a whale in heat. She glanced over at the CD player on the counter and saw the disk's cover: *Whale's Mating Song*. Yep, just as she'd thought.

Candles and incense burned everywhere, enough to make any fire marshal quake in his boots. Not one inch of the walls or floors were exposed; all were covered with brightly colored throws, rugs, tapestries, ropes strung with glittering bangle bracelets, handwoven blankets and plants, plants, and more plants. The place felt like a miniature jungle . . . inhabited by a sultan . . . and whales. Definitely weird.

What the hell did Danielle Lamont sell in here?

A beaded curtain was swept aside and the garish brunette from the charity ball appeared. Tall and slender to the point of thinness, she entered the room with a dramatic flourish, bringing with her a cloud of fragrance that smelled suspiciously like "a California brushfire," as some locals affectionately called marijuana smoke.

It took her a moment to focus on Savannah; then she gave her a peaceful though a bit empty-headed smile.

"Welcome to Danielle's," she said with a grandiose gesture that encompassed her domain. She glanced up and down Savannah's sensible though unremarkable angora sweater and light wool slacks. "May I help you find something . . . special? Something to express the *wild* woman in you?"

"I beg your pardon?" Savannah had to admit that the wildest she got when it came to apparel was that tiger-striped teddy from Victoria's Secret.

"The *wild* woman," Danielle said. "We all have one, just waiting inside, waiting to be released, to express herself with total joy and abandon!"

Lifting her multibangled arms over her head, she spun around several times. The brightly painted sheer fabric that she wore draped casually around her body floated with her, emphasizing the graceful movement. The tiny bells sewn to the end of her skirt jingled as she moved, and Savannah couldn't help grinning. A wild woman, indeed.

"Actually, I'm not here as a customer," she said.

"Ah, that's too bad. We could have had fun playing dress-up. I have so many lo-o-ovely things."

"Maybe some other time," Savannah said, feeling the urge to lose herself in this woman's mystical world. It would be fun, acting like little girls who were exploring the treasures in Grandma's attic trunks.

So she did know what Danielle Lamont sold here, after all. She sold fantasies.

"My name is Savannah Reid," she said, pulling her badge from inside her sweater, where she kept it on a chain. "I'm the detective who's investigating the murder of Jonathan Winston. I was hoping I could ask you a few questions . . . about Jonathan . . . about the fashion industry."

Danielle's hazy smile faded and her eyes instantly became alert and guarded. "About where I was the morning in question?" she said.

Savannah smiled and nodded. "I'll probably get around to that, too."

"Come on," Danielle said, waving her toward the beaded curtain. "I have a little cubicle that we use for tarot readings. We can talk in there."

Savannah found herself in a charming nook that held two comfortable overstuffed chairs, a small table covered with a lace cloth, and an antique lamp whose shade had been draped with an embroidered fringed scarf of a delicate rose color. It gave the space a romantic pink glow.

"What would you like to know?" Danielle said, settling into one of the chairs.

Savannah took the other seat and glanced down at the deck of cards on the table with their strange but beautiful pictures. "I'd like to know when I'm going to meet that tall, dark, handsome stranger who's going to sweep me off my feet."

Danielle laughed. "Wouldn't we all."

She reached across the table and covered the cards with her right hand. Closing her eyes for a moment, she seemed to be concentrating; then she cut the cards and looked at the one she had selected. "This week," she whispered in a deep, mysterious tone.

"What?" Savannah leaned closer.

"I said, 'This week.' You're going to meet a tall, handsome stranger . . . let me see. . . ." She squeezed her eyes closed again and scrunched her face into a grimace with the effort. ". . . probably within the next forty-eight hours."

Savannah laughed. "Yeah, right."

Opening her eyes, Danielle gave her a mock-indignant frown. "You doubt the cards?"

"You believe them?"

"Damn right. And if you know what's good for you, you will, too."

Savannah stared at her, wondering if she was serious or putting her on. She decided it was a bit of both.

"What else do you want to know?" Danielle asked, deftly running the deck through her fingers.

"I want to know who murdered Jonathan Winston."

Fumbling briefly, Danielle dropped one of the cards to the table. They both caught their breath when they saw the twisted face of evil looking up at them.

Danielle chuckled dryly. "The Devil. How appropriate. There's your answer, Detective Reid."

"Could you possibly be a little more specific?"

With a sigh, Danielle placed the cards on the table and leaned back in her chair, arms crossed over her chest. "The only way I would know who killed him would be if I had done it myself. I didn't. I'm sorry I can't solve your case for you, but if you want to know anything about Jonathan Winston, the man, I'm the one. A walking encyclopedia."

"You knew him well?"

"We were friends, enemies, business partners, and lovers, not necessarily in that order. Yes, I knew him well. What do you want to know?"

Savannah thought for a moment. "Was he a good man?"

"He was good in bed. Very good, in fact. But that's probably not what you're asking." She pursed her bright orange lips thoughtfully. "Morally speaking, I'd say Jonathan was a good guy, when it was convenient. But then, I've always thought that, for most of us, morality is based on convenience. Don't you think so, too, Detective?"

"I'd like to say you're wrong, but . . ." Savannah pulled her notebook from her purse. "Can you think of anyone who had a grudge against Jonathan, who might have wanted to kill him?"

"Yeah, me. The son of a bitch ripped off some of my best designs and made a fortune from them. I took him to court. I won the case, but the court costs were so high that it nearly broke me. With Beverly's money behind him, he hardly even felt it. So, who's to say who won and lost." She shrugged. "*C'est la vie.*"

"But you've already said you didn't kill him."

"I didn't. Other than me . . . it could have been Beverly. Being his wife and all, I'm sure she had plenty of motives. Or it could have been the guy Beverly's been seeing."

"Do you know who that is?" Savannah asked, staring down at her notebook.

"No, but I suspect that you do." She leaned closer and lowered her voice. "Who is it, Detective? Everybody in town is dying to know."

Savannah smiled and ignored the question. "Can you think of anyone else?"

"Could have been Fiona, his ex. I took him away from her years ago, and she never got over it. She divorced her second husband last year, and I heard she was after Jonathan again."

"Anyone else?"

"Nobody I can think of right away. He gambled a lot, you know. Drank, chased women. He did all kinds of things that might have gotten him shot. Jonathan was charming and smart, but he wasn't all that wise, if you know what I mean."

"Just a couple more things," Savannah said, realizing that she needed to end the interview and get back to the station. It was nearly three. "You said you two were lovers?"

"That was years ago, long before he ever laid eyes on Beverly. I was all done with him by the time he met her. We were going to be this great designing team, knock the rag business on its ass. But he took the designs, my heart, and ran. End of partnership."

"You sound pretty bitter."

"I am."

Savannah looked directly into her eyes and saw more pain and hurt than bitterness. But you never could tell.

"Where were you, Danielle, the morning he was killed, around four?"

"Sitting right here, doing a tarot reading."

"A tarot reading? Who would be interested in having their future told that early in the morning?"

"Me. I was doing a layout for myself."

"Then you were—"

"Alone? Yeah," she said wearily, "I was alone. In other

words, I have no alibi, Detective. Ain't life a bitch? Come to think of it, it was a lousy reading, too."

Yes, life *was* a bitch, Savannah agreed as she sat outside Captain Bloss's office, waiting for him to acknowledge her existence. She had been sitting there so long that she believed her tailbone had become rooted to the miserably uncomfortable chair.

She felt like a naughty kid, waiting outside the principal's office to get a lickin'. The punishment she could take, but the suspense was killing her.

For the hundredth time she ran down the list of possibilities. Drawing and quartering could probably be ruled out, along with the firing squad at dawn. There hadn't been any public floggings in San Carmelita since the late 1800s, so that wasn't too likely.

He might give her an official reprimand, which would be a permanent black mark on her otherwise spotless record. But on what grounds? Insubordination, maybe. But, then, he would have to enter it all into the files, and she didn't think he would want the business with the tape and the chief on paper.

"Reid."

She jumped and nearly dropped the magazine that she hadn't been pretending to read.

Bloss stood in his doorway, looking so pleased with himself that she reinstated drawing and quartering on the list of possibilities.

Silently, she followed him into the office and watched as he closed the door behind them.

"Sit," he said, pointing to the rusty folding chair.

The command irked her. Deeply.

"Shall I roll over and play dead, too . . . sir . . . ?" she asked sweetly.

He didn't even react. That wasn't a good sign. He must have something really rotten planned for her. Maybe scrubbing the men's john with a toothbrush?

"I'll make this short and sweet, Reid. Then you can be on your way," Bloss said, plopping down in his chair. "There's no point in prolonging it. I don't think you enjoy my company any more than I do yours."

"I sincerely doubt it . . . sir," she said. "Thank you, sir."

He picked up a paper from his desk and shoved it in her direction, along with a pen. "I'd like you to read and sign this, Detective. Now."

"What is it?" she asked, her eyes scanning the unfamiliar document. A sick jolt went through her as the title at the top snagged her attention.

NOTICE OF TERMINATION

"Termination? Termination of what?" she asked, hardly able to breathe.

"Your job, Detective . . . or should I say *Miss* Reid. It's my sad duty to inform you that you are fired."

A cold rage swept through her, overriding the initial shock. "Oh, yes," she replied evenly, "I can see that you're all broken up about it."

"Hey, you're a good detective, Reid. I hate the idea of losing you like this."

The sarcastic smirk on his face made her want to crawl across the desk and feed him his front teeth. "You can't do this. I'll fight you to hell and back on this. I was only trying to do my job and find a killer, and—"

"I'm sure you were doing a fine job, Reid," he said in a condescending tone. "I have no problem at all with the way you were handling this case."

"Then what . . . ?"

She quickly scanned the rest of the document, looking for the grounds for dismissal.

" 'Failure to meet physical requirements set by the SCPD? What the hell is that supposed to mean?"

He drew a deep breath, leaned back, and stuck his thumbs inside his belt. "It means, to put it bluntly: You're too fat."

"Too . . . what are you talking about? You're kidding, right?"

"I would never kid about another officer's career ending, Reid," he replied. "But, according to the results of your last physical exam, your body fat ratio exceeds department regulations by quite a bit."

"Of course it does. I'm female. Women naturally have more body fat per pound than men. We have boobs, in case you hadn't noticed. And a few other curves that you fellows seem particularly fond of. I hate to tell you this, but these ain't muscle." She pointed emphatically at her cleavage. Only after the words had left her mouth did she realize how unladylike this defense must sound.

Screw it. This wasn't the time to worry about Southern gentility.

He glanced at her generous bustline, then averted his eyes. "Miss Reid, this isn't open for discussion. The decision is final."

"This is ludicrous! I am not *fat!*"

He picked up another paper from his desk. "This is a statement from the departmental physician. He says he warned you that you needed to drop the excess weight as soon as possible."

"Of course he did. He's been telling me that crap for years. Doctors always—"

"Then you've had ample warnings and many opportunities to go on a diet. The department must insist that its officers be in tip-top shape. You aren't. You refuse to be. That means you're out. Now sign the paper and let's both get on with our lives."

Savannah stood, staring down at him, the termination notice in her hand. Slowly, deliberately, she began to crumple it in her fist.

"This has nothing to do with my weight, and you and I both know it. You're kicking me off the force to cover your chief's ass. You gave me this case because you thought I'd be a nice, submissive girl and do whatever you said. Now that I won't, I'm out."

She paused and took a deep breath, steadying herself against the desk. "Well, it isn't going to happen. I will *not* take this lying down, Bloss. I'll go to my union; I'll take you to court; I'll even talk to the media if I have to. You people just made a very bad decision, and it's going to cost you. Just wait and see."

Throwing the wadded paper at him, she marched to the door. He jumped up from his desk and intercepted her before she could open it.

"Just a minute, Reid. I'll need your gun and your badge."

"Oh, God . . . spare me the 'Dragnet' routine."

He slammed his hand against the door, preventing her from leaving. "I mean it. Now."

Reluctantly, she reached inside her shirt and pulled out the badge. With one jerk she broke the chain that was holding it. "Here you go . . . sir," she said, dropping it on the floor at his feet. "If it represents this town's police department and the men who run it, I'm not interested in wearing it anyway."

"Your gun . . ." He held out his hand.

"My gun is not departmental issue. It's *mine*. I bought it; I registered it; I have a license to carry it. And until you can pull enough strings to get my permit revoked for some equally petty reason, I'll just keep it. Anything else, Captain . . . sir?"

"Yes. Unless you want to make your life more complicated than it is right now, I'd suggest you keep your unfounded suspicions about the chief and Mrs. Winston to yourself. Get my drift?"

"Captain Bloss, thanks to you I am now a civilian. I can talk to anyone about anything I damned well want. And you, Captain, may go screw yourself and the mangy mule that brought you into this town. It was a much better city without you."

In a daze of shock and fury, Savannah walked through the building, down corridors and through doors that she had grown to love over the years. She hadn't gotten married, even though she had been tempted several times. She hadn't had kids, even though she was crazy about them. She hadn't thought it fair to subject a family to the kind of stress her job created. Her job. Everything had been for the job.

And now?

Now what?

As she left the station and headed for the parking lot, half of her brain was already formulating the attack strategy. Talk to her union steward, hire an attorney, prepare her case . . .

But the other half couldn't think, couldn't even begin to assimilate the fact that her life had just changed, completely, maybe irrevocably.

Oh, she'd meant what she'd said to Bloss. She would fight them tooth and nail. They'd be sorry they ever made an enemy of Savannah Reid.

But, for now, she just wanted to get the hell out of this place.

The half of her brain that was still frozen in shock was going to thaw out any minute now.

And even though she didn't want to think of herself as a weak person or a cry baby, she wanted to be at home when she fell apart.

CHAPTER TEN

For years Savannah had struggled to exorcise all those pesky demons of guilt from her spirit. Guilt about every bite she ate, guilt about not exercising enough, guilt about weighing thirty pounds more than the charts said she should. It hadn't been easy. Devils don't surrender their power over a soul without a fight.

Her battle had been a virtual Armageddon, but she had finally done it. She took great pride in knowing that, in spite of a society that insisted that every woman look like an anorexic teenager, she had the confidence to accept her own body. She had lived guilt-free for years, loving food, loving life, loving her own flesh and blood . . . all of it.

So it was a shock to her psyche when she opened her refrigerator door and found all those vexing demons back again to torment her.

"You shouldn't eat the rest of that Black Forest cake," they said. "That's how you made yourself *fat* in the first place, you idiot, you glutton. Show a little self-control, for Pete's sake. Eat some lettuce instead."

"I don't want lettuce. I want chocolate!" she said, grabbing for the cake. "Get thee behind me, Satan!"

"We would, but there isn't room! That chocolate is going to wind up there on your behind, too. Your butt's already the size of a barn."

Strange how one little thing, like getting fired from a job you loved for being fat, can ruin your day, she thought.

"Too bad it didn't ruin your appetite," one of the demons whispered.

"Oh, shut up!" She slammed the door closed and walked into the living room with the entire cake box in one hand and a tablespoon in the other.

Most people in her position would be getting totally plowed at a local bar, she rationalized, trying to feel a little self-righteous. At least she was feeding her sorrow, rather than trying to drown it. That *was* better . . . wasn't it?

So tomorrow I won't have a hangover, she thought. *I'll just weigh five pounds more*.

Other than devouring the cake, she hadn't decided what to do with herself for the remainder of the evening. She was all cried out. Her eyes were swollen nearly closed and her head ached abominably. She didn't think she would be able to concentrate on a movie or television show. Reading a book was definitely out; she doubted she could even see straight.

She could go on to bed, but it was only seven-thirty and she was certain she'd never be able to get to sleep.

Like an answer to an unspoken prayer, a knock sounded on her front door. It was the old shave-and-a-hair-cut knock. Dirk.

"If you came back for the rest of your cake, you're too late," she said when she opened the door and saw him standing there. "I just polished it off. You can lick the box if you like."

He gave her a suggestive grin that made her giggle in spite of her agony.

"Come on in," she said. "I look like hell, but—"

"You look fine, kid. Don't sweat it," he said, his tone far more sentimental than his words.

"Are you off duty?" she asked.

He nodded.

"Want a beer?"

He nodded again.

"So am I," she said as she handed him the bottle and plopped down on the sofa beside him. "Off duty, that is, permanently."

"So I heard. Damn it, Van, I still can't believe it."

He set the beer on the coffee table—she had never been able to teach him to use a coaster—and turned to face her. She couldn't recall ever seeing him look so upset, and she was touched that she was the reason.

"What the hell happened?" He reached over, took her hand in his, and squeezed it.

"I got canned. Bloss said I was too fat, but I—"

"I heard the reason they gave, but we all know it's a pile of bullshit. Come on; what *really* happened?"

Savannah wanted to blurt it all out, to tell him everything from beginning to end. This was one of the most difficult things she had ever faced, and not being able to share it with anyone she loved was driving her crazy.

But intuitively she felt she should wait at least twenty-four hours. She should give herself a cooling-off period, and then she would be in a better frame of mind to make rational choices.

"I'll tell you all about it, Dirk. Really I will. But for right now I just want to think about something else. *Anything* else. Okay?"

"Okay, but before we close the subject, there's just one thing I want to know."

"What's that?"

"Is there *anything* I can do to help out? Anything at all."

That did it. She had been able to hold back the tears for at least half an hour. But the sweet, compassionate tone of his voice and the unaccustomed softness in his expression was her undoing. Covering her face with her hands, she began to sob with renewed fervor.

So much for having cried it all out. The well wasn't dry after all.

"No, no-o-o-thing. But . . . but . . . thank you," she added between hiccups.

"Ah, come on, kiddo," he said, putting one hand on her shoulder and giving her the same sort of shake a naughty puppy gives his master's slipper. "Don't do that. It can't be that bad. There's gotta be something I can do. You just name it."

Suddenly she realized that what she needed most was human contact. Just to be close to another person for a few minutes. Cleo and Diamante were nice, but they just didn't cut it when things were this bad.

"Do you mean it? Anything?" she asked with a loud sniff.

He pulled a tissue out of his pocket and handed it to her. She didn't dare look too closely to see if it had been pre-blown-upon. His heart was in the right place.

"Sure. What is it? You need somebody to go tear Bloss another asshole? We can jump him in an alley; I'll hold him down and you can beat the shit out of 'im. Sound good?"

"Oh, yes, Dirk, perfectly lovely," she replied with subdued enthusiasm.

"Not what you had in mind, huh?" He actually seemed disappointed with her reaction.

"Not exactly. I was hoping for something a little less macho."

"Like?"

"A hug."

He stared at her for so long that she thought he might have suffered a minor stroke. Of course, she had figured he might be surprised at her request. In the five years they had been partners they had eaten together, snoozed in a cramped car together, fought, argued, and laughed together. She had even pitched an ice-cold Coke all over him for calling her a "dame," but they had never hugged. Never even come close.

"Really?" he asked, looking both shocked, pleased, and scared at the same time.

"Yeah. I feel like shit. I need a hug and my granny is in Georgia."

"Your granny?" He seemed insulted. "You want me to hug you the way your grandma would?"

"I don't care, damn it. Just be my friend and hug me and tell me that I am . . . or was . . . a good cop, and that I'm not fat."

"Oh, Van," he said, holding out his arms to her. "Come here, honey. Of course you aren't fat. You're a hell of a lot of woman, but I've never once thought of you as fat."

She scooted toward him on the sofa and melted into his embrace. It felt much better than she had even hoped. His arms were hard, muscular, and warm as they folded around her. He mashed her to his chest in an overly vigorous bear hug, then rocked her gently, as though she were a kindergartner who had skinned her knee while jumping rope. She found she liked the dichotomy of gentle and rough.

After soaking in the comfort for a few moments she pulled back and looked up at him. "Is that really true?" she asked, her wounded ego needing to hear it one more time.

"Let's put it this way," he said with a deep, sexy growl, "a lot of words come to mind when I think of the way you're built, kid, and none of them are anything like 'fat.' "

Again she snuggled into his masculine warmth, breathing in the pleasantly combined scents of aftershave, tobacco, the freshness of outdoors, and man. She hadn't realized how much she had missed enjoying the opposite sex.

At one time, not that long ago, she had allowed herself the other hedonistic pleasure that made life worth living—other than food. And while she hadn't exactly been what Gran would call "a maiden of ill repute," she had compiled a lengthy list of delicious memories to warm her on a chilly night.

Why she had denied herself the real thing in lieu of memories, she wasn't sure. Too busy, she supposed. Too involved with that damned job . . . for all the good it had done her in the long run.

Her arms stole around his neck, and she could feel him tense for a few seconds. Then his own hold on her tightened, pulling her closer.

"And you're a good cop, Van," he said, his voice husky, "the best I've ever known . . . other than me, of course."

She giggled. "Of course."

His big hand moved slowly up her back. She wished she was wearing one of her new satin robes, something prettier than her old terry-cloth standby. Although, judging by his accelerated respiration, Old Faithful wasn't doing so badly either.

"Savannah," he said, burying his face in her hair. "I don't think we should . . ."

His breath felt warm and moist against her neck. She leaned her head back, giving him better access.

"Then don't think," she replied breathlessly.

Part of her couldn't believe what she was doing. She was sitting on her sofa, dressed in her old ratty robe, her eyes swollen, her nose like Rudolph's, her hair stringing down around her face . . . and she was trying to seduce Dirk. Good ol' Dirk, her buddy, her *compadre*, her companion in arms.

Not anymore, she thought sadly. Immediately her sense of urgency soared.

She reached up to touch his hair, and she felt him cringe. He was so sensitive about his thinning hair, so self-conscious. But he didn't need to be. It was much nicer to touch, much softer than she had ever thought it would be.

Looking up at him, she was overwhelmed with an unexpected, overwhelming urge to kiss him. His lips were right there, inches from hers.

She had never noticed before how full and inviting his lower lip was, what a pleasant contrast it was to the rest of his rugged face.

Or maybe it was the cherry brandy in the Black Forest cake she had just devoured.

Whatever the reason, she wanted to be kissed. By Dirk. Now.

Lifting her face to his, she brushed her lips lightly across his. The contact set up an electrical charge that flowed through her body and settled into some rather intimate, decidedly feminine areas.

"Kiss me, Dirk," she said, her own breathing as ragged as his. "Please, I really need it."

For a moment he bent his head, as though he was going to. She closed her eyes, waiting, anticipating.

But when nothing happened she finally opened her eyes to find him staring at her, looking perplexed and maybe even a little hurt.

"I know you do," he said.

"What?"

"I know you need it." He gave her another hug, shorter than the others, then gently pushed her away. "But . . . but I'd rather wait."

"Wait? For what?" she asked. "We're all alone. We've known each other for years. It isn't as though we haven't thought about this a thousand times."

"I know," he said as he rose from the sofa. "I know you're hurting, you're feeling insecure about yourself, and you probably do need to have some guy wrestle you on that mattress of yours for a few hours. It'd probably cure what ails you."

"So, what is it you're waiting for?" she asked, completely confused. In her thousand fantasies, things had never played this way. He had never said no.

Dirk smiled knowingly, bent down, and gave her the kiss she had asked for . . . but he placed it on her forehead.

"I know you need it," he said as he walked to her door. "But you've always been really special to me, Van, and I think I'd like to wait until you need *me*."

Savannah couldn't think of a thing to say as she watched him walk out the door and close it quietly behind him. In the empty space he left behind she felt more alone than ever.

And she found that the well of tears *still* wasn't dry.

Savannah awoke from the first shallow stages of sleep with a start. The phone. It was that damned phone again. For hours she had lain in bed, counting sheep, trying to get to sleep. Actually, she had been counting heads, rolling from a guillotine, most of them wearing faces that looked remarkably like Bloss's. She had found the image more soothing than fleecy, gymnastic sheep.

Glancing at the new digital clock that had replaced the broken one, she groaned. It was a quarter to four. She had been asleep for ten whole minutes. Whoopee.

"This had better be a wrong number," she mumbled into the phone. "Because if I know you, you're dead meat."

"Savannah, it's me, Atlanta! I have got the *neatest* surprise for you! You're not going to believe this, really!"

Savannah seriously considered hanging up the phone without saying another word. But if she did, the kid would just call back again, and she didn't think her system could stand hearing that shrill ring again so soon.

"Atlanta, I was asleep. I just had the *worst* day of my life, I'm exhausted, and I don't want to talk to anyone. Not even you."

"No, no, you don't understand. This is fantastic! You're gonna love this; trust me."

"No, Atlanta, *you* are the one who doesn't understand. I *hate* chipper, happy, bouncy people who wake me up in the morning. *Hate* them. But *you* are waking me up in the middle of the night, and you're chipper and bouncy. That's much worse."

"Savannah, guess what I've done? Come on, just try."

"Good night, Atlanta."

"No, wait! You're going to be so surprised. Guess where I am?"

"Where you are?" Fatigue was muddling her brain again, and she could hardly concentrate. "I suppose you're there. Right?"

"Wrong."

"Wrong?"

"Yeah . . . Savannah, I'm here!"

"Like I said, you're there in—"

"No, I'm here in California at LAX! I just flew in on the red-eye flight. Mom said I could come out here and live with you! She even paid for my ticket. Isn't that just totally cool?"

Savannah lay, staring up at the ceiling, her mouth hanging open, her jaw slack. She didn't blink. She didn't breathe. It was one shock too many. Her circuits had been completely blown.

"There's just one thing . . ." She could hear the voice, as though from far away. ". . . I bought some really neat clothes on my layover in Denver, you know, in those cute little gift shops, and I don't have any more money on me, you know, for a cab. So . . . could you come get me? Could you, Savannah? Savannah? Sava-a-a-annah!"

Fortunately, Savannah's anger brought its accompanying shot of adrenaline, so she had no trouble staying awake while negotiating the maze known as Los Angeles International Airport.

She considered parking in one of the forbidden, sacred, "white" zones and sticking her police ID card in the window. But she was still far too bitter to want to affiliate herself with any police force at the moment, even for the convenience of free parking.

After stashing the Camaro in one of the quickie lots across the street from Atlanta's terminal, she made her way through the parking structure to the elevator. Ordinarily she would have used the steps, but tonight she wanted to avoid as many challenges as possible.

Stepping through the sliding doors, she found herself inside the small enclosure with a couple of rough-looking teenaged boys. The color of their jackets and bandannas and the name of the football team on their caps identified them as members of one of the more violent L.A. gangs.

The older of the two flashed her a less-than-genuine smile, then began to look her up and down with predator's eyes, taking in every detail from her watch to her purse and the gold chain around her neck.

She had been sized up before, while playing decoy in robbery stings. She knew the look.

"Don't even think about it," she said in a low, menacing tone as she slid her hand inside her jacket, where she kept the Beretta. She had no intention of drawing the gun unless she had to, but the gesture was one every street kid knew.

He took a step back from her and toward his friend. His expression and his body language told her that he had gotten the message, but she wanted to be sure.

"I'm not kidding," she said. "If you knew how goddamned mad I am right now, you wouldn't even want to be in this elevator with me."

The doors opened, and they hurried out as quickly as they could without losing their cool.

She felt the letdown, the relief surge through her body, leaving her weak in the knees. Over the years she had been in similar situations many times. But she had never gotten to the point where it didn't scare the shit out of her. Maybe now that she wasn't a cop those experiences would become rarities, instead of the norm.

As she hurried into the terminal, she scanned the area for a dark-haired, blue-eyed Southern beauty, standing alone and forlorn . . . one she wanted to hug, then strangle.

Instead she saw a teenager who had her sister's eyes and face, but whose hair had been bleached and dyed an impossibly bright shade of red. Her figure had filled out considerably in the past six months, but unlike Savannah, it had been in all the right places.

And she was hardly alone or forlorn. Four guys in gaudy, pimp attire hovered around her, like buzzards over an old prospector on his last gasp. Damned vultures. They hung around the airport, trying to recruit any young kid who looked like she had just arrived via turnip truck.

But what distressed Savannah most was that Atlanta was giggling and mincing with them as though she was surrounded by a bevy of eligible gentlemen beaus. Her peals of laughter echoed all the way across the room, and Savannah watched in horror as the girl placed her hand on one of the guy's shoulders and gave him a friendly nudge.

Good God! she thought. *Can't she just tell by looking at that guy that he's got the creeping crud?*

"Atlanta! Atlanta!" she shouted, not caring that a dozen people were staring.

"Savannah!" The girl let out an ear-piercing squeal of delight as she threw down her suitcases and ran to Savannah, arms outstretched.

Savannah gave her a hearty hug, keeping one eye on the luggage, lest it sprout feet and walk away.

"What were you doing, talking to those jerks?" she said as she walked across the room to retrieve the bags from the floor. She gave the guys her best evil eye. "You've got to be careful, kid. You're in the big city now."

Atlanta stood, her lip stuck out, pouting like a four-year-old who hadn't gotten her favorite flavor Popsicle. "Gee, Savannah, the first thing you do is yell at me and start bossing me around. Why do you think I left Georgia?"

"I'm not sure," she replied, motioning her toward the large glass doors. "Why *did* you leave?"

"Oh, it's a long story. I'll tell you all about it on the way home."

"I'm sure you will," Savannah muttered as she anticipated the drive ahead, Atlanta nattering happily in her ear. She was too tired to breathe, let alone listen to worthless babbling and try to insert the proper "Oh, really? You don't say. Hmm-mm-mm."

This just wasn't going to work; she could tell already. With a sinking feeling, she watched yet another streetworn guy in a garish white suit and hat saunter over in their direction.

"Hey, hey . . . beautiful ladies," he said, slathering the charm on thick. "Do you have a ride to where you're going? Do you need a place to stay, a nice dinner maybe?"

Atlanta smiled and opened her mouth to respond; Savannah shoved the suitcase at him. "I'm a cop, asshole, and this is *my* little sister," she told him. "Get the hell out of my face before I bust you."

The guy seemed to evaporate before their eyes.

"God, Savannah, you are *so* rude!" Atlanta pursed her too-red lips petulantly, reminding Savannah of when she had been caught eating Mama's lipstick. Somehow the expression had been a lot cuter then. "Why did you say that to him? He was just being nice."

"Being nice, my hind end," Savannah said, forging ahead and out the sliding glass doors.

"But he offered to buy us dinner."

"Yeah, and do you know how you would have been expected to pay for it?"

She shrugged. "He acted like it was his treat."

At the curb Savannah handed Atlanta the smaller of the two bags and punched the button on the pole to change the traffic light. "He's a pimp, Atlanta. So were those other guys you were talking to. They were trying to pick you up, recruit you. Got it?"

Atlanta's mouth opened wide; then she snapped it shut. "Well, I be . . ."

She seemed surprised, but not exactly indignant. In fact, she didn't look nearly as appalled as Savannah would have liked. Any decent Southern belle would have swooned at the very thought.

The girl reached up and fluffed her hair with one hand, in a gesture that looked like a bad impression of Mae West. She smiled coquettishly. "Gee, then they must have thought I was pretty cute or, you know, sexy. . . . I mean, if they wanted me to be one of their girls . . ."

It was Savannah's turn to be amazed. "No, 'Lanta," she said, shaking her head, "you've got it all wrong. You don't have to be cute to be a hooker. That's just in the movies. In real life all you have to be is young and stupid."

One look at her sister's face told Savannah that she had been wrong about the ride home. She wasn't going to have to listen to Atlanta's chattering after all. No, the drive was going to be long, cold, and very silent.

CHAPTER ELEVEN

As Savannah rounded the final corner to her house, she glanced down at her watch. Seven-thirty. There was hardly any point in going back to bed now. She had always found it next to impossible to sleep in the daytime, even with thick window-shades and a satin mask.

Glancing at Atlanta, who sat beside her, still pouting, Savannah could see that she was far from sleepy, too. The little booger had probably snoozed several hours on the flight. Atlanta had never had any problem sleeping, day or night, horizontal or vertical.

"This visit of yours is going to be pretty long and miserable," Savannah said, "if you and I aren't even speaking to each other."

"Well *you* started it." Atlanta crossed her arms over her chest and pushed out her chin. "You're not any better than Mom. Neither one of you gives me any respect."

Savannah whipped the car into the driveway and cut the key. Leaning her forearms wearily against the top of the steering wheel, she said, "In the first place, Atlanta, respect isn't something that you are given on demand. Respect is something you earn. And—"

"But I *have* tried to earn your respect."

"Yes, you have. And I do respect you a lot more than you realize. I think you're an intelligent, funny, and kind person. You're also an extremely talented singer."

"And cute."

Savannah smiled and nodded. "Yes, much too cute for your own good. It's a problem all of us Reid gals have . . . that and an overabundance of boobs."

"And humility," Atlanta added with a giggle. "We're far too humble."

"Ah, yes, of all our countless virtues, humility is the greatest of all."

As Savannah climbed out of the Camaro, she experienced the first fleeting moment of happiness and levity she had felt for the past three days. Maybe this wouldn't be such a burden after all, having the kid around for a while.

"So, how long do you intend to vacation here in the California sunshine?" she asked, helping Atlanta pull her bags from the trunk.

"Vacation? Oh, you thought this was a vacation?"

"Yes . . ." Savannah felt her throat closing.

"Oh, no, it's a *lot* better than that! Mama said I could actually *live* with you! She's going to be sending all the rest of my stuff next week. Isn't that great?"

"Wonderful," Savannah replied, slamming the trunk closed

with a bit more force than was required. "Did it occur to either you or Mama to call and discuss it with me first?"

"Sure. I told her we should phone you, but she said it would be better to surprise you."

"Yes, I'll bet she did."

This wasn't the first time Mama had gotten rid of one of the brood by shipping them off to her. Mama had a damned good reason for not calling first; she knew Savannah would say no.

Making a mental note to call her mother as soon as possible and delay the shipment of all the "stuff," Savannah hefted two of the suitcases and led Atlanta up the walk to the house.

"Your place is kinda cute," Atlanta observed, "like a little dollhouse. I was expecting something newer and bigger, but this will do."

"Gee, I'm so relieved," Savannah muttered, wondering how many times she could hear the adjective *cute* without barfing.

As they approached the porch, she was startled to see someone standing there in the shadow of the bougainvillea: Beverly Winston.

Savannah glanced back over her shoulder and saw the burgundy Volvo parked in front of her house. She had been so occupied with Atlanta that she hadn't noticed it before.

"Mrs. Winston," she said, setting the luggage on the porch. "I'm surprised to see you here."

Beverly Winston offered her hand and an apologetic half smile. "I have to talk to you, Detective Reid." She glanced Atlanta's way and looked uneasy. "It's very important . . . and private."

"Yes, of course. I understand."

Savannah turned to her sister. Like anyone who thinks they

might get to hear something they shouldn't, she looked eager and curious.

"Let's go inside," Savannah said, unlocking the door. "You and I can talk in the living room. Atlanta . . . you can watch television in my bedroom . . . you know . . . for a while. . . ."

"Sure, no problem." Again the lip protruded, even farther this time. She stomped into the living room, where she pitched the suitcases onto the floor. "I can take a hint. I'll get lost. Just like home," she added under her breath as she disappeared up the stairs.

"Teenagers," Savannah said, shaking her head. "I wish we could just put them on ice the day they turn thirteen, and not thaw them out until they're . . . oh . . . about thirty."

"The world would be a simpler place, to be sure," Beverly replied. "But far less pleasant or exciting."

Savannah offered her a chair and a cup of coffee. She accepted the seat but declined anything to drink.

"No, thank you. I want to get straight to the point and tell you why I'm here."

Savannah sat on the sofa beside her, forcing herself not to sit on the edge of the cushion. But it wasn't easy to pretend that nothing out of the ordinary had happened in the past couple of days.

Why would Beverly Winston approach her? Hadn't she been fired for going after the councilwoman? Savannah thought Beverly would have been relieved to be rid of her. A hundred possibilities were racing through her head, none of which made any sense.

"First of all," Beverly began without preamble, "I want you to know I think it is deplorable that you were terminated, and I've told Norman so in no uncertain terms."

"Thank you," Savannah said, studying the woman's face. She looked sincere enough, for all the good it did Savannah.

"And, if you'll help me, I promise to do everything in my power to see that you're reinstated." She paused and stared down at her hands, which were folded demurely in her lap. "To be honest, I'll do everything I can, whether you help me or not. I feel really horrible about what's happened to you."

Savannah was touched by her obvious concern, but even if the councilwoman could pull strings and get her her job back, she wasn't sure she wanted it.

"I appreciate your offer," she said. "But I make it a practice not to foist myself off on anyone who isn't pleased to have my company. I don't think I want to work for the SCPD anymore, even if you could arrange it. I'm sorry; I don't want to appear ungrateful."

Beverly looked disappointed but nodded her understanding. "Neither would I. They've treated you very badly. You deserve much better."

"Well, it appears I'm going to have lots of free time to find better," Savannah said, only half panicked. "Meanwhile, how can I help you?"

"I want you to continue to investigate the case."

Savannah hesitated, confused. "I'd like to, but . . ."

"Then do it, unofficially, on my behalf. I'll pay you whatever you feel your services are worth and, of course, all your expenses."

"Do you mean you want to hire me as a private investigator?"

"That's exactly right." Leaning toward her, Beverly Winston looked Savannah squarely in the eye, and Savannah could see the depth of her pain and frustration. "Savannah, I didn't kill Jonathan. I don't know who did. And I need to know."

She sighed and leaned back against the sofa, her personality suddenly deflated. "I don't know if you believe me or not, but it's true. In my own way I really did love Jonathan. I had fallen out of love with him long ago, but I will always have a deep affection for him. The person who did this horrible thing to him has to be caught and punished. Will you help me?"

Savannah began to weigh mentally the pros against the cons. A private investigator. In all the years she had been in law enforcement the thought had never once crossed her mind.

"How about the police?" Savannah asked. "They'll be continuing their investigation and—"

"They think I did it, or had it done. Even Norman thinks so. That's why you were fired, Savannah; because they were afraid you were going to nail me. They're going to conduct this investigation in the most politically correct manner possible. And that may or may not lead them to the truth. I can't take that chance. That's why I need you."

When Savannah didn't respond Beverly leaned over and placed her hand on Savannah's forearm. Savannah was surprised at the degree of energy that radiated from the woman, warming her with just a touch.

"Please, Savannah. Please do this for me."

Savannah smiled and shrugged her shoulders. "Oh well, sure. What the hell? It's not like I had anything planned for the next twenty years."

Fiona O'Neal had once been a beauty, but it hadn't been last week . . . last year . . . or any time in recent history. Savannah watched the woman from the other side of the smoke-choked bar as she finished performing her second set of the evening. Her choice of material had been predictably cliché, the usual Top Forty. But she had delivered each song in her own throaty, bluesy style that made the most simplistic lyrics sound deliciously sensual and provocative. Her hand and body movements were infinitely graceful and seductive.

Glancing around the bar, Savannah could see that the singer's melodic aphrodisiac was working its magic on male and female alike. Some of the guys in this place were definitely going to get lucky tonight.

With her shimmering, waist-length red hair and slight figure, Fiona looked much younger from a distance than up close, Savannah realized when the singer walked past her table on the way to the rest room. Her pale complexion, with its sprinkling of freckles, was as Irish as her brilliant, cobalt blue eyes. But her skin also showed the wear-and-tear of a life lived hard. A life that would probably end early unless its habits were amended pretty soon.

As Savannah waited for Fiona to leave the rest room, she took a sip of her virgin margarita and tried not to grimace; it just wasn't the same without the tequila. But, although she was no longer a cop and didn't have to abide by the department's policies, she couldn't throw aside years of discipline and allow herself to drink while "on duty."

Wearing a fresh coat of makeup, lips newly glossed, Fiona emerged and walked over to a table in the corner of the room near Savannah. She dropped onto the chair, her stage grace gone, the fatigue showing through as she bent over the generous drink the waitress had delivered: at least three fingers of scotch or whiskey.

Savannah left her own table and approached Fiona's, mentally rehearsing her new introductory speech. The old standard: "Hello, I'm Detective Savannah Reid with the San Carmelita Police Department, and I'm investigating so and so . . ." wouldn't wash. What the hell was she now, anyway? A private investigator, God forbid? Didn't she need a license or something for that?

"Fiona?" she asked as she slid onto the chair across from the singer. Fiona nodded tiredly. "May I talk to you for a moment?"

The woman hesitated, then said, "I really don't like to talk much between sets. I need to rest my voice and—"

"I understand. I used to sing a bit myself."

She brightened slightly. "You did?"

"Not professionally. Let's just say that being a world-famous singing star was one of the careers I was intending to have . . . after becoming a go-go dancer and a stewardess, but before being an Academy-Award winning actress."

Fiona took a deep slug of the liquor and closed her eyes for a second as it burned its way down. "How old were you when you were making all these plans?"

"About fourteen."

She nodded. "That explains a lot. But a go-go dancer?"

"Hey, it was the sixties. Didn't you want to put on a pair of white boots, a miniskirt, and a crocheted top and dance in a cage?"

Fiona smiled, but even then her face was tinged with sadness. "I must have been a bit older than you. I wanted to wear a poodle skirt and be Connie Francis."

A momentary lull in the conversation gave Savannah a second to reconsider her alternative introductions, but she didn't need any.

"You're the lady cop who's investigating Jonathan's murder, aren't you?" Fiona said, dropping any pretense of a smile.

"Uh . . . I was," Savannah replied.

"You *were* investigating it, but now you're not?"

"No, I mean I *was* a cop. I'm still investigating the homicide."

Fiona scowled. "That's a little confusing."

"For me, too." Savannah leaned forward on her elbows and looked into Fiona's dark blue eyes. She saw no deceit or evasiveness, only the profound emptiness that accompanies a deep depression. "Can you help me, Fiona? You loved the man once; you were married to him. Who do you think might have killed him?"

"Oh, I *know* who killed Jonathan. And if you'd been investigating this case for more than ten minutes, you'd know, too. It's pretty obvious, don't you think?"

"Sorry, but I don't assume that anything is obvious in a situation like this. Who do you know did it?"

"Beverly, of course." Fiona pulled a pack of extra-length cigarettes from her purse and stuck one between her glossed lips. With her lighter poised an inch from the cigarette's tip, she said, "Do you mind?"

"Well, yes, actually I—"

Too late; she had already lit up. She took a deep draw, released the smoke over her shoulder, and leaned back in her chair. Savannah could tell that the single thread of rapport that had been between them at first was broken. Fiona's blue eyes reflected her sudden suspicion and defensiveness.

"Why do you think it was Beverly?" Savannah asked, pushing in spite of the guarded posture.

"Because he told her he was coming back to me. We fell in love, again, and he asked her for a divorce so that we could get married. He told her he had made a mistake by leaving me in the first place, that he had never stopped loving me and he couldn't live without me anymore. She kicked him out of the mansion and told him she would kill him before she would give him a divorce. I guess she meant it."

"How do you know all of this?"

"Jonathan told me."

Savannah sat quietly for a moment, toying with the salt on the top of her margarita glass. "You said you were in love with Jonathan and intended to remarry him. I know you must have trusted him, but how could you be sure he was telling you the truth?"

"Because he couldn't have faked it. The fear I saw in his eyes the few weeks before he was murdered . . . it was real. And then, there was the bodyguard. Why would anyone hire a big, high-priced bodyguard unless they really needed one?"

"A bodyguard?" Savannah pulled her notebook from her purse and flipped it open. "Tell me about him."

"You haven't heard about Ryan?" Fiona said with a slight crooked smile. "Well, you don't know what you've missed." She assumed a brief, dreamy look, staring away into the smoke-filled haze. "I was madly in love with Jonathan, always will be, but I have to admit . . . that Ryan What's-His-Name was the most gorgeous man I ever laid eyes on. Just before the murder he was everywhere, watching over Jonathan, just like he was hired to do. But after the murder, poof, haven't seen him since."

"Do you think he had anything to do with the killing?"

Fiona glanced at her watch and rose from the table. "All I know is, he was supposed to have prevented it," she said, somewhat bitterly. "Looks like he didn't do a very good job."

Name: Ryan Something
Occupation: Bodyguard (but not too good at it)
Physical Description: Knock 'Em Dead Gorgeous

Not a lot to go on, Savannah told herself as she dragged her tired body across her threshold. Ah, home at last. In ten minutes she would be soaking in lavender-scented suds, holding a steaming cup of coffee, fortified with a wickedly generous splash of Bailey's and heavy cream.

Yes, indeed, she thought, there was nothing on earth quite like the bliss of walking through the door of your own little cottage, to be greeted by—

An empty pizza box on the floor, smeared with tomato-sauce stains, mozzarella strings hanging over the edge and onto her favorite Oriental rug. One more step and she would have been standing in it.

The radio playing a station she had never heard, featuring a style of music that she fondly referred to as "that rap crap." The volume high enough to severely rattle her new speakers, not to mention her nerves.

Diamante and Cleopatra seemed to share her distaste; they sat in her floral wingbacked chair with their ears laid back, tails twitching bad-temperedly. Cleo's whiskers were tinged red—pizza sauce, no doubt.

That did it! Nobody fed her animals junk food . . . nobody but *her*, that is. The stuff could kill them!

"Atlanta!" she called, trying to be heard above the irritating voice on the radio, who was encouraging his listeners to "Whip that bitch in line. . . ."

"Up he-e-ere," a sweet voice replied.

Savannah punched the power button on the stereo and momentarily reveled in the silence. Then she heard a splash . . . and some humming . . . another splash.

"Why, that little . . ."

She hurried up the steps, two at a time. The kid was in *her* bathtub! Soaking in *her*—

"Wait a minute," she told herself, pausing at the top step.

"Of course she's taking a bath in your tub. It's the only tub in the house. Where else would she bathe?"

She gritted her teeth as another pseudo-operatic arpeggio drifted out to her.

"Share, Savannah," she told herself. "Be a nice girl and share your things with your little sister."

"Wow, this lavender gel stuff is really cool. I wish you had more," trilled the angelic voice, followed by the rather rude, farting sound of an empty plastic tube being squeezed for its last drop.

Damn. So much for the lavender bath.

"I'm so glad you liked it," she replied with equal sweetness. But the words had a bitter, saccharine aftertaste in her mouth. Exactly *why* was it her mother had said she couldn't hit her little sister?

"I was looking forward to taking a bath myself," Savannah ventured, leaning wearily against the bathroom door. "Are you going to be done any time soon?"

"Sorry, but I just got in. Beat you to it, huh?"

"Yeah, seems so," she muttered as she turned and trudged down the stairs.

In the kitchen she made several other discoveries that sent her blood pressure soaring a few more notches. The array of empty food containers and dirty dishes strewn across the counters gave silent testimony of how Miss Atlanta Prissy-Pot had spent her day. Eating. Not *cooking*, mind you: There wasn't a pan or a mixing bowl among the mess. Why go to the trouble of making a meal when there were so many yummy snacks to choose from?

With a lump in her throat Savannah surveyed the ruins of her treasured stashes. The carnage lay everywhere: deflated chip bags, crumpled candy wrappers, empty guacamole and French onion dip containers and—!

Dear God! Was nothing sacred?

There . . . in the sink . . . lying on its side . . . was the soggy, dripping carton that had once held her beloved Ben and Jerry's Chunky Monkey Ice Cream!

Savannah opened her mouth to scream, but nothing came out. She'd definitely have to get physical with the kid.

As visions of woodsheds danced through her head, she whirled around, ready to stomp back up the stairs and offer her sister a slight attitude adjustment. But the phone rang.

She wasn't in the mood to talk to anyone about anything. But, on second thought, she *was* unemployed, without an income, with a new—and obviously voracious—little mouth to feed. This wasn't the time to play the hermit.

"Hello-o-o," she said in her most charming, butter-wouldn't-melt-in-my-mouth tone.

She was glad she had answered it; the caller was Beverly Winston, wanting to know how things were going.

"Do you know anything about Jonathan hiring a bodyguard?" she asked her. "A Ryan somebody?"

"Only that his first name was Ryan," Beverly replied, "and he was gorgeous."

"Hmmm . . . so I've been told. You wouldn't have a last name on him, would you? Or maybe the name of his agency?"

"Sorry, no. Jonathan and I weren't exactly on speaking terms when he hired him. A bodyguard . . . to protect himself from me . . . can you imagine?"

"How do you know it was protection from you?"

"He said so, made sure everyone knew it." Savannah heard Beverly draw a long, shaking breath. "To be honest, I think it was just one of Jonathan's stupid games to embarrass and hurt me. He knew I didn't mean it."

"Didn't mean what?"

"That I was going to kill him. It was just a figure of speech, you know. . . ."

Savannah twisted the phone cord around her index finger and tried to imagine Beverly Winston saying those words, figuratively or otherwise. "Beverly, did anyone else hear you make that threat?"

"Oh, sure. I said it in front of the entire country club one evening last month. Not smart, huh?"

Savannah thought of the next detective who would be assigned the case. Bloss would have to appoint someone. And that somebody would have to conduct some sort of investigation. He would be sure to run across at least some of the same information she had. And all paths seemed to lead back to Beverly Winston.

"No, Bev," Savannah said softly, "I'm sorry, but I'm afraid you're right. It wasn't too smart."

CHAPTER TWELVE

"Are you mad at me, or what?" Atlanta stood with her hands on her slender hips, an indignant pout on her freshly scrubbed face. She stared down at Savannah, who sat in the middle of the living-room floor, surrounded by stacks of Jonathan Winston's private papers.

"Ah . . . what?" Savannah pulled her attention away from the task at hand and glanced up at her younger sister. Then did a fast double take. Damn! The kid was wearing her terry-cloth robe. Old Faithful on someone else's body. Even worse, a much thinner body.

"I want to know if you're mad at me. I've been standing here for five minutes and you haven't said a word to me." She flounced over to the sofa and stretched out on it, carefully arranging each fold of the robe to best accentuate her newly curvaceous figure.

Dear lord, Savannah thought, *was I ever that vain?* The resounding answer was, "Yes, maybe more." Which was probably why she found the behavior so irritating.

"I'm not trying to ignore you, Atlanta," she said with as much patience as she could muster. "But, whether it looks like it or not, I'm trying to work here."

"Once a cop, always a cop," the girl replied in a singsong tone, rolling her eyes heavenward.

"Not necessarily," Savannah muttered. She supposed she should tell Atlanta that she had been canned. But she had always taken a small comfort in thinking the kid looked up to her, and she couldn't quite bring herself to climb down off the pedestal yet.

"What are you looking for?" Atlanta asked, exhibiting more interest than Savannah would have expected.

"A gorgeous guy named Ryan."

"Really?" She perked up and leaned over the coffee table, looking down at the mess on the floor. "Want some help?"

A refusal was on the tip of Savannah's tongue, but she swallowed it. Why not? She had been staring at these papers so long, her eyeballs were about to roll out onto her cheeks. Might as well put some of that youthful energy to use.

"Okay, get down here on the floor and help me. If you help me find something, I'll buy you a carton of your own Chunky Monkey . . . since you already ate all of mine," she added rather mournfully.

"Oh, sorry." She slid off the sofa and onto the rug beside Savannah. Glancing up at her, Savannah was surprised to see that she appeared genuinely remorseful. Not suicide-watch sorry, but mildly repentant. "Was that like . . . your favorite or something?"

"Everything that has calories in my kitchen is my favorite, 'Lanta. Don't worry about it. Just ask next time before you eat me out of house and home, okay?"

"Okay, what are we looking for, really?"

Savannah tossed her a stack of canceled checks. "Anything with a Ryan on it. Or maybe the name of a business that sounds like it could be a security service or something like that. I don't know what the guy's last name is. He was my victim's bodyguard, and I figure if he guarded his body, he must have paid him something for it."

"He could have paid him cash."

Savannah sighed. "I can think up discouraging thoughts like that all by myself, dear heart."

"Well, cheer up; I have some good news." She began to shuffle through her stack, while Savannah did the same.

"Really?"

"Yeah, I think I've got a job already."

Savannah was astounded. All that eating and she had found time to job hunt, too? Maybe she had underestimated this kid.

"Doing what?"

"Going on dates."

Alarm bells went off in Savannah's brain. No. Surely not . . .

"What do you mean, going on dates?"

"I saw it in the paper. The ad said they wanted attractive young women to escort gentlemen around town, go to fancy parties with them, show them the sights, stuff like that." She paused to fluff her hair, which Savannah could swear was a couple of shades brighter than it had been last night at the airport. "I've got an interview at three o'clock tomorrow afternoon with the lady who runs the agency. It's called Twilight Paradiso. That means 'Twilight Paradise.' Romantic and classy, huh?"

She didn't wait for Savannah, who was still trying to recover her composure, to say anything before nattering on, full steam ahead. "Which reminds me . . . can I borrow some money to get a new outfit? I don't have anything sophisticated enough, and I can't take anything out of *your* closet because you're so much bigger than me now that you've gained weight."

"Of course not," Savannah replied dryly, picking up another stack of checks and shoving them at her.

"Does that mean, 'Of course not,' I can't wear your stuff, or 'Of course not,' I can't borrow the money?"

"Both."

"Oh."

Savannah set her work aside for the moment. This parenting stuff took a lot more intense concentration than she would have thought. "Atlanta," she said, considering her words well before speaking. The last thing she wanted under these circumstances was to alienate the girl again as she had in the airport. "I'm going to tell you something, and I need you to believe me, whether you want to or not."

She said nothing, but nodded.

"These escort services—they aren't what you think. You won't just be going on nice dates to nice places with nice gentlemen. Those are fronts for prostitution. You would be expected to do a lot more than just walk into a high-society ball on their arm. Believe me. I busted dozens of them back when I worked vice."

Savannah watched as a series of emotions crossed her sister's face: irritation and self-righteous indignation, followed by some sappy look that was probably supposed to be benevolent understanding born of infinite wisdom.

"Sa-va-a-annah," she said with a gentle shake of her head, "you are *so* suspicious. But I understand why; it's because you're a police officer and they pay you to be suspicious. But this is the *real* world, with *real* people in it. This is *my* world, and it's very different from yours. Believe it or not, in *my* world not everyone is a criminal."

Savannah dropped the checks and stared at the girl, dumbfounded. The *real* world? What the hell was she—?

"I don't hold it against you, Savannah," she continued, in that insipid, condescending tone that made Savannah want to reach over and pull out a handful of her overprocessed hair. "You can't help being the way you are. But you have to learn to trust my judgment. I'm far more mature than you realize. For instance . . . it occurred to me that this might not be legitimate, so I asked the woman, right out, if I'd have to do anything dirty with the guys. And she said, 'Of course not, dear.' She called me 'dear.' I think she's from England or France . . . someplace where they have those fancy accents. She said that all I had to do was go on the date for three hours for a hundred and fifty bucks, and after the date whatever I did was my own business."

"And what do you think you're going to be doing . . . after the date?"

With a demure batting of her lashes Atlanta dipped her head and smiled coquettishly. "I'll just shake his hand and tell him what a nice time I had. Unless he's cute, of course, and then I might let him kiss me."

"A kiss? You're going to give him a little kiss?" Savannah's control snapped. "So, tell me, Miss Priss, how do you feel about blow jobs, group gropes, bondage, and anal sex?"

"Wh—wha—what?" She shot up from the floor, canceled checks fluttering around her like a flock of startled pigeons in a city park. "Savannah! You—you have a filthy, filthy mind! Why, I never heard such a . . ."

Her voice trailed away as she disappeared up the stairs, the long ends of the robe's sash dragging behind her.

"Atlanta!" she shouted after her. "Atlanta Reid, don't you go anywhere near that place tomorrow! You hear me, girl?"

"What are you going to do?" she yelled back. "Take a switch to my backside?"

"I might. You get too big for your britches, I just might do that! Don't you go thinkin' you're too grown up for a whoopin'. I could still bend you over my knee and set your bee-hind afire!"

Savannah heard the exaggerated Southern accent in her own voice and flashed back to her mother saying the same words to her. Obnoxious words, to be sure. But they made a lot more sense at that moment than ever before.

Feeling sad and defeated, she shook her head. No, Atlanta didn't need a "whoopin'." She needed some common sense. And, unfortunately, that wasn't something Savannah could just open the top of her head and pour in. The only way a person learned was through trial and error. Experience had to teach her, and Experience wasn't nearly as compassionate an instructor as her mother or family. She would learn that the hard way.

"Damn," she said tiredly as she stared down at the scattered checks with bleary eyes.

Through the haze of fatigue and unshed tears, Savannah saw it . . . there on the floor at her feet. A check . . . made out to one Ryan Stone. In the lower left corner on the memo line Winston had scribbled two words. "Personal Protection."

"Well, Mr. Ryan Stone," she said softly, "my little sister found you for me."

But as Savannah looked up toward the staircase, she didn't feel even half the thrill she usually felt when she experienced a breakthrough like this.

Somehow, with her younger sister sobbing upstairs, this minor victory didn't seem to matter nearly so much.

The little white lies that Savannah had been forced to tell in the course of law-enforcement duties had bothered her. But without the instant access afforded by her badge, she'd had to resort to a garbage-truck load of big, rotten, black ones. Her tongue was definitely in mortal danger, not to mention her soul.

In the past twenty-four hours she had acquired a bevy of new relatives. Just now she had told the woman at the apartment office that she was Ryan Stone's sister, in order to gain admittance through the security gate. She had been his aunt when finagling his address, and his ex-roommate for the telephone number.

There were definite handicaps in being a civilian. But in spite of the challenging odds, she had persevered all day and here she was, approaching Ryan Stone's apartment. She glanced down at her watch. Nine P.M. Not too bad. It had only taken her twenty-six hours to find him.

The complex was one of those Southern California hillside developments that seemed to defy the law of gravity. Perched precariously on the steep slope, it provided its occupants with breathtaking views of the town and the Pacific.

Savannah contemplated exactly how breathtaking the experience might be in the midst of an earthquake. Would the building stop rolling when it hit the courthouse below, or just keep sliding—taking everything with it—until it reached the town dock and the water?

As she formulated her theory, she glanced around at the immaculately kept, romantically lit pool, surrounded by full palmettos that waved in the night breeze with a paper-crisp crackle. They, too, were illuminated with blue, pink, and gold accent lights, buried in the lawn and shining upward through the foliage.

Nice place. She considered the feasibility of becoming a

bodyguard instead of a private investigator. Being overweight didn't appear to disqualify one for the position, judging from the potbellied Neanderthals she had seen escorting celebrities on television. Hell, a few more Black Forest cakes, a bit more facial hair, and a shirt that was two sizes too small around her midriff . . . such a minor investment to begin a new business.

Remembering what Beverly and Fiona had said about Ryan, she wondered if her preconception of the gorilla bodyguard might be an ill-founded, stupid prejudice. One could always hope.

In the corner of the complex she found Stone's apartment. The prime spot, she noted. Perfect view, close to the pool, a tad more secluded than the others. So, he had good taste in apartments. She still wasn't ready to let go of her prejudices just yet.

As she neared the door she saw an off-white square, stuck into the jamb. It was an envelope. A beautiful, square piece of elegant stationery—with her name on it.

"Ms. Savannah Reid" had been written across the front in fine, sweeping penmanship with what appeared to be an antique fountain pen, judging from the distinct calligraphic quality of the strokes.

Ryan Stone, Bodyguard to the Rich and Fashionable, was a class act, she decided, no matter what he did for a living.

She rang the doorbell, then pulled the envelope from the jamb. If it had her name on it, it must be for her. As she waited, she didn't really expect him to answer. Mr. Stone wasn't at home. Or, if he was, he didn't intend to make an appearance. This envelope, whatever it contained, was all she was going to get this time out.

Carefully, her curiosity rising by the moment, she opened the envelope and looked inside. It looked like . . . yes, it was . . . an engraved invitation.

The gracefully scripted words requested the pleasure of her company for dinner the following evening at Chez Antoine, her very favorite restaurant in the world.

Did he know somehow? Or had it been a lucky guess?

Her question was soon answered as her eyes skimmed the rest of the card, which went on to say that he had ordered the Salmon Mousse, prepared just the way she liked it, and her favorite bottle of Beaujolais.

Realizing that she had been standing there for several minutes with her mouth hanging open, Savannah shoved the card into its envelope and hurried back down the path toward her car.

As she drove away, her pulse was racing at a much higher speed than the brisk walk would have accounted for. She was both flattered and flabbergasted. Only this afternoon had she found out where this man lived. Last night she hadn't even known his name. How the hell did he know her favorite restaurant, entrée, and wine? The thought was exciting, even titillating . . . but unsettling, nevertheless.

What else did Ryan Stone know about her?

CHAPTER THIRTEEN

Savannah sat up in bed and switched on the lamp, bathing the room in a romantic, rosy glow. Long ago she had discovered that a woman's skin looked its best by candlelight, and second best was the soft light of a pink bulb.

Picking up a piece of paper that lay beside the phone, she ran her finger slowly along the edge. It was "his" number. She hadn't called it earlier, because she had wanted to surprise Mr. Stone with her visit. And she hadn't called when she had returned home because . . .

Well, she wasn't exactly sure why.

Several times she had dialed a couple of the numbers, then hung up the phone, like a shy eighth-grader too bashful to return a boy's call.

This is dumb, she told herself. *More accurately, you are dumb.*

He's a lead in a murder investigation, for Pete's sake, not your date for the prom. Just call him, accept the invitation, and be done with it.

After mentally rehearsing what she was going to say and clearing her throat a couple of times, she took the plunge and punched in the appropriate numbers.

After the fourth ring she heard the line pick up and a deep, wonderfully sexy voice say, "Hi . . ."

"Hi," she replied quickly and efficiently—except for that one damned croak in the middle of the word. Those cursed frogs always appeared in her throat when she was nervous.

She started to tell him who she was, but she was cut off by the rest of his sentence, ". . . this is Ryan Stone. Sorry I missed your call, but leave a message at the beep and I'll get back to you."

Damn. A stupid answering machine.

She was sitting here in her bed with sweaty pits, cold palms, and a dry mouth . . . for a machine.

After waiting through what she thought must be the longest beep in the history of the modern world she cleared her throat again and said, "Yes, ah . . . hello, Mr. Stone—croak, gulp—I'd be glad to meet you tomorrow evening at Chez Antoine for dinner. See you then."

It was only *after* she had hung up that she realized she hadn't told him who she was. Oh, well, he could figure it out. How many women had he invited to Chez Antoine tomorrow night?

The moment she turned out the lamp, the phone rang, scaring her half to death. She scrambled for the light, reached for the receiver, then froze. Something told her it was "him." But it couldn't be. He didn't have her unlisted number . . . did he?

Bounding out of bed, she grabbed her robe and hurried downstairs, trying not to wake Atlanta, who was in the guest room. She'd let her own machine answer it and she would listen in.

By the time she reached the kitchen, her message had finished. After the tone the deepest, sexiest voice she had ever heard reached for her . . . stroked her . . . velvet smooth in the darkness.

"I'm so glad you called, Savannah," he said, verbally caressing her name. "I'll be looking forward to spending some time with you. I'm sure we'll have many things to talk about. I'll send a car for you a little before eight. Until then, good night. Sleep well."

She paused and leaned against the doorframe, her knees weak, her blood having rushed to the nether regions of her body. Dear God, a man with a voice like that could simply *talk* her into an orgasm.

Sleep well? Not bloody likely after hearing that!

She flipped on the light, rummaged around in a drawer, and pulled out a couple of C batteries. The two cats stood at her feet, looking up at her with confused and eager eyes.

"No, it isn't dinnertime," she said. "Go back to sleep. You two shouldn't have any problem; you've both been spayed." She tossed one of the batteries toward the ceiling, then snatched it out of the air. "While I, on the other hand, have all my parts, and they are in excellent working order. Unfortunately, tonight . . ." she added with a sigh.

Turning out the light, she headed up the stairs, fresh batteries in hand and the residue of Ryan Stone's deep, sexy voice still running hot and liquid through her body.

Savannah wondered when Stone's driver would call to get her address. But as the vintage silver Bentley pulled into her driveway at seven-forty-five the next evening, she realized . . . among the other bits of information he had compiled about her, Ryan Stone knew where she lived.

The elderly driver, dressed in full chauffeur livery, stepped out of the car and hurried up the walk to greet her. Doffing his cap, he revealed a head full of hair as sleek and silver as the automobile he drove. Although he wore no trace of a smile beneath his neatly clipped gray mustache, his pale blue eyes twinkled as he greeted her.

"Good evening, madame," he said in a melodic, if a bit theatrical, British accent.

Stifling a giggle, Savannah thought he sounded like the proverbial butler who always did "it" in the old mystery movies. "Good e-e-e-vening," she replied, trying to mimic his accent, but what came out resembled a bad impression of Boris Karloff.

"My name is Gibson, madame, John Gibson. Mr. Stone has asked me to escort you to the restaurant. Is there anything I can do to make you more comfortable?" he added as he opened the door and graciously handed her into the backseat.

"Ah . . . no, thanks. This is fine," she said, sliding across the soft, supple leather. As she settled back against the cushioned seat, she breathed in the scents of leather, something rather masculine that might have been the chauffeur's cologne, and the distinct perfume of a rose.

To her right she saw the source, a beautiful white rose in full bloom, tucked into the gold-plated bud vase attached to the windowpost of the car. Nice touch.

The driver climbed into the front seat, manipulated a few buttons on the burled wood dash, and started the engine. It purred, barely audible above the soft classical music that filled the car.

"Just relax then, madame," he said, "and enjoy the ride."

"Oh, I will," she replied as she sank lower into the seat and closed her eyes, allowing her spirit to float and absorb the elegance, the ambience. For the next fifteen minutes she intended to forget all about Jonathan Winston, his murderer, and asinine departmental politics. She slipped off her high heels and buried her toes into the plush gray carpet. "Ah, yes, Gibson," she said, "I most certainly will."

"Savannah! You look *wonderful* this evening. What have you done to yourself, mademoiselle?" Antoine exclaimed as she entered the foyer of the restaurant and walked over to the reservations desk.

Antoine was a tiny man, barely a few inches over five feet, with suspiciously black hair and a pinched face. Definitely not a handsome man, by European or American standards. But what he lacked in stature and good looks he more than made up in vibrancy. Over the years that she had frequented his restaurant they had built quite a rapport, based upon mutual admiration, harmless flirtation, and a common love of great food.

"You are meeting a lover tonight, no?" he said, his eyes trailing down the front of her dress. She had especially chosen this silk wraparound because the sapphire blue accented her eyes and the deep vee gave a hint of softly rounded femininity. She had a great set of boobs and didn't mind who knew it—one of the advantages of being a bit overweight.

"No, Antoine," she said, "I am not meeting a lover. This dinner is strictly business."

He shook his head and clucked his tongue. "What a shame! What a terrible, terrible waste!" The playful gleam in his eyes told her he didn't believe her. Perhaps the corresponding glint in her own eyes had given her away. The French could always tell.

"And who is the lucky man who gets to do 'business' with you tonight, Savannah?" he asked as he offered his arm and escorted her in courtly fashion toward the dining room.

"Who said it's a man?"

"You would not wear that dress for another woman," Antoine replied assuredly. "I am right, no?"

She laughed. "You are right, yes." Looking for a man who might be classified as "gorgeous," she peered between the potted palms and around partitions of sparkling beveled glass and brass, into the cozy cubicles that encouraged intimacy and fostered romance.

"Actually," she said, "I'm supposed to meet a Mr. Ryan Stone. He may be here already."

"Ah, Mr. Stone," Antoine said, nodding with a sage smile. "Of course. He arrived half an hour ago. He is there, at the end of the bar."

With her pulse pounding in her ears, Savannah could hardly hear Antoine as he told her that he would prepare her favorite table and seat them right away. Nor did she feel the light kiss he pressed to her knuckles before taking his leave.

At the far end of the highly polished, inlaid oak bar sat the man Antoine had indicated. Had Savannah been looking at him through a telescope, her tunnel vision wouldn't have been more complete. The world narrowed down to that one figure—that very tall, moderately dark, and excruciatingly handsome figure—who was turning his head in her direction.

Their eyes met, a silent introduction was made, he rose from his stool and began to walk toward her.

It was when he touched her hand that Savannah fell absolutely, positively, completely ass-over-tea-kettle in lust.

"How did you know where I live?" she asked. Now that she had seen him, she was more curious than indignant. He could know what bra size she wore and she wouldn't give a damn. In fact, she would be glad to tell him . . . *show* him.

He leaned one elbow on the table with all the casual grace of an aristocrat who had arrived at such a high pinnacle of society that he no longer needed to obey its rules.

"I followed you home from the station," he said, his green eyes twinkling with mischief.

"You tailed me?" In spite of the blinding infatuation, her professional ego was wounded. She had always prided herself on being able to spot a tail.

"That's right." He reached for his wineglass and took a sip. She tried not to think about how full and sensuous his lower lip was, or how nice it would be to feel it against her . . .

"And my phone number?" she pressed, trying to distract herself.

He laughed. Damn, he had dimples, too; cute, deep dimples. Even cuter than hers, she had to admit. And that jawline! He could model for a shaving commercial with a chin like that.

"Actually," he said, "I don't have your phone number."

"But you called me after I—"

"Yes, but I have that new call-back feature from the phone company. You know, you punch the right buttons and you can call the person who most recently phoned you."

"That's cheating."

"True, but how about you? I suppose you used the Department of Motor Vehicles to find out where I live. Cops have it easy; all those resources at their fingertips."

Savannah bit her lower lip and toyed with the handle of her fork. "I'm not a cop at the moment," she said. "I'm on sort of a permanent suspension, so I don't have all those great resources either."

"I know," he said, looking sympathetic, "I heard. I just thought you would still have access to . . . well . . . never mind."

"Is there anything you *don't* know about me?" She was starting to feel a bit uncomfortable. Was he a bodyguard, or a private investigator, or what? He seemed far more clever than the average hired muscle.

"I don't know why you're continuing to investigate Jonathan Winston's murder after the department fired you," he said. "Are you just tenacious or—?"

"I have my reasons," she replied. "They aren't important. Why have you been investigating *me?*"

"I have my reasons." His smile mocked her. "And they *are* important."

"What are they?"

Rather than be shocked by her bluntness, as she had expected, he laughed. "Okay, so we're going to lay it all on the line, huh?"

"I've always found that to be the best way in the long run. Saves a lot of time."

"All right." He took his last bite of the Salmon Mousse and wiped his lips with his napkin. "I'm interested in you for a couple of reasons. Primarily because I think you can help me find out who killed Jonathan Winston. I was supposed to be protecting him and—"

"Where were you at four that morning?" she interjected.

"Is that the time of the murder?"

She nodded.

"I was home, sleeping."

"Alone?" She reminded herself that it was a legitimate question, which had nothing whatsoever to do with the fact that she had a burning desire to know if he had a girlfriend or not.

He smiled. "Do I need an alibi at this point?"

"Not really," she answered honestly.

"Then I decline to comment until I do. Shall I go on?"

Not exactly the answer she had been hoping for, but . . . "Yes, please."

"I left Jonathan at the showroom about eleven o'clock the night before. His idea, not mine. By then he had polished off a considerable amount of Scotch and wasn't showing any signs of stopping. I offered to give him a ride home, but he said he wanted to stay awhile longer. When I told him he was foolish to consider driving any time soon he told me he didn't intend to. Someone was coming by to . . . visit. He said they would take him home."

Suddenly Savannah forgot all about the attractiveness and animal magnetism of the man sitting across from her. Her pulse quickened as she considered the intriguing possibilities.

"Who? Do you know who he was expecting?"

He smirked, and she realized how much he enjoyed baiting her like this. She didn't care. Let him have his fun; she'd get even sooner or later.

"Yes," he replied.

"Yes?"

"Yes, I know. He told me."

She waited another five seconds that felt like an eternity. "Well? Damn it, who?"

"He didn't mention any names."

Her stomach sank as though she'd swallowed a boulder along with her dinner. "But you said . . ."

"I said he didn't mention any names. But he did say he was expecting his wife."

"His wife?" Her stomach sank lower. "His wife. Oh, great; as we say in Georgia, that's just peachy."

CHAPTER FOURTEEN

By the time Savannah had finished a forty-five-minute phone call to her union steward she was ready to just go hang herself and get it over with. She stood, fuming, in her kitchen, hand still on the receiver.

"I'm sorry, Ms. Reid," he had said in a less-than-remorseful tone, "but I've pursued every possibility and there's nothing I can do. Perhaps if you were to drop about thirty or forty pounds in the next couple of months, I could ask them to reconsider and . . ."

Thirty or forty pounds in two months! Obviously this guy had never dieted in his life. Probably one of those scrawny-assed, pencil-necked geeks who basically disappeared if they turned sideways.

Let him eat rice cakes and celery, drink chalky 280-calorie milk shakes, or go to a dieting center run by anorexic, self-righteous twenty-year-olds who claimed that their slender figures were due to eating overpriced TV dinners that tasted like sawdust and running ten miles a day.

And, of course, if you lost three and a half pounds the first month, you gained back five the next month. Gee, it was so much fun, the dieting game. Wonder why so many people found it difficult to drop those unsightly pounds?

From where she stood Savannah could see into her backyard, where Atlanta lay, stretched out on her favorite Betty Boop beach towel, "catching some rays." The teeny, tiny red bikini left little to the imagination. Savannah wondered if the residents of the apartment complex across the alley were enjoying the view.

The phone rang and she jumped. God, her nerves were tight these days.

Beverly Winston wanted to know how things were going, so Savannah told her about Ryan. She also asked her about the large bank withdrawals that Jonathan had made recently.

"I have no idea," Beverly replied. "Not that he ever asked my permission when conducting his business, but usually I would have known if he was dealing in sums that large."

"Did he have any other savings accounts?"

"Not to my knowledge."

Savannah thought back on what Ryan Stone had said about Jonathan's expected visitor the night he was murdered. "Beverly, tell me something, and please, don't lie. It's very important that I know the truth."

"Okay; shoot."

"Did you go to Jonathan's showroom the night he was killed, or that morning?"

"No, not at all."

"Then why would he have told Ryan Stone that he was expecting a visitor, his wife?"

Beverly was silent for a long time; then she said, "This probably isn't that important, but I do have one bit of information that might interest you. I was going through some of his papers and I found that he had changed the beneficiary of his sizable life-insurance policy."

"I would assume it was you," Savannah said, "if he had no children."

"It had been. But a month ago he reassigned the benefits to his first wife, Fiona. Maybe *she* was the wife he was expecting that night."

"Maybe," Savannah said thoughtfully. "I guess I need to speak to Mrs. Winston Number One again."

This time Savannah decided to visit Fiona at home, rather than work, to see another side of the woman. She was surprised at how different that other side was.

Had Savannah encountered her on the street she wouldn't have recognized this unkempt, sickly looking woman as the one who had been singing the other night with the sultry voice and the seductive moves.

With her hand poised, ready to knock on the screen door to the shabby little apartment, Savannah saw Fiona O'Neal, sitting on the floor of her living room, surrounded by cardboard boxes, arms around her knees, rocking and sobbing. Her beautiful, long red hair spilled around her, a stringy, tangled mess.

Her simple cotton shirt looked as though she had slept in it, but her eyes looked like two burned holes in a blanket, as Gran used to say. Savannah estimated that she probably hadn't slept well for a very long time.

"Fiona?" she asked softly. No one cried like that unless they were truly, deeply hurting. Savannah couldn't help feeling a rush of pity toward her. "Fiona, it's Savannah Reid." She pressed her nose to the screen. "Do you need help? May I come in?"

With a loud sniff Fiona focused on Savannah, seeing her for the first time. Her crying momentarily subsided and she brushed the ratted hair from her face. She said nothing, but she nodded.

Savannah opened the door and stepped inside. The tiny room reeked of alcohol, cigarette smoke, and unchanged cat litter. Savannah fought the urge to hold a scented handkerchief over her nose as she walked over to Fiona and sat on a threadbare recliner near her. The room was sparsely furnished, with only a few of the most basic necessities. Cardboard boxes, piled with paperback books of every genre, lay everywhere. At Fiona's feet was a roll of packing tape and a pair of scissors.

The kitchen appeared to be full of cardboard boxes, too. Apparently, Fiona O'Neal intended to move. Soon.

"Fiona, what is it?" she asked, feeling the need to probe gently. If she pressed too hard, the woman would close up, and she wouldn't find out anything.

"Nothing," Fiona replied between sobs. "I mean, nothing new. I just get to thinking about Jonathan sometimes and . . ."

Her voice trailed away as her sobs renewed.

"Did you love him that much?" Savannah asked.

"More than anything. I always did, from the first moment I met him."

Fiona picked up a nearly empty whiskey bottle from the coffee table nearby and took a long drag from it. Then she did the same for the cigarette that dangled between her fingers.

The sunlight, which poured through the living room's one window, was less kind than the dim lights of the nightclub. Its brightness exposed the sallow color of her translucent skin, the dark circles and wrinkles around her eyes, the nicotine stains on her teeth and the fingers of her right hand. Makeup and dim lighting had done a lot to conceal just how tough Fiona O'Neal's life had been to date.

But the record of those difficult years was there, plainly written on her face for all to see.

"He was coming back to me, really, he was." The fingers that held Fiona's cigarette were trembling. "We were saving money so we could leave this damned place. We almost had enough; then we were going to run away, away from Beverly, away from the fashion industry and all of its sharks, away from the people who were suing him over nothing."

"That's what Jonathan was running from, but how about you, Fiona? What were you trying to escape?"

Fiona thought for a moment, took another slug of whiskey, and stubbed the cigarette into the Las Vegas ashtray on the coffee table. "Who knows?" she replied, visibly closing off.

"You do," Savannah replied; "you know."

Fiona looked uncomfortable, as though she was unaccustomed to sharing her innermost secrets.

"All right," she said. "I was running from dreams . . . old dreams that are never going to come true. I was going to be a successful singer someday. Make a lot of money, go on national tours, appear on talk shows, play to sold-out audiences three times a week. But now I know that isn't going to happen. If it hasn't by now, it isn't going to. I'm not exactly getting younger by the day."

Savannah nodded but refrained from saying something inane and mundane about never being a go-go dancer. Fiona wasn't talking about the passing fancy of a naive adolescent. Hers was a life's dream that had died and taken a large part of the woman's spirit with it.

"What were you running *to*, Fiona?" she asked.

"What do you mean?"

"Everyone who's running from something is also searching for something. What were you hoping to find at the other end?"

Fiona sniffed again, then reached for a box of tissues that sat on top of a pile of sheet music on a nearby end table. "A life with Jonathan, just the two of us, like it was in the beginning, before *she* came along."

"Beverly?"

"No, Danielle. She's the one who took him away from me. We had a good home until she decided she wanted him. She wasn't all that sexy, but she seduced him by telling him that they were going to be this world-famous designing team."

"But it didn't work out?"

"Of course not. Danielle didn't have an ounce of talent on her own; that's why she needed Jonathan. She stole all of his best designs, then threw him away."

Savannah did a quick mental check and found contradictory information in the files. "I thought Danielle sued Jonathan for ripping off *her* designs. And won."

Fiona shrugged and blew her nose. "Well . . . they don't call it 'blind justice' for nothing."

Since the conversation was going so smoothly Savannah decided to press her luck a little farther. "Where were you and Jonathan intending to go when you ran away?"

Wrong move. Instantly a wariness appeared in Fiona's eyes, and she drew back several inches, crossing her arms over her chest.

"We hadn't decided exactly," she said.

"Is that where you're moving to now?" Savannah waved a hand, indicating the stacks of boxes.

"No," she replied, but Savannah could tell she was lying.

"There's no point in me being there without Jonathan. Or anywhere, for that matter."

Savannah didn't like the sound of that, or the look in Fiona's eyes when she said it. At that moment Savannah began to be concerned about Fiona O'Neal's mental state. She was obviously deeply depressed, possibly suicidal.

Savannah wished she could help, but she sensed she had already alienated her.

Oh, well, she had blown it; might as well make it a complete bust. "You say the two of you were saving money to leave. . . . Can you tell me where that money is now?"

Fiona's disposition temperature gauge plummeted from cold to freezing in an instant. "No. I can't."

"You can't tell me because you don't know or you won't because—"

"I can't, I won't; take your pick." With fidgety fingers she lit another cigarette. "Why did you come here today anyway?"

"I wanted to ask you a couple of important questions. I understand you're the beneficiary of Jonathan's life-insurance policy."

"That isn't a question," Fiona replied. "Aren't you really asking why?"

Savannah nodded.

"Because he loved me best. I've already told you that. But it doesn't really matter now. With him being murdered, the insurance company is going to take forever to come through with any of it. I'll probably be too old to spend it; if and when I get it, that is."

Thinking that over, Savannah agreed. She had seen cases like this drag on for years as the insurance company conducted its own investigation. So she changed the subject with her second big question of the day. "Jonathan told someone that you were coming to the showroom to pick him up that night. Did you go?"

Fiona looked shocked for a moment, as though Savannah had knocked her breathless with an unexpected tap to the diaphragm. But she quickly recovered. "Who told you that?"

"It doesn't really matter."

"Ryan, that bodyguard guy—I'll bet *he* told you. Huh?"

"Did you go, Fiona? Were you there later that evening or during the night? In the morning?"

Fiona's face registered nothing but pure defensiveness and anger. "I didn't kill Jonathan. I don't know who did. That's all I'm going to tell you." She rose on unsteady legs and walked to the door. "I'd like you to leave now, if you don't mind. I have a lot of packing to do . . . unless I'm under some sort of order not to leave town."

"Not from me," Savannah said, thinking that if the officer assigned to this case didn't get out here and at least interview Fiona O'Neal, he might lose a valuable lead.

Not that she gave a damn, Savannah decided as she walked out of the dark, stale apartment and into the fresh air and sunshine. To hell with the department. It wasn't like they were going to conduct an honest investigation of the matter anyway.

At this poiint, why should she care?

Like Fiona, Savannah had held a dream very dear to her heart for years. Nothing so grandiose as a Top-Forty singer, or a jiggling, giggling go-go dancer. Those dreams had been as brief as her adolescent love affairs. In her heart Savannah had only wanted to be a cop. A good cop who helped decent people and nailed the bad ones. A simple dream, but it was all she had.

She knew how Fiona felt, having that dream die unexpectedly, in a split second, and being helpless to resuscitate it.

But unlike Fiona she didn't intend to run away. She was determined to stay right where she was and hold her ground. Until her heart found another dream to pursue.

How strange, Savannah thought as she walked into the office of the recently departed Jonathan Winston; even after the body was gone that eerie feeling remained in a room where someone had been murdered. She was extremely aware of it: that weird sense that the room wasn't empty, as a room should be when no one was in it. That inexplicable feeling that you weren't alone, even though your eyes and ears said you were. The natural peace of the place was gone, and an unsettling sort of agitation seemed to radiate from the very walls.

Long ago she had decided that this was what people meant when they believed a house was "haunted." Unlike her more metaphysical friends, however, she didn't believe the actual person was still there, doing the haunting. Instead, she theorized that the structure served as a kind of battery. Somehow it absorbed the energy of those extremely strong emotions emitted by a person who realized they were about to die in an unnatural, violent way.

Usually Savannah avoided going into a place like that alone. Especially alone and at night. But she didn't want to run into the newly appointed investigator on the case, since, legally, she no longer had any right to trespass on a murder scene. She hoped that, since it was after midnight, he was home watching TV in bed or snoring.

Fortunately, she still had a key to the back door, given to her by the janitor. Bloss hadn't asked her to return any of the things she had taken with her regarding the investigation. She supposed that if Bloss and the chief were intending to sweep it under the carpet, they wouldn't be particularly concerned about collecting potential evidence.

Dr. Jennifer Liu had been in the office with her lab crew. Squares of the carpet had been removed, as well as swatches of fabric from Jonathan's desk chair, which was covered with blood. The splattered portion of wall had also been excised, revealing the inner studs, insulation, and wiring. Fingerprinting dust covered everything—white on the dark surfaces, black on the light. Dr. Jennifer was thorough.

Being extremely careful not to disturb anything, Savannah crept over to the file cabinets. She pulled a pair of surgical gloves from her pocket and put them on before she tried to open the first drawer. All the drawers on the left side of the cabinet were locked, and a search of the contents of his desk revealed no keys. If Dr. Liu or the detective in charge had examined the files' contents, they had made certain that no one else would. Or, she surmised, the investigation might be so stalled that no one had even gotten that far.

Fortunately, the drawers on the right opened freely. Inside, Savannah found what she had been looking for: the company's ledgers. She wanted to compare the figures she would find there with Jonathan's personal accounts, which she still had at home.

Still feeling as though someone were watching over her shoulder, she decided to take the ledgers into another part of the building to study them. She would have loved to have taken them home with her, but she was pressing her luck already just by invading a cordoned area as a civilian. There was no point in poking her head *all* the way into that noose.

In what appeared to be a sewing room she sat at one of the long tables that was covered with cloth patterns, fabric remnants, sketches, and half-constructed garments. Apparently Jonathan had been working on a swimsuit line when the process had come to an abrupt halt. On a rack, which ran the length of one wall, hung dozens of exotic bikinis made of leopard and tiger prints, gold and silver spandex, and scandalously sheer laces.

Nice, she thought, *if you're a size three*. She hadn't bought a bikini since exceeding size nine. *Oh, well, they never make the tops large enough for a* real *woman anyway*.

Pulling her notebook and pen from her tote bag, she opened the first ledger and began to take notes. Unfortunately, she had never been much of an accountant, so she didn't understand everything she was looking at. But a couple of things were clear even to her untrained eye.

Jonathan's company hadn't done well at all in the beginning. She figured it was Beverly's money that had kept him afloat during those early days, because the records indicated heavy losses . . . too heavy for most individuals to bear.

Suddenly there had been a large influx of funds that didn't appear to come from the meager company profits. A private investor, perhaps? She couldn't be sure; there was no notation to indicate where the money had come from.

Then, the past year, business seemed to have gone through the roof. The rise in orders had been phenomenal. Apparently Jonathan had come up with some fantastic designs, or at least some highly successful marketing strategies.

Now she knew how he could afford to make all those enormous withdrawals.

However, two weeks before his death the company's assets had shown a substantial drop, coinciding with the largest of his transactions. He had pulled enough funds out to cripple even a healthy business.

Savannah chewed her bottom lip thoughtfully as she scribbled the details in her notebook.

Maybe what Fiona had said was true. Perhaps Jonathan was cashing out to run away with her. Skipping town with all the loot was certainly more financially lucrative than sticking around and having to split everything fifty-fifty with the old-ball-and-chain in divorce court.

As she was making her last notations, Savannah felt a cold draft, as though someone had opened a door or window nearby. But she decided that was silly. Glancing at her watch, she saw it was one-thirty A.M., and the place was empty except for her . . . and Jonathan Winston's residual terror, which had seeped into the walls along with his spilled blood.

Even here, in a room on the other side of the building, she could feel it: that distinct feeling of another presence, the acute sensation of being watched.

She snapped the notebook closed. It was time to call it a night and get the hell out of this place.

As she gathered the ledgers and her belongings and stood to leave, a figure caught the corner of her eye, a human figure. She spun around, her heart in her throat, her hand on the Beretta under her sweater.

But just as she was about to pull the gun, she realized that the figure was nothing more than a mannequin, wearing a skimpy gold lame rhinestone-studded bikini.

"Atta girl, Annie Oakley," she chided herself, "you almost shot a dummy. Better go home while you still have most of the cards in your mental deck."

A second later something crashed down on the back of her head with so much force that she saw, more than felt, the pain. It exploded through her body with a shower of fiery lights, bursting across the velvet blackness of her mind.

Savannah had only one cognitive thought after she hit the floor, where she lay, paralyzed from shock and pain: *Gee, they're right! You really* do *see stars!*

Then every one of the blazing meteors fell, burning itself out on the way down, and all that remained were the soft black heavens.

CHAPTER FIFTEEN

"You son of a bitch!" Savannah yelled, reaching up and grabbing the man standing over her by the front of his shirt. With all her strength she pulled him down onto the floor beside her, then rolled on top of him. One well-placed karate punch to the chest and she could feel and hear his breath leave him in a whoosh.

But there was another one, right behind her. He grabbed for her, trying to pin her arms behind her back.

"Let go of me, you bastard!"

Instinctively she used whatever method of defense was at hand and threw herself backward, knocking him off balance, then rammed the back of her head into his groin.

Both she and he let out screams of pain as the blow connected—he, because she had squashed his gonads, and she because her head was already throbbing from the whack she had taken.

"Savannah!" The guy beneath her struggled to throw her weight off him, but she gripped him tightly with her knees and prepared to give him another punch. "Damn it, Savannah, it's me, Mike Farnon. Will you get the hell off me . . . please."

"Mike?" Slowly his features began to come into view: the slightly crooked nose, the cleft in the chin, the bushy eyebrows, the patrolman's blue uniform. "Mike Farnon?"

She shook her head to clear it, then decided to never do that again. The pain was nauseating.

Reaching around to the base of her skull, she gently felt the swelling that seemed impossibly large.

"Why?" she groaned. "Why did you guys hit me on the back of the head?"

Slowly she turned to see Jake sitting on the floor behind her, his hands cupped over his crotch, his face green. Although his eyes were slightly bugged and infinitely alert, he didn't seem to be breathing.

Again, she inquired, "Why? You damned near knocked my fool head off! What the hell did you do that for?"

Mike twisted sharply to the side and rolled her off him. She hit the floor with a thud that sent lightning bolts of pain through her head.

"Damn it, Savannah," Mike said as he sat up and unbuttoned his shirt, checking the karate-chopped area for damage. A dark bruise was already beginning to swell. "We didn't hit you. What are you talking about?"

"But . . . but . . . ?"

She looked around at the now-familiar sewing paraphernalia, the tables, the swimsuits hanging on the wall rack, the sunlight coming through the windows.

The sunlight?

"What . . . ? Oh, God, I'm so confused. What's going on?" she said, burying her face in her hands.

Jake seemed to be slowly recovering; at least he was moving, sort of. He scooted, crablike, over to the nearest wall and rested his back against it. He still didn't appear to be breathing very often.

"We're as confused as you are," Mike said, wincing as he massaged his bruised rib cage. "All I know is that we were walking our regular beat and saw the back door open, so we came in to check things out. You were lying there on the floor, groaning, moaning, rolling around and holding your head. When we tried to help you out you went ballistic on us. Goddamn, where did you learn to do that judo shit? Are you a black belt or what?"

"When I was on a beat in Hollywood. And it's karate, not judo."

"Oh, great. I feel *so* much better now." He turned to Jake. "You gonna live, buddy?"

Feebly, Jake nodded.

"You gonna be able to service your old lady? 'Cause if you're not up to it, I can . . ."

Jake's color improved instantly, from sick green to an angry red, but he still hadn't recovered his gift of speech.

Slowly the facts began to sink into Savannah's battered brain, along with a semitruckload of guilt.

"I'm sorry, guys. Somebody gave me a whopper of a whop upside the head . . . last night, I guess. I must have been unconscious for hours and didn't realize time had passed. I thought you were the ones who hit me. Gosh, I'm really sorry."

"You . . . you . . . should be," Jake croaked as he found his voice and a smattering of composure. "Shit, you really got me good."

"If it's any consolation, it hurt me as much as it did you," she said, gently palpating the platypus egg on the back of her head.

"I . . . I sincerely . . . doubt that," he replied.

"What were you doing in here last night?" Mike asked as he rose to his feet and helped Savannah to stand.

She could tell by the reproachful look in his eyes that he knew she was off limits.

"I had to check out some things, Mike," she said, glancing over at the table where she had been working. "Some ledgers . . . which are gone now . . . along with my notebook."

"You aren't really supposed to cross the line," Mike said in a half-apologetic tone. "Captain Bloss told us you'd probably sneak in here. He told us to bust you if you did."

"Then I guess you'd better get on with it," she said, turning around and offering him her wrists for cuffing. "Because if you don't do it now, I'm going to walk out that door and head for the nearest hospital. I think I'd better get an X ray or two and see if anything's cracked."

Instead of cuffing her he slapped her on the back. She gasped at the pain. "We're not going to run you in, Savannah; what do you take us for, anyway? We're not gonna, are we, Jake?"

Jake shook his head.

"See there," Mike continued. "He won't even charge you with assaulting a police officer, huh, Jake?"

Again, he shook his head.

Savannah felt a bit of relief wash through her system, but it certainly wasn't enough to dull the pain in her head.

"Community General, here I come," she muttered as she leaned over and gingerly picked up her tote bag from the floor.

"Are you up to driving?" Mike asked. "If you aren't, we could give you a ride down there."

"No, that's all right. You stay here and take care of Jake."

"Who did this to you?" Mike inquired as he walked her to her car, behind the building. "Did you catch a look at him?"

"No, but I know one thing for a fact," she said as she climbed into the Camaro and hooked her seat belt. "Whoever whacked me was solid, flesh and blood. 'Cause I'll tell you right now: No ghost could hit that hard."

As Savannah lay, neglected and in agony, in the tiny cubicle delineated by blue curtains that rode on overhead rails, she had a horrible thought that made her, if possible, even more miserable: *Damn! I don't heave health insurance anymore. I'm going to have to pay for this!*

She had been forced to fill out reams of stupid forms that asked more personal questions than the application for the police force. Next she had received a cursory look-see by a guy whom she was sure was the hospital custodian, wearing the facade of a white jacket and a stethoscope around his neck.

Then Mr. Clean had shoved her onto a gurney in this depressing cubicle and the staff of Community General Hospital of San Carmelita had promptly forgotten that she existed.

"Hey," she called feebly as she heard a pair of rubber-soled feet squeak by, "hey, there's somebody dying in here. Does anyone out there care?"

Apparently not. One dark corner of her scrambled brain reminded her that their lack of interest might have something to do with the code blue that was occurring two cubicles down, or the car-accident victim who was screaming at the top of his lungs and bleeding all over the place. Just on the other side of the sheet her neighbor sounded like a teenager who had swallowed too many baby aspirins and was being forced to puke her guts out. The flimsy curtain did nothing to screen the liquid, gagging sounds or the nauseating stench.

Ah, the romance, the ambience, the service . . . and for this they would expect to be paid more than the price of a five-star hotel, including gourmet room service. By the time they were finished with X rays and assorted tests half her savings would be gone.

"Never get sick again," she muttered to herself. "Never have an accident, never get shot, perforated, mutilated, or folded, and never, never get whacked on the head again. You're a poor person now, and poor people can't afford the luxury of getting hurt."

Just when she had decided that she would grow old and die there on the gurney, with no one even aware of her presence until she started to stink, the blue curtain was pulled open a few inches and a decidedly masculine hand, bearing a perfect yellow rose, slipped inside.

For a microsecond she forgot the pain in her head. "Ryan?" she said, unable to believe this turn of events.

"May we come in?" a voice asked, the hand still offering the rose.

We? Who was we? It didn't matter; she nearly cried with relief. She wasn't alone anymore. Someone she knew and liked was here. Someone cared.

"Sure," she said; "please do."

The curtain opened wider, and she saw that her visitor was, indeed, Ryan Stone in all his urbane glory. And he had brought John Gibson with him. They were both dressed in casual clothes;

at least casual compared to Gibson's chauffeur livery and the designer suit Ryan had worn at Chez Antoine. They looked as though they had both just stepped off the green of a Beverly Hills country club.

"We heard that a friend of ours was under the weather," Ryan said as he walked to the gurney, handed her the rose, and placed a quick kiss on her cheek. "So we thought we should drop by to cheer you up."

"But . . . how did you . . . who told you that I . . . ?" Savannah might have been able to figure out the puzzle herself, except that half of her brain was frozen in panic that Ryan Stone was seeing her in such a disheveled condition.

"And these are also for you, ma'am," Gibson said, his tone formal but his pale blue eyes friendly. He handed her a box of Godiva raspberry truffles—her very favorite confection in the world—and a small gold-and-black bottle of her favorite perfume, First by Van Cleef & Arpels.

This time she couldn't hold back the tears. They spilled from her eyes and ran down her cheeks and into her ears, streaking whatever traces of mascara and liner she might still be wearing.

"All right," she said, "enough of this. Tell me how you know everything about me. You're just a little too resourceful for a bodyguard and a chauffeur. Who are you?"

Ryan smiled, reached down, and brushed the hair away from her face. "I'll tell you everything, I promise." He lowered his voice and leaned closer to her. "But this isn't really the place, if you know what I mean."

Curious as she was, she had to admit he had a point. If she could hear every gag and gargle from the girl getting her stomach pumped in the neighboring cubicle, this wasn't exactly a high-security setting.

"Now, what have they done for you so far?" Ryan asked.

"One guy took my blood pressure and temperature, then stuck me in here."

"How long ago?"

"Centuries."

"Let me see where it hurts."

She rolled onto her side and pointed to the back of her head.

"Good God! No wonder. He didn't exactly hold back when he hit you."

"When *who* hit me? Who's 'he'? Do you know who did this?"

"I have a pretty good hunch."

"Who? Who?"

Ryan laughed and patted her hand. "You sound like an owl. I'll tell you all about that, too, later. For right now, let's just get you taken care of." He turned to Gibson and nodded.

In an instant Gibson had pulled a tiny cellular phone from his pocket, along with a credit card–sized computer for storing personal information. He looked up a number, then dialed.

"Hello, John Gibson here. I'll have a word with Dr. Weinberg." A momentary pause. "Yes, Harold, how are you, old chap? Oh, not well at all, I'm afraid. A close friend of mine is lying here in your emergency ward, gravely injured, and your staff has been extremely negligent in attending to the dear girl."

He listened briefly, then continued, "Ah, that's wonderful, Harry. I'm so very pleased. See you soon; you *will* be down right away then? Splendid." With a quick snap of the wrist he closed the phone and lowered the antenna. "Well, that's settled nicely. Dr. Weinberg will see you personally, Ms. Reid, so you needn't worry anymore."

Savannah couldn't believe her ears. Dr. Harold Weinberg! "Isn't he the chief of staff here?" she asked, trying to recall the details of a story she had heard, recounting the idiosyncracies of the arrogant, tyrannical Dr. Weinberg.

"He is now," Ryan said, "but Gibson knew him when he was a wet-behind-the-ears intern. It was during the war, wasn't it, Gibson?"

"It was, indeed. But on to happier topics." He nodded toward Savannah.

"Oh, yes," Ryan said, picking up the cue. "As soon as they release you from this place, Gibson will drive you home in the Bentley and I'll follow with your car."

"And then you'll tell me what's going on?"

He laughed, picked up the rose, and tickled her chin with it. "Once we have you tucked into your bed, nice and comfy, if you have the energy, I'll tell you all about it."

If you crawled into bed with me, I'm sure I'd have plenty of energy, she thought. But with Gibson standing there, the picture of dignity, and the almighty Dr. Harold Weinberg on the way to examine her, Savannah decided to put the thought on hold. At least until her head wasn't throbbing and she was wearing something sexier than a damned hospital gown.

He was in her bedroom. Ryan Stone was sitting on the end of her satin chaise lounge chair, only a few feet from the bed where she lay, finally wearing a sexy silk robe and feeling like a woman. And they were alone.

Savannah was in heaven.

Or she would have been if the medication Dr. Weinberg had given her had kicked in yet.

"It's bad, huh?" he asked, the picture of masculine magnificence and paternal concern, a combination that had always been her undoing.

"Yes, very bad. But answer some of my questions and I'll feel much better."

"So, fire away," he said, leaning forward, his elbows on his knees. "Let the interrogation begin."

"Who are you, really?" She wanted to know, but she was afraid she wouldn't like the answer.

"First of all, my name really is Ryan Stone."

"Let me guess; that's the only thing you've told me that *is* true."

He laughed, deepening his dimples. "Not at all. Everything I said about how beautiful and intelligent you are—that was all true, too."

"Gee, thanks." She could feel her cheeks blushing a hot pink . . . the ones on her face, too. "But how about what you told me about you?"

"Such as?"

"That you run a bodyguard service."

He shook his head. "That's not what I said. I don't usually function as a guard; I generally conduct investigations. Jonathan Winston was a rare exception."

"Why him?"

"Because he was a friend of a friend of Gibson's. And, besides, his story intrigued me."

"How so?"

"He first came to me, asking me to gather evidence that his wife was cheating on him. I told him I didn't do matrimonial disputes—far too grim a way to make a living. Later he returned and begged me to be his guard for a few weeks. He said he had gone out and gotten the evidence himself of his wife's infidelity. He had confronted her, and he was convinced she would try to kill him."

Savannah mulled that one over for a moment. "What was so intriguing about his situation?"

"He was lying to me, plain and simple, and I wanted to know why."

"Lying . . . about his life being in danger?"

He shook his head. "No, I believed that part—he was obviously a nervous wreck. But I didn't buy the bit about it being Beverly."

"Why would he say it was?"

"He was furious that she was being unfaithful to him. He wanted to hurt her. I believe he figured that if he was going to get killed, he might as well get even with her after the fact by having her blamed for it."

"That's pretty nasty."

"Hey, the fury of a man scorned. Of course he was having his own affair, but that was all right. Typically male, huh?"

"Afraid so." She paused to mentally categorize and file this new information. "Then why did you leave him that night, if you were supposed to be guarding him?"

"He insisted. To be honest, I think he wanted to take care of some business and he didn't want me around to witness it. I also think he was about to skip town . . . travel arrangements being made, lots of over-the-phone banking, stuff like that going on. More than once he ended conversations abruptly when I walked into the room."

"But how about his fear? If he really thought somebody was about to pop him, wouldn't he have wanted you holding his hand every minute?" *I know I would*, she added silently.

"For some reason he seemed less afraid those last two days. Almost cocky. I think he was getting ready to make his own move and thought he had things under control."

"Mmm . . ." She tapped her fingernails on the table, thinking. "Who do you suppose the killer is, a professional?"

"I don't know who he is, but I don't believe he's a pro. He's too sloppy."

"We haven't been able to catch him yet. He must not be *that* sloppy."

"So far he's just been lucky. But if you and I put our heads together, we might be able to put a halt to his winning streak."

"You mean like . . . work together on this?" The very thought both thrilled and confused her. The possibility of spending that much time with him was intriguing. Deliciously intriguing. But the professional in her cautioned her to take one careful step at a time. For all of his charm, the fact was she didn't know Ryan Stone from Adam. As far as she knew, he could have been the one to bop her over the head last night. Which reminded her. . . .

"You said you might know who whacked me. I'd be very interested in having his name and address."

He smirked. "I'm sure you would. But I'm afraid I can't be that accommodating. Would you settle for a physical description?"

"Would I?" She sat up in bed, eyes blazing, then groaned and sank back against the pillow. "Yes, I would. I would *love* a physical description. Because if I *ever* get a hold of him, I'm going to whup the living snot out of him. I'm a civilian now, and I can do that sort of thing . . . as long as I don't get caught."

Ryan laughed, then became somber. "Then try this on for size—tall and skinny, about six-three, one-hundred-seventy pounds, long blond hair, dirty, thin on top, goatee, heavy metal T-shirt—"

"About thirty-five, teeth missing in the front, wears a heavy chain for a belt?"

"Yeah; you know him?"

Adrenaline, like liquid fire, pumped through her veins.

"I know him. He's that cracker who said he wanted to buy my Camaro. That son of a bitch! The next time I see him I'm going to knock the rest of his scraggly teeth so far down his throat, he's going to have to chew with his asshole!"

CHAPTER SIXTEEN

"Where did I put that hot water bottle?" Savannah asked as she searched the miscellaneous drawers, closet, and cubbyholes in the guest room. Hoping that something either cold or hot—she had decided to try both—on the back of her head might reduce the swelling, as well as the infernal pain.

"Someday, I swear, I'm going to get organized. I'm also going to stop muttering to myself like an old lady."

For the tenth time in the last few minutes she glanced over at the unmade bed, proof that Atlanta had at least spent the night there. They hadn't touched base—not really—since their big fight. The temperature between them had been unseasonably chilly, their exchanges formal and overly polite.

To her knowledge Atlanta didn't even know she had been hurt or had spent the night away from home. Savannah had called from the hospital to explain her absence at about ten o'clock this morning, but there had been no answer. She had left a message on the machine, but it had still been there when she had arrived at the house.

And there was still no sign of Atlanta.

Savannah tried not to even think about it, let alone panic. God knows, her head couldn't take any added strain. But the thought of a girl as pretty and as naive as Atlanta running around Southern California scared her half to death. It was a toss up which brand of trouble she would dive into first.

Ah ha! There it was, shoved into the back of the vanity's lower drawer. The all-purpose hot water bottle, cold water bottle, enema, douche bag. She hadn't used it in years, so it kicked up a bit of dust as she pulled it out, along with its various attachments.

Just as she was about to close the drawer something caught her eye—a flat gold box. A very nice garment gift box with tissue spilling out one side.

What was this? A present long forgotten? She was forever poking things into strange places, then finding them later and being delighted with her "new" treasure.

A bit of black lace peeking out hinted at something naughty and nice. For some reason she instantly thought of Ryan.

Pulling the box out, she lifted the lid and found a pair of almost there, G-string panties, made of high-quality black lace and satin, as well as a matching garter belt and stockings. "What the . . . ?" A gossamer-thin chemise of soft, rippling chiffon completed the costume. Pure, elegant, slutty . . . and it *wasn't* hers!

That meant—

Oh, lord, she didn't want to think what that meant.

She could have happily waited another twenty years to know that her sweet, innocent little sister wore this sort of garb. But if she had seen it in Atlanta's suitcase, or in one of the drawers with her other lingerie, she wouldn't have been so concerned.

This stuff had been hidden. And was in a gift box. And since some of the how-to-launder tags were still attached, she assumed it was new.

To the best of her knowledge Atlanta hadn't had enough money to buy something like this since she had arrived. That only meant . . .

She searched the box for a receipt—anything—and found a white card. Scrawled across it, beneath the embossed name of the store, were the words:

To Atlanta,
A rare and delicate Southern beauty,
At the beginning of a long, fulfilling career.
Forever yours,
Max

"Savannah! What are you doing?" The shrill voice shattered her nerves, and she dropped the box, spilling its contents onto the floor.

She spun around—a movement that cost her dearly—and saw Atlanta standing in the doorway, her face as dark as a Mississippi River thunderstorm.

"You *are* just like Mom!" the girl shouted. "Neither one of you have any respect for my privacy!"

She ran into the room, scooped the lingerie from the floor, and shoved it back into the box. Holding it tightly against her chest, she began to cry. "You had *no* right, going through my stuff like that! This is *my* room and—"

"Wait a minute!" Savannah held up one hand in a gesture

reminiscent of her traffic cop days. "Just hold on a gall-darned minute. I'll have you know that this is, first and foremost, *my* house. Every inch of it. I bought it, I make the payments on it, and I'm the one who's going to have to put a new roof on it next year."

She slammed the drawer closed with her foot. "You," she continued, "are a guest in *my* home. My home, my room, my vanity, and my drawer. Got it?"

Atlanta plopped down on the unmade bed and stuck out her lower lip in a petulant pout.

"Furthermore, you are a minor in my home, temporarily—I hope—under my guardianship. And while I do respect your right to your privacy, I don't expect you to abuse that right by hiding things from me. Privacy is fine, but we're talking secrets here, and people only hide things they're ashamed of."

"You're wrong!" Atlanta shoved the box under the blankets. "I'm *not* ashamed of anything. I just know that you're so straight and hung up about things that you wouldn't approve of me developing a relationship with an older man. So I had to—"

"An older man? Just how old is this Max guy, if that's his real name? And what the hell is he doing giving you crap like that?"

"It's expensive lingerie, not crap."

Savannah recalled the feel of the heavy silk between her fingers. "All right, it's expensive crap. Now, who is this guy?"

"I'm not going to talk to you about him. I have something very beautiful with him, and talking about it with you would make it seem dirty or something."

"Very beautiful?" Savannah couldn't comprehend the depth of this girl's naïveté. How had she managed to live for sixteen years without learning anything about the world and its scumbag inhabitants? "You've only been here a couple of days! How can you have something beautiful with *anybody* that quick?"

"Max and me, we're soul mates. We've been lovers before in a previous life. I knew it the minute I saw him, and so did he. But you wouldn't understand anything like that, because you aren't a spiritual person. You're probably a young soul. In fact, I'll bet this is your first time around."

"Around what?" She shook her head, trying to clear it. This was getting more bizarre by the minute. "Look," she said, carefully reining in her anger, "I don't know who this man is or what has happened between you, but I can tell you now that, whatever line of bull he's given you, he doesn't have your best interests at heart. And if he's been sexual with you in any way, he's a criminal. You are still under age and that makes it child molestation."

Atlanta grabbed one of the pillows from the bed, buried her face in it, and began screaming hysterically. At first Savannah was alarmed; the kid appeared to be completely unhinged. Had she suffered some sort of nervous breakdown? Did sixteen-year-olds have nervous breakdowns?

Then Savannah remembered having witnessed this sort of spectacle before—when Atlanta was younger, say, about three. This wasn't soulful agony, resulting from emotional trauma. This was an old-fashioned temper tantrum.

"Atlanta, stop that! You're overreacting."

Instantly the hysterics ceased and the room was silent. The pillow lowered, and Savannah was looking into two of the angriest eyes she had seen in ages, even counting the ones that had been sighting down a gun barrel.

"That does it," Atlanta said with deadly calm. "I hope you're proud of yourself. I loved you. I trusted you. And you've violated me. Thanks to you I'll never be able to love or trust another human being again."

Savannah had heard enough. As Gran would say, her can

was full—way full and overflowing. "Sure you will, 'Lanta," she said with equally cold sarcasm. "You'll trust that Max pervert, who's just out to get into your pants. At least I hope that's all he's after. But you won't trust anyone who truly loves you, unless they're kissing your cute little butt and telling you everything you want to hear."

"Shut up, Savannah! You don't even know Max. How can you say things like that about someone you don't even know?"

"Just answer me a couple of questions. Is he over twenty-one?"

Reluctantly, she nodded.

"Over thirty?"

Again.

"Has he screwed you yet?"

"No!" She pulled herself up into that haughty pose that Savannah was quickly learning to despise. "He has *not!* He says he has too much respect for me to just *take* me like that. He wants to wait until the time is right, a really romantic time, when he can make it special for me. He said so."

She paused and fluffed her hair, striking what she probably thought was a sexy pose, but Savannah found the look overt and foolish. The kid didn't know the first thing about the subtleties of feminine sensuality.

"For now," Atlanta said, a dreamy look in her eyes, "Max says he just wants to worship my body from afar. He wants to record my beauty for all the world to enjoy. He says every woman will envy me and every man will want me."

"That son of a bitch has talked you into posing for him, hasn't he? He wants you to do nude shots and—"

"No, he doesn't. Max said I didn't have to show anything I didn't want to."

"Didn't have to . . . ? You've already done it? You've posed for this jerk?"

"He isn't a jerk. He's a very nice man who helped me realize that I should be proud of my body. Nudity is healthy. Only those who are ashamed of their bodies feel the need to cover them up."

"How about good old decency and modesty? Those are healthy, too, you know."

Savannah's strength left her in a wave that traveled from her head to her feet, then seemed to flow out onto the floor around her. If she didn't lie down soon, she was going to fall down.

"Atlanta, I was assaulted last night," she said, holding her hand to the back of her head, which felt as though a worker for Cal Trans was drilling into it with a jackhammer. "And I—"

"You were assaulted? What do you mean?"

"I mean one of the bad boys knocked me in the head and I was unconscious for several hours."

"Oh, mercy! That's awful! Are you all right?"

Savannah felt a passing wave of relief to see that the girl wasn't so self-centered that she couldn't appreciate someone else's misfortune. Maybe there was hope for her after all.

"Can I do anything for you? I mean, do you want me to warm up some soup for you or get you some ice cream?"

Savannah's heart melted. This was the Atlanta she remembered with so much affection, the considerate, loving little girl who had rubbed her neck and brushed her hair when she was a child. This was the Atlanta who had seemed to disappear with the onset of puberty, to be replaced with the vain, egocentric, bubble head whom she had been living with the past few days.

Savannah walked over to her sister, sat on the edge of the bed, and put her arms around her waist. Holding her close, she said, "Thanks, sweetie, but I'm all right. I just need to lie down."

She pulled back and looked down into her sister's eyes, which were wet with unshed tears. "But what I want more than anything," she continued, "is for you to be safe and happy. I love you, 'Lanta. I don't want you to get hurt. And, whether you'll believe me or not, you're very close to getting badly hurt. Some of the mistakes you're about to make can have lifelong repercussions."

Atlanta pushed her away and rolled to the other side of the bed. "You need to trust me more, Savannah. I'm not stupid, you know. I can take care of myself, if you'll just leave me alone."

"Stay away from him, Atlanta, or I swear I'll bust him for messing with a minor." Considering her current lack of status with the SCPD, Savannah knew the threat was as empty as a race horse's bladder, but Atlanta didn't know that. "I will; I'll do it. If I even get wind of you seeing him again, he's in the slammer. And you should see what they'll do to this 'soul mate' of yours in prison. Even the least desirables of our society hate child molesters."

She had scored that time; she could see the fear mixed with rage in Atlanta's eyes. Maybe, just maybe, it would work.

"If you ever did anything like that . . ." Atlanta said, her voice shaking with fury, "if you ever put a friend of mine in jail, I swear, I'd hate you forever."

The animosity in her words took Savannah off guard. She had bluffed the kid; now the kid was bluffing back. Or maybe she was serious. Either way, now wasn't the time to back down.

Savannah looked her squarely in the eye and said, "Okay, if that's the way you feel. I can live with it."

With a studied nonchalance that was one hundred percent a facade, Savannah rose from the bed and left the room. It wasn't until she was safely ensconced in her own bed that she allowed the mask to drop and herself to cry.

"Mom, you *have* to take her back. I'm not kidding, Mom! If you think you had problems with her there, you should see the kind of trouble she's into here! I'm serious, Mom. Mom, you'd better—"

Beep! Click. Dial tone.

That damned answering machine of her mother's always ran out of tape before she ran out of wind. Angry, she hung up the phone, picked it up again, and punched redial.

Buzz, buzz, buzz, buzz . . .

"Yeah, yeah, yeah, it's busy, all right. Takes half an hour for that stupid fossil to rewind."

She tried again. This time she got through.

"Hi, this is Shirley Reid. I'm sorry I'm not home to take your call but . . ."

Savannah drummed her fingers on the kitchen counter, waiting for the rest of the message and her beep cue.

"Mom, really, call me back about Atlanta. We have to figure something out right away. This *isn't* going to work! And by the way, Mom, you really shouldn't say your name on your machine. And it's best not to tell them that you aren't at—"

Beep. Click. Dial tone.

". . . at home. Shit."

CHAPTER SEVENTEEN

Savannah knew she should be home in bed, not only because Dr. Weinberg had told her to stay there, but because she felt dizzy, queasy, and ready to throw up all over the interior of the Camaro. Not good; she had just had it reupholstered.

She rolled down the window, just in case.

Doctor's orders or not, headache and nausea aside, she simply couldn't stay in that bed another minute. Somewhere out there in the big, bad world was a stringy-haired, scraggle-toothed blond who had chosen the wrong broad to bop. She and he had a little rendezvous with destiny, known as payback time.

A *rendezvous with destiny*, she played the words over in her mind, enjoying the melodrama of the phrase. *Savannah Reid, Private Investigator—the streets and its criminals never sleep . . . and neither does she.*

She would like to, she quickly amended, *she just never gets the chance*.

Rounding the corner on Laurel Street, she pulled into the gas station where she had last seen the unkempt gentleman in question about a week earlier. She had come out of the adjacent convenience store, peach-flavored Snapple in hand, to find him with his head stuck through the driver's window of the Camaro, looking around.

"Hey, you!" she called. "You wanna get the hell outta there?"

He gave her a sullen, sarcastic smirk and a leisurely once-over that made her skin crawl. She could smell the stench of stale beer from ten paces away.

Turning his head aside, he spat a long brown stream of tobacco juice through the gap where his two front teeth had once been and onto the ground in front of her car door.

"How much you want for it, babe?" he asked, jabbing a greasy thumb in the direction of the car. "I'd be glad to take it off your hands."

She walked up to him, trying to breathe through her ears instead of her nose. "It isn't for sale. Please move away from the car."

The puzzled look he gave her told her that he wasn't accustomed to being told what to do by a woman. Either that or he wasn't bright enough to comprehend the details of the demand.

In case it was the latter, she repeated herself. "Get away from my car. Now."

"What'cha gonna do?" He grinned broadly. "Gonna call the cops?"

She reached inside her sweater and pulled out the badge on its chain and held it up for his perusal. "Don't have to."

He hadn't appeared surprised to see the badge, and even then she had registered and filed away the fact. Usually people weren't expecting a woman in street clothes to be a police officer. There was almost always that moment of silence as they readjusted, trying to reconcile their preconceptions of her with their idea of what a cop should be. Apparently she didn't fit most stereotypes.

But this guy hadn't needed those few seconds to shift gears, and she had briefly wondered why.

After a couple of more offers to buy and refusals to sell, he had meandered off into the sunset, marking territory with ill-aimed tobacco squirts along the way.

"Hey, Savannah!" a friendly voice called from inside the open garage bay. "She sounds like she's runnin' good!"

She pulled the Camaro next to the water and air hoses at the side of the building and cut the key. "Of course she is; I've got the best mechanic this side of the Mississippi."

She climbed out of the car and walked into the garage, where Ray March hung over the fender of a 1956 Chevy. Ray enjoyed a well-earned reputation for being good with old cars. Everyone in town brought their classics to him because they knew he would treat them with the special love and attention they deserved.

"How are those new brakes?" he asked, stopping to wipe the sweat from his forehead with a shop towel.

She could tell by the fact that his red hair was standing practically on end that the Chevy wasn't cooperating.

"When I step on the brake pedal the car stops. Every time, not just when I'm headed up a steep hill."

"Whoa, big improvement."

"I'm not complaining."

"Then what are you here for?"

Savannah laughed and tugged at the sleeve of his overalls. "To buy you a cup of coffee and chat for a minute . . . not about cars."

"Oh, okay. Sorry, but you learn to expect the worst in this business."

A few minutes later she and Ray were sitting in the primitive waiting area amid piles of National Tattlers, empty soft-drink cans, and wadded candy wrappers. On the wall above them were posters of classic automobiles with less-than-classic females sprawled across the hoods, legs spread and butt cheeks and boobs hanging out of skimpy costumes. Their eyes were empty, giving the illusion of being brain dead, but horny—some guys' idea of the perfect woman.

A chill went through Savannah; she could almost see Atlanta in one of those pictures, wearing the outfit she had found.

"Thanks for the coffee," Ray said, lifting the Styrofoam cup in a toast. "What can I do you for?"

"Did you notice the last time I was in here, about a week ago, I had a bit of a tiff with a guy out front?"

"Yeah, actually, I did." He nodded thoughtfully. "I was gonna come out and see if you needed help, but you seemed to be handling it fine all by your lonesome."

"Thanks; I appreciate the thought. Do you happen to know that guy?"

"Not by name, but I've seen him around from time to time. One nasty-lookin' cuss." He grinned at her and winked. "You know, Savannah, if you're looking for a man, I know a bunch of dudes who'd love to volunteer for the job. You just let me know and I'll give you a list."

"You're all heart, Ray, but I'm afraid my interest in this guy isn't social."

"Mm-m-mm, police business, huh?"

She shook her head and swallowed hard. "Kinda. Can you think of any way for me to get hold of him?"

"Let's see. . . ." He stared down into his coffee, as though searching for an answer. "Like I said, I don't know his name, but I've seen him driving an old classic. I believe it was . . . yeah, it was a Studebaker Golden Hawk. He hasn't really done anything with it. Last time I saw it, he had a couple different colors of primer on it. A waste of a great car."

"A Stude Hawk . . . there can't be many of those running around."

"Not many at all. I know where you might get a lead on the car—the local chapter of the Studebaker Club. I'll give you the president's number. He's a nice guy by the name of Duke Wallace. Just tell him Ray sent you, and be sure to have him show you his car." A fanatical gleam lit Ray's eyes. "See, Duke's got this *incredible*, beautifully restored Avanti. You won't belie-e-e-ve that car! It's got . . ."

"Boy, that fella's sure popular," Duke Wallace drawled in a rich Louisiana accent that made Savannah momentarily homesick. "Yer the second person to call me 'bout him jist today."

Savannah stood by, watching him polish the Avanti's graceful ebony curves with a baby's diaper. Ray was right; the car was incredible.

On the other hand, Duke appeared to have confined his body work to vehicles. He sported a potbelly that lapped over his belt, nearly hiding the enormous, silver N.R.A. buckle. Impressive. Apparently he had been working on it for a while. He looked as though he was probably pushing sixty.

"Oh, really?" she asked, following him across his garage while he collected a handful of cotton swabs from a jar.

"Yep, this other gentleman was by 'bout an hour ago, askin' the same thing: 'Where's that guy with the Hawk?' Yep, that there's exactly what he asked me, same as you."

With a groan and a remarkable display of butt crack, he squatted and began to clean the minute particles of dust between the wire rims with the swabs.

Good lord, Savannah thought, *I'm not that conscientious with my own ears.*

"What did this man look like?" she asked, with a feeling that she would know the answer.

"The guy with the Hawk or the gentleman who was askin' after him?"

"Both."

"Well, one's a whole lot prettier than t' other. The fella with the Hawk . . . now he looks like he fell outta a big tall Georgia pine tree and hit ever' branch on the way down. But the other 'n . . . now you'd like him. He's one of them tall, dark, and handsome sorts with nice manners. A real ladies' man. And you shoulda seen what *he* was drivin'! It was a—"

"A Bentley."

"Yep, that's right. How'd you know that?"

"Just a guess," she replied dryly. It seemed that Ryan Stone was one step ahead of her all the time. And, considering the length of his legs, that was a long way. "How about the other one? Do you know where I can find him?"

He shook his head. "Sorry, but I'll have to tell you the same thing I told that gentleman. That fella ain't part of the Studebaker Club. He didn't ask t' join, and we didn't exactly invite him. We don't cotton to trash like that in *our* club. Besides, it's a cryin' shame how he's treated that Hawk. It's ugly as he is."

"Do you have any idea where he lives or works?"

"Nope. Don't see him 'round that much."

"Can you think of any way I might find him?"

Duke looked up at her, suddenly suspicious. "You shore do wanna find him bad, lady. What'd he do? Did he go and do you wrong?"

"Let's just say he attacked me, and I want to get even."

"Boy, I hear ya, Sis." He tossed the used swabs into a nearby garbage can. Savannah half expected him to take out some dental floss and attack the grill. "I'll tell ya right now, where you and me come from we don't have as much of this meanness as they do here. We take care of it ourselves, we do. Right away. Then it don't happen again. A man don't mess with another man's womenfolk, not more 'n once, that is."

Savannah didn't necessarily agree with him. She could remember quite a bit of "meanness" going on, despite self-appointed guardians of the law such as Duke Wallace. But she thought it better to keep her opinions to herself for the moment. The rebel flag on the garage wall and the N.R.A. buckle were the deciding factors.

"Here's my phone number," she said, handing him one of her old business cards with the station number and her extension crossed out and her home number written above.

"You're a police lady?" he asked with the expected amount of surprise.

"Nope. Used to be."

"My, my . . . I never did cotton to the idea of havin' women policemen. Didn't seem right somehow." He shook his head sadly. "But you seem like a real nice lady, so I'll do what I can to help you out. We're havin' a big barbecue this Saturday, downtown at the park. I'll ask around and see if anybody else knows where this guy is. Fair enough?"

"Fair enough."

As she walked out of the garage, she could have sworn she heard him whistling "Dixie."

Old Confederates never die, she thought. *But the odd one does move to California and restore Studebakers.*

It took all kinds.

Dirk had invited Savannah out for dinner. All she could eat.

That meant happy hour at the Bench.

She sat in a corner booth of the sports bar and watched him raid the goodies table for the fourth time. When he returned to their booth he was carrying two tiny paper plates, grossly overburdened with cheeses, crackers, meatballs, ribs, and some strange, breaded, deep-fried things that didn't warrant close scrutiny.

"Dig in, kid. I wanna get my money's worth," he said, nodding back at the table. "They've got sissy food, too, you know."

To Dirk, "sissy food" consisted of anything that hadn't recently said, "Moo." Fruits and vegetables definitely fell into that category, along with pastas and whole grain products.

Having already consumed her fill of celery and carrot sticks, dipped in ranch-style dressing, she had decided to give it up and just eat later. So much for dinner out with Dirk.

She hefted the one token margarita that had granted her access to this cornucopia and took a sip. Dirk was safe; he knew she would only have one if she was driving later. Savannah was Dirk's idea of the perfect date: cheap.

During the next half hour he finally managed to worm it all out of her: the whole sad story of the demise of Detective Sergeant

Savannah Reid . . . even the part about the videotape. He was incensed.

"I knew there was a lot more to it than that. Why didn't you tell me about this before? I could have jumped in there and—"

"Because I didn't want you to jump in there. You would have just gotten yourself fired. Then we'd both be out of a job, and we couldn't afford to go out on the town . . . like this."

She waved an arm, indicating the threadbare bar with its big-screen TV, whose picture rolled every few seconds, and the once-elegant stained-glass windows on either side of the door. Unfortunately, an overzealous bouncer had attempted to eject a rowdy patron through the one on the right. The broken glass and stretched lead were bowed outward, roughly in the shape of a human body. Savannah and Dirk had been coming here for years, and for as far back as she could remember the TV had rolled and the glass had bowed.

"True," he said, not quite comprehending her underlying sarcasm, "but hell, that's what being partners is all about."

"Thanks, Dirk, you're a doll."

"Sh-h-h . . ." He cast a furtive glance at the bar-stool jocks that lined the place, wall to wall. "Don't say something like that in a place like this. Jeez, a guy's got a reputation to uphold, you know."

"Sorry, I got carried away."

"Seriously, how can I help? Name it, you got it. We'll get you back on the force somehow. We have to."

"Do you miss me?" she asked in her sexiest tone.

"Sure I do. Hell, I'm going through nail-polish fume withdrawal."

She drew a deep breath and braced herself, knowing he wasn't going to like what he was about to hear.

"Don't fight for me, Dirk. At the moment I don't want back on the force. I miss you, too, but the rest of the bullshit I can do without."

"You're kidding! You're just going to roll over and play dead? That isn't like you, Van."

"I don't see it that way. I'm beginning to think they did me a favor. This ain't so bad, Dirk. Really. It has its drawbacks, sure. But overall, I think I could live with the thought of being my own boss, of not having to deal with the stiff white shirts."

He sat for a long time, fingering a lump of cheese on a saltine. Finally he cleared his throat and said in a husky voice, "Fine; then I guess you won't need me anymore. No problem."

She wanted to reach across the table and squeeze his hand, but in a macho sports bar frequented by jocks and cops such a blatant display of affection was unacceptable.

"That's where you're wrong," she said. "I do need you . . . just not to help me get back on the force. I need you really bad. Atlanta's in deep shit and she doesn't even know it."

"Your kid sister? The little one?"

"Yeah, she's out here with me now. And she ain't that little anymore. That's the problem."

"Okay," he said, reassuming his air of importance. "Lay it on me. What do you need?"

"Tell me anything you know about a kid-molesting, pervert photographer named Max."

He stared at her for a few seconds, mouth open. Then he shook his head. "Shit, if she's mixed up with Max, she *is* in trouble."

CHAPTER EIGHTEEN

Savannah reached into her mailbox and pulled out a handful of bills, a couple of letters, and a Victoria's Secret catalog. The thrill she felt upon receiving the flyer made her wonder if maybe she should get a life. Victoria had great undies, but this shouldn't be the highlight of her day.

Ah . . . another, higher highlight . . . a fine parchment envelope with "Savannah" written across the front of it in that elegant, flowing penmanship she had admired before.

She couldn't wait until she got into the house to open it. What would it be this time? An evening at the Greek Theater? A weekend at the Biltmore? A week on a cruise ship to—

Down, girl; get real! she cautioned herself. But her hand was shaking, nevertheless, as she pulled out two sheets of paper. Unfolding the pages, she read the first one, a letter that had been written with the now familiar fountain-pen flourish.

My dear Savannah,

Here is a little present for you from Gibson and me. We wanted you to know we were thinking of you and wishing you all the best.

Affectionately,
Ryan Stone & John Gibson

The following page had only three typed lines. She stared at them for a long moment, wondering what Ryan had intended.

ERIC BOWMAN
1453 Chestnut Ave. #245
San Carmelita

Could it be? she wondered. Was this the name and address of her attacker? Somehow she knew it was. How typical of Ryan to beat her to the punch like this.

How could he have located the guy so quickly when she was still working on it? Amazing! She had to give him one thing: He was a hell of an investigator. Having always been proud of her own skill, she had to admit that he might even be better at this game than she was.

Might. Probably not, but maybe.

Feeling lighter on her feet than she had in days, Savannah strolled on into the house. After finding Ryan's note, her interest in the Victoria's Secret catalog had taken on a whole new perspective.

But the momentary reprieve ended when she saw Atlanta curled up on the end of the sofa, the telephone cradled against her cheek, a look of love-lust dulling her eyes.

Brain dead and horny, just like those chickie-poohs on the

posters. She was also wearing a gold satin jacquard robe, Savannah's newest acquisition. First old faithful, the terry-cloth robe, and now the one she had been saving for a special occasion.

Okay, she had to admit she'd been saving it a long time; lately special occasions had been few and far between. But that wasn't the point.

Atlanta was so absorbed in her conversation that she didn't even notice Savannah at first. When she did she jumped, mumbled something in the way of a quick good-bye, and hung up the phone.

Savannah didn't need Ryan's fancy call-return feature to know who had been on the other end of the line. But if she confronted her sister again this soon, the kid would only dig her heels in that much more deeply. Convinced that Savannah was nothing but a cosmic killjoy, Atlanta would automatically assume that anything her big sister didn't want her to do must be something pretty wonderful.

Besides, Savannah had an ace up her sleeve named Dirk, and he had promised to drop by in a little while to assist Savannah in giving her sister a dose of reality therapy.

"I'm expecting a guest," Savannah said as nonchalantly as possible. "Please go upstairs and get dressed."

"I'm dressed," she muttered, reaching for the television remote control. She flipped on MTV, propped her bare feet on the coffee table, and stared sullenly at the screen.

"You aren't dressed. You're wearing *my* robe. In the future I would appreciate you at least asking before you borrow my clothes. Now, please go take that off. My partner, Dirk, is going to be dropping by any minute, and since you've never even met the man, I don't think it's very ladylike to greet him wearing lingerie."

Atlanta's lethargy vanished and she jumped up from the sofa. "Well, excu-u-u-use the hell outta me! I didn't realize you had gotten stingy in your old age. Here's your stupid old robe."

Standing in the middle of the living room, Atlanta whipped off the robe and threw it on the floor at Savannah's feet. Wearing nothing but a skimpy pair of panties and an equally tiny bra, she turned and began to stomp up the stairs.

Once she had gotten over her initial shock Savannah couldn't help noticing that something was quite different about Atlanta's skin color. Usually she was fair, with an ivory complexion like Savannah's. But now she looked more orange than ivory, and the pigment seemed to be blotchy and uneven. Especially on her rear end, which she was wagging conspicuously from side to side.

"Hey, 'Lanta," Savannah called, unable to resist. The girl was already most of the way up the stairs; all Savannah could see were her feet, which paused briefly in midstep. "Nice sunless tan you got there. But your ass is all streaky. Maybe you'd better slap on some more of that orange crap."

The feet pounded on up the stairs and down the hall. The guest bedroom door slammed, rattling the entire house. From the corner of her eye Savannah saw Cleopatra and Diamante scurry out the back door. "Wimps," she called after them. "Can't handle the heat, huh?"

She scooped up her robe from the floor, caressed the satin for a moment, then laid it lovingly across her favorite chair, entertaining a brief but vivid fantasy about Ryan Stone. Something about tying him to her bedposts with a pair of silk stockings and running the satin slowly over his naked body. A special occasion. Yes, she needed a special occasion. Badly.

Alternative electrical devices just weren't cutting it anymore. If this dry spell continued, she'd have to buy stock in Energizer.

Sinking onto the sofa, she switched off the television, picked up the phone, and dialed Beverly Winston. She set a time with her to meet the next day to discuss her progress. Savannah decided not to mention her little bash on the head or the lead on Eric Bowman over the phone. She'd wait until she could see Beverly face-to-face and gauge her reaction. Not that Beverly Winston had especially readable reactions. Quite the contrary.

No sooner had Savannah hung up the phone, leaned back on the sofa, and closed her eyes for a momentary break, than a shave-and-a-haircut knock sounded on the door.

Dirk had arrived with the ammunition. She sighed . . . a weary warrior. "Take cover all ye beasts: furred, fish and fowl," she said. "Round two is about to begin."

"I asked Dirk to do a little research for me," Savannah said to Atlanta, who was once again curled into the corner of the sofa. This time she wore skintight jeans and a black halter top. Wow . . . big improvement. But she wasn't looking lust-besought. She appeared grandly pissed.

"Dirk is very good at research," Savannah continued. "I think you'll find that what he discovered is fascinating."

Sitting on the footstool in front of Savannah's chair, Dirk produced a manila envelope and handed it to Savannah. He looked a bit uncomfortable, and she was certain it had nothing to do with his awkward seating arrangement. Dirk wasn't good at family squabbling—probably why his wife of twenty years had divorced him.

She reached into the envelope and pulled out some photographs and documents.

"Let's see what we have here. . . ."

Savannah could hear the sarcasm in her own voice and she hated it. Until Atlanta had called her from the airport that night she had considered herself a pretty nice person. Since when had she turned into a caustic bitch?

"Recognize this gentleman?" she asked, placing the mug shot of a rather seedy but marginally attractive man on the coffee table in front of Atlanta.

Savannah watched her sister's face closely. Her orange skin quickly faded to a sickly gray. She did know him, whether she would admit it or not.

"This guy just got out of prison a year ago. He was in for statutory rape, using minors for pornography, pandering, good stuff like that. His name is . . ." Savannah turned the photo over and read the back. ". . . Maximillian Turner. Of course, he's also known as Max Russell, Mark L'amore, and Michael Lovejoy." She turned to Dirk. "Kinda overt, don't you think, like Trixie Delight?"

Dirk cracked a grin, but one look at Atlanta told Savannah that she didn't get the joke. She still appeared to be suffering from shell shock at seeing her soul mate in a police mug shot.

Savannah decided to keep the ball rolling. Reaching into the envelope again, she produced a dozen or more photographs of young women, wearing little or nothing, posed in extremely compromising and demeaning positions. She fanned them out on the coffee table in front of her sister.

"I thought you should see some of the photographs that were used in evidence against Max-Mark-Michael. The authorities seized them when they raided your pal's 'studio.' He's quite the little artiste, huh?"

Savannah knew she was about to strike a low blow, but she

had to make her point with Atlanta for her own mental health and safety. She chose a particularly abusive and graphic photo of a girl, chained to a whipping post, wearing bondage garb and a terrified look on her young face. The photo was in color, and dark red welts showed clearly across the girl's white breasts and buttocks.

"Her name was Cindy and she was fourteen when that was taken," Dirk told her, averting his eyes from the photograph. "The marks on her . . . they weren't done with makeup. They're for real. Two days after Max was convicted Cindy threw herself out a window downtown. Her suicide note said it was because she had lost the only man she had ever loved."

He paused, waiting for his words to sink in, before he added, "She didn't look very pretty at all when they scraped her up off the sidewalk and into a body bag."

"By the way . . ." Savannah continued, pouring all available fuel on the fire, ". . . when Cindy testified at Max's trial she told the court that he had said she was the most beautiful 'woman' he had ever photographed. That every man who saw her pictures would want her; every woman would envy her."

"You're lying!" Atlanta swept the pictures onto the floor and jumped up from the sofa, her eyes blazing. "He didn't tell her that! He didn't! He doesn't say that to everybody. I *know* he doesn't!"

"He also told her that she had a rare and delicate beauty," Dirk said, the calm tone of his voice a direct contrast to hers, "that a sweet, sexy woman like her really touched his heart."

"Shut up!" She started to cry, shaking her head in denial. "Why are you guys lying to me?"

"We aren't, 'Lanta, and you know it," Savannah replied, feeling the tears begin to well up in her own eyes. "He invited her up to his apartment to watch the sunset and eat ice cream. Then he screwed her. She was fourteen, Atlanta. A baby."

"Damn you, Savannah! I *hate* you for doing this! I really, really *hate* you!"

Savannah rose and hurried over to her sister, arms outstretched. "I'm sorry, sweetheart," she said, choking back her sobs as she reached to hug her. But instead of folding into her embrace Atlanta pushed her away. "I don't want to hurt you like this, but I don't want you to wind up like Cindy. And this Max creep will chew you up and spit you out, honey. He doesn't care about you, no matter what he said or did. A guy like that only cares about himself."

Still shaking her head and crying hysterically, Atlanta ran up the stairs and into the guest room, again, slamming the door behind her.

Savannah stood in the middle of her living room, arms and heart empty. She liked to think of herself as a pretty tough broad, but this was just one thing too many. Much more of this and she was going to just "cut her strings and go straight up," as Gran would say . . . whatever the hell that meant.

Dirk rose from the footstool and walked over to her. Sliding his arms around her shoulders, he folded her against his big, warm bear chest. "You had to do it, Van," he said. "She's feelin' pretty rotten up there right now, but she'll be feelin' a lot worse if she keeps hanging around that scuzball."

He patted the top of her head as though she were a cocker spaniel. It felt remarkably good. "You've warned her; now the rest is up to her."

"She hates me," Savannah said with a sniff, her face buried against his shirt. "My little sister hates me."

Good ol' Dirk, Savannah thought as she leaned back and looked up at him. He didn't seem to even notice that she was getting tears all over the front of his clean shirt. Now that was a friend.

"Naw . . . she doesn't hate you. She just hates the truth that you told her. And right now she's too young to know the difference."

"I appreciate you coming along for this," Savannah said as she and Dirk climbed the stairs to the veranda of the old Victorian-style house.

San Carmelita had been built with citrus money at the turn of the century, and this section of town had been restored beautifully. The brass plaque on the front lawn stated that this house, as with many others on Santa Barbara Street, had been declared a California historical landmark.

"Nice place," she admitted reluctantly as they approached the door with its beveled and stained-glass oval window. "I have to admit I would have felt better about this if he'd had his 'studio' off some dark alley in a tough part of town."

"Why's that?" Dirk rapped on the door with the heavy brass knocker in the shape of a horseshoe.

"Because criminals should look, talk, act, and live in bad places so that we can tell at a glance. Nowadays they're getting so 'respectable' that you can't tell the difference."

Dirk knocked again, and Savannah was quiet for a moment, bracing herself for the coming confrontation. It felt good having Dirk beside her again, especially for something this emotional. She had to admit she really hated working alone.

The door opened and a beautiful young Asian woman opened the door. Dressed in a red silk kimono, her black hair flowing past her hips, she was incredibly striking. The only imperfection in an otherwise blemishless appearance were her eyes.

They were empty, lacking the life and sparkle that should be there, considering her youth.

She looked like the girls whose photographs were in that manila envelope of Dirk's.

"May I help you?" she asked in a blatantly sexual tone that sounded flat, a little too practiced.

"Yes, we're here to see Maximillian," Savannah said. "He's an old friend of ours."

"Is he expecting you?" she asked. "Do you have an appointment?"

Savannah laughed. "No, no, we don't need an appointment to see Max. Just tell him that Betty and Marco are here. He'll want to see us, believe me!"

"Betty and Marco . . . okay, wait here."

The girl disappeared for a moment down the dark hall, leaving them standing in the doorway.

A while later a man walked out of what appeared to be the parlor and into the foyer. Savannah could see him through the transparent segments of the leaded glass. In spite of his expensive suit and haircut he looked like a punk . . . a vampire of the worst kind.

Her stomach turned as thoughts ran, unbidden, through her brain, thoughts of what he might have done to her sister. Thoughts of how good it would feel to make him pay for what he had done with a bullet between the eyes.

Although Savannah had never once had to kill or even shoot a human being in the course of her law enforcement career, she had to admit she didn't think she would be irreparably traumatized by taking this child-molesting pervert out.

As he approached, Savannah was struck by what a small man he was, probably no more than five-four, and she doubted he weighed much more than a hundred pounds. What did her sister see in this guy?

The moment he opened his mouth, Savannah had her answer.

"Good morning, good morning," he gushed. "And how can I be of service to you two today?"

He flashed a mouth full of perfectly capped teeth that gleamed against his perfectly suntanned face. His skin had a familiar orange glow to it, but apparently he was more skilled at spreading it on than Atlanta.

Savannah supposed that a naive sixteen-year-old girl might be awed by the flash. She remembered being embarrassingly easy to impress at that age.

"We need to have a word with you . . . in private," she added, dropping her voice. "It's very important, and I don't think you'll want to talk about it here on your porch . . . if you know what I mean."

"Yeah," Dirk interjected, "there are just some things that a guy doesn't want his neighbors to know about his private life, like—"

"Okay, okay, come on," he said, beckoning them inside. His charm and effervescence fizzled like an old seltzer tablet, and Savannah wished Atlanta could see him now.

He hurried into the parlor, and they followed. The room had been beautifully decorated with Victorian furnishings that were from the same period as the house. A bit overly ornate, but in keeping with the times. Brocade diamond-tucked sofas, love seats, and chairs; marble-topped tables, Oriental rugs, and almost everything trimmed with lace or covered with doilies.

"So, Marco . . . Betty," Max said, not bothering to offer them a seat, "what's this all about?" He stood with his arms crossed over his chest defensively. The gesture wrinkled both his suit and his facade of composure.

"It's about you being up to your old tricks—so to speak—again," Dirk said, pulling his badge from his pocket and flipping it open. "And I'm not Marco. She just calls me that sometimes for fun."

"I don't know what you're talking about." His face flushed and a muscle in his jaw began to twitch. "Do you have a warrant or something?"

"Not yet. I was hoping we wouldn't have to resort to that. Don't get me wrong; I'd love to put you back in the joint where you belong, but I don't want to embarrass the young lady in question unless I have to. Get my drift?"

Savannah watched his eyes carefully. She detected a hint of uncertainty when Dirk referred to the "young lady." *God,* she thought, *he's got more than one, and he doesn't know who Dirk is referring to.*

"I repeat, I don't know what you're talking about. But I don't see any need for anyone to be embarrassed about anything," he replied with a half-nervous, half-cocky grin. "And I don't think we have anything else to talk about."

"Oh, but we do." Savannah stepped forward, invading his comfort zone. "That is, you and *I* have things to talk about. Could you leave us for a moment?" she asked Dirk. "Just wait for me in the hall. I'll only be a minute."

"No problem." Dirk nodded to Max. "Nice chatting with you. I'll be leaving you in my friend Betty's capable hands. Good luck, sucker," he added as he walked out the door.

As soon as Dirk had left, Savannah discreetly slipped her hand inside her jacket and produced the Beretta. A half second later Max the Perv's back was plastered to a mahogany wainscoted wall, the end of the gun's barrel pressed tightly against his jugular.

"I'm going to tell you a couple of things, Max, and you need to listen really good. Got it?"

He nodded ever so slightly, staring down at the gun.

"You've been messin' with a pretty young thing named Atlanta. You know . . . Atlanta?"

Again he nodded.

"Well, 'Lanta is my baby sister, and I don't cotton to havin' a forty-year-old degenerate like yourself fool around with my little sister." Her voice was smooth, taking on an even heavier than usual Southern accent. But her eyes were only inches from his, and the deadly intensity registered there was unmistakable.

"Let me tell you something else that you need to know: I'm from Georgia. Now that's *below* the Mason-Dixon Line. And down there we see things differently than you Yankees. We don't always do things by the book."

She paused and began to trail the barrel of the gun slowly down the front of his shirt, dragging it over each pearlized button.

"Don't get me wrong: I'm not going to put a sheet over my head and burn this pretty house of yours down. I mean, it's not like I'm a vigilante or anything like that. But if you *ever* . . ." She punctuated her words by sharply gouging him in the ribs with the gun. Then she slid it down to his zipper area and a tad lower. She could smell his terror in the sweat that was beginning to run down his face. "If you *ever* even look in my sister's direction, I'm going to personally shorten parts of your anatomy that are probably already woefully inadequate. 'Cause where I come from that's the way we handle dirty ol' men like you who mess with our pretty little girls."

Slowly she withdrew the pistol and replaced it in her shoulder holster.

The instant the gun was no longer a threat the fear disappeared from his face and fury replaced it.

He lifted one fist, shook it in front of her, and said, "You bitch! Don't you ever point a gun at my—"

He never got to finish his statement, because she snatched his fist out of the air and gave his wrist a vicious twist that instantly brought him to his knees. He let out a scream of pain as she gave it one more quarter turn for emphasis.

"Have it your way," she said. "I won't need a gun to accomplish what I want to with you. Maybe I'll just twist that little Vienna sausage of yours off with one hand and feed it to you with the other."

As abruptly as she had grabbed him, she released him. He sagged to the floor, groaning and rubbing his wrist, which was already beginning to swell and turn blue. Every trace of arrogance and cockiness was gone from his face. Only pain, fear, and anger remained.

Maybe he had gotten the message.

She left him there on the floor, holding his wrist, which looked as though it might be broken, and joined Dirk in the foyer.

He raised one eyebrow and said, "Is he still alive? I heard him yell."

"Oh, yeah . . . he's still kickin'," she replied.

She took Dirk's arm, and they walked out the door and down to his car.

"But let's just say," she added, "that unless he's ambidextrous, his sex life may not be too satisfying for a month or so."

"So, what's next?" Dirk said as they climbed into his car.

Savannah hesitated for a moment, actually enjoying being inside the old jalopy again . . . with Dirk. She felt good about what had just gone down. As a cop, she would never have threatened someone like that. But as Atlanta's avenging big sister, she was satisfied that she could live with the memory of scaring Max the Perv so bad that he'd wet his fancy britches.

She gave Dirk a bright smile and giggled. "Ah, hell . . . while I'm on a roll, let's go after that bastard who whacked me in the head."

CHAPTER NINETEEN

"Tell me again, exactly why is it that we have to wait for this Ryan Stone guy to show up?" Dirk said as they sat behind the Seaview Apartments, keeping an eye on the battered old Studebaker parked in the lot across the alley.

Savannah had often wondered at the wisdom of the owners who had given the complex its name. Here on the far east side of town there wasn't so much as a whiff of sea air, let alone a sea view. And unless the predicted "Big One" rearranged the better half of California's geography, there wasn't likely to ever be a sea view from this property.

"Because he gave me the name and address. And when I called to tell him we were coming over here he offered to help. Plus, I wanted to ask him a few more questions before I go splitting this guy's head. I need a plan—like how many clefts I should put in his skull—before I strike the first blow."

Dirk gave her a questioning look. "Geez, you really are on a roll, aren't you? I've never seen you quite so revved, Van. I have to tell you, it's kinda sexy."

She replied with a growl and took her bottle of red nail polish from her purse.

The low, sensual purr of a motorcycle caught her attention. Peering down the alley, she saw a fully outfitted Harley-Davidson coming toward them. The rider wore black leathers and a silver helmet that matched the black-and-silver trim on the bike. Something about the wide set of the shoulders and the slender waist and hips tipped her off as to who might be under that helmet.

"Oops, never mind," she said as she stuck the polish back into her purse. "I do believe Mr. Stone has arrived."

"*That's* your buddy?" Dirk asked in a sarcastic tone that Savannah instantly recognized.

Ha, ha! Dirk was jealous.

Wait until you see him with his helmet off, she thought. But while her heart was thumping at the thought of seeing Ryan again, she was uncomfortable having him and Dirk meet. She wasn't sure why.

Okay, she suspected why, but she didn't want to think about it. The words "When Worlds Collide" kept bouncing around in her brain.

Ryan brought the bike to a halt beside Dirk's car, next to Savannah's window, and killed the engine. He took off his helmet and ran his fingers through the thick, dark waves that fell almost to his collar. Before, when Savannah had seen him, he'd had his mane slicked back in a G.Q. look. She sucked in her breath and tried not to ogle. Heavens . . . he looked even better mussed up.

"Hi," he said, grinning down at her as he peeled off the leather gloves. "Am I late?"

"Yeah," Dirk mumbled under his breath so that only Savannah heard. She didn't expect him to like Ryan. He had an aversion to any man who had more hair than he, and that included a rather large percentage of the male population.

"Nah, we're just early. See, we don't have a life." Savannah nodded toward the Harley. "Subtle," she said. "Blends right in with the neighborhood."

"Better than the Bentley," he replied, climbing off the bike and stowing the helmet and gloves. "Actually, this is Gibson's. He let me borrow it."

"Gibson's?"

"Yep." He laughed. "There's a lot more to the Brit than meets the eye."

"No kidding."

Beside her, Dirk cleared his throat, and she realized she had been excluding him from the conversation. In fact, she had all but forgotten his presence.

"Oh, ah . . . Dirk Coulter, this is Ryan Stone. Ryan—Dirk."

"A pleasure, I'm sure," Ryan said, leaning into Savannah's open window.

"Yeah, right." Dirk refused to make eye contact with him but continued to stare straight ahead at the battered van. "Now that you've shown up, maybe we can get this over with?"

Discreetly, Savannah reached over and pinched him hard on the ribs. He jumped slightly and gave her a dirty look.

She turned back to Ryan. Lord knows, he was a lot easier on the eyes and in a helluva lot better mood.

"How did you find out about this guy, anyway?" she asked. "I didn't even tell you where or how I'd met him."

"You want to know my secrets, huh?"

His voice was deep and sultry, his tone flirtatious. She could feel Dirk's disapproval radiating in giant waves around her, even as her own body melted like a lukewarm bowl of gelatin.

"Yes," she said, trying not to stumble and croak over the frog in her throat. "All of them."

"I have a contact on the streets who knows someone, who saw a scrawny blond guy in heavy-metal regalia driving away from the back of the showroom in a classic Studebaker Golden Hawk. Let's just say I took it from there."

Dirk gave an unpleasant snort. "The guy got nailed because he was driving a weird vehicle. Take a lesson, pal."

This time Savannah was sure Ryan must have heard him, but he didn't rise to the bait. Instead he glanced quickly up and down the Buick, lingering a moment on the avalanche of fast-food wrappers littering the backseat and floorboards. At any given time one could look into the rear of the Buick and tell what Dirk had eaten for dinner the past two weeks. Sequence could be determined by the varying degrees of decomposition of any remaining organic materials.

"Just what do you think we're going to accomplish by confronting this guy?" Dirk said. "We don't have a search warrant. Our potential witness is a friend of a friend of yours—whoever you are, Mr. Stone—so we can't even think about arresting him."

"I just want to know, okay?" Savannah said, her temper rising along with the intensity of her headache. The painkiller she had taken earlier was beginning to wear off, and she wasn't supposed to pop another one for two hours. "I want to look into his eyes and see if he's the one who bopped me. I'll know. And if he is, I'm going to be all over him like stink on a roadkill skunk until I find a way to nail his butt to the nearest jail wall."

"I can certainly understand that," Ryan said, nodding approvingly. "Can't you, Detective Coulter?"

"Sure, of course I can." Dirk pulled the keys from the ignition, opened the door, and stepped out. "Let's go have a little 'close encounter' with your scrawny, heavy-metal dude," he grumbled. "And we'll find out how good a detective you are, Mr. Sherlock Stone."

It was him.

Savannah knew the moment he opened the apartment door and focused on her with beer-bleary eyes. Not that she recognized him as her attacker. She had never actually seen the assailant; he had merely been a movement in her peripheral vision.

But the look of shock on his face when he saw her told Savannah more than she needed to know. She was more to him than just the lady with the neat Camaro.

"Why?" she said, stepping into the doorway, forcing him back.

"Why . . . what?" He glanced quickly from Dirk to Ryan, then back to Savannah.

"Why did you crack me on the head last night?"

"I don't know what you're talking about."

Savannah sighed. "If one more creep tells me that he doesn't know what I'm talking about today, I swear, I'm gonna smack him. Now . . . I'll ask you again, and you'd better think long and hard about your answer. Why did you attack me last night?"

This time he didn't reply; he just stood there, beer can in hand, bare chest, bare feet, his jeans riding low on his skinny ass, giving her the same smirk that she had slapped off many faces during the course of her life. Admittedly 98 percent of those had been in the first ten years, but she hadn't forgotten how it was done.

"You hit the wrong person last night, Mr. Bowman. I'll do whatever is necessary to see that you spend some time behind bars. Because nobody lands me in the hospital and gets away with it. *Nobody!*"

She saw a momentary flicker of fear cross his face, and she realized she had practically screamed the words at him. Having meant every word she had said, Savannah could see that he was at least intelligent enough to know when a threat was real.

A second later his cool look slid back in place. "Lady, I don't know who you are or what you're talkin' about. But I'm watchin' a great rerun of 'Gilligan's Island' in here, and you're makin' me miss the good part."

Ignoring the sarcasm, she decided to take a stab in the dark and see if she could hit something vital.

"Also, I know that you killed Jonathan Winston. And by the time I'm done I'll have proven that, too."

Bull's-eye! A direct hit.

She heard him catch his breath and hold it, and she saw the color drain from his face.

My *god*, she thought, not believing her luck. *He did it!* She shot a look at Dirk and Ryan. They seemed as surprised and pleased as she at this new revelation.

"I didn't kill nobody," Eric said, his voice shaky, all traces of cool gone. "And I didn't do anything to you either, 'cept ask you if you wanted to sell your car. You fuckin' cops think you can go around givin' people shit all the time. Well, I know my rights, and unless you got a warrant or somethin', you can't hassle me."

Having stated his case, Eric Bowman slammed his door in their faces.

Savannah had to employ all of her self-control not to jump up and down and giggle manically as they walked back toward the alley.

Finally, a break in this damned case! A break that might eventually lead to an arrest, that might lead to a conviction, that, ultimately, might lead to vengeance! Ah, life was sweet.

"He's lying, he's lying," she told Dirk and Ryan, who were both jockeying for a position beside her. "That little weasel is lying through his snaggley yellow teeth."

"You sure about that?" Dirk asked.

Dirk always took some convincing.

"Sure she is," Ryan supplied with a one-up grin.

"Oh yeah, and how do you know so much about it, smart guy?"

"Easy. You could see it in his eyes, his body language. Besides, she never said a word to him about any of us being cops."

When Savannah returned home that evening she found the atmosphere in her living room chilly and ominously quiet—like the silence after a storm, or before a storm, or in between. It was hard to tell.

Atlanta sat on the end of the sofa, which she had apparently staked out and claimed with squatter's rights. The room reeked of nail polish and remover. She had her feet propped on the arm of the sofa, cotton wedged between her toes, and was performing a meticulous pedicure.

Savannah thought she looked like a duck who had waddled through a cotton patch with sticky feet. But, astute as she was, she decided it might be best to keep the observation to herself.

"Hi," Savannah said, testing the waters.

Stony silence.

When the girl glanced up, then returned to her toes, Savannah could see that her eyes were badly swollen from crying.

Savannah's heartstrings twanged with a discordant zing. Poor kid. She had done some less-than-savvy things recently, to say the least, but she was paying for them. Thank God, the price didn't appear to be so high as to ruin her life.

"Tough day, huh?" she said as she walked over to the sofa and sat on the other end.

"Yeah, you could say that," Atlanta muttered, dabbing some Coral Sunset Ultra-Frost on her pinkie toe.

"Wanna talk about it?"

"Nope."

"Okay."

So much for communication.

Diamante jumped onto Savannah's lap and forced her head under her mistress's hand, wanting to be petted. The gesture almost brought tears to Savannah's eyes. At least somebody in the house was glad to see her. Gee, it just wasn't all that much fun coming home these days.

"Did I get any messages?"

"Nope."

"Mail?"

She said nothing but pointed toward the end table with her polish brush.

Oh, joy. A stack of bills. Just what she needed right now.

"Damn it, 'Lanta," she said, her patience snapping, "I did what I thought was best . . . for you, that is. Can you give me that, at least?"

Her sister looked up at her, swollen, slitted eyes glaring. "You won! Okay? He won't even talk to me on the phone now. Hung up on me *five* times today. Gee, I wonder why. Could my big sister have maybe gone to visit him and waved her badge under his nose? Could that be why he's afraid to talk to me, even for a minute?"

"I don't feel as though I've won anything, Atlanta," she said, her anger dissolving in the face of her sister's pain. She reached over and touched the girl's shoulder. "If I've lost part of your love for me, then nobody's won."

She was relieved when Atlanta didn't shake her hand away. Instead, she laid the polish aside, turned around, and held her arms out to her sister. Savannah wasted no time in pulling her into a warm embrace.

"You didn't lose my love," the girl said between sniffles. "I still love you."

"Good." Savannah's own tears began to flow, wetting her sister's hair as she rocked her in her arms. "I'm so glad. I love you, too, baby."

Again Atlanta sniffed, then pulled away and scowled at the smudge on her right big toenail. "I'll always love you, too, Savannah," she said, licking her thumb and running it lightly over the mussed polish. "But right now I really don't like you very much. You understand, don't you?"

Savannah sighed. "Sure. I understand. No-o-oo problem."

Finally the day had ended—some days seemed *never* to end—and Savannah had intended to turn in early and curl up in bed with a good romance novel. A bit of escapism never hurt anyone, she reasoned. But once she was enveloped in her new Laura Ashley sheets, skin softened by a long soak in a lavender-scented bath, her body caressed by the ivory silken folds of a lusciously decadent teddy, her cats curled warmly on either side of her feet—Savannah realized that there was no way in hell she could relax.

With a groan she plunked the romance novel onto the nightstand and leaned over the edge of the bed until she was nearly standing on her head. Feeling the blood rush to her face, she tried to see past the spots that were rapidly forming in front of her eyes as she groped for what she fondly called her Rat Maze.

The Rat Maze consisted of a two-by-three-foot rectangle of purple foam core board with small hot pink stick-on notes all over it. When trying to keep mental track of the countless people, events, evidence, etc., involved in a case, she used this self-made tool to keep it all straight.

Even with this little invention of hers, she still felt as if she was struggling to find her way through a difficult maze, but, inevitably, she was searching for a particular "rat," and it was worth the effort when she finally nailed the dirty rodent.

In the top row she listed her possible suspects, those who had motive and opportunity. Her practiced eye scanned the inventory of potential culprits in this particular maze.

Beverly Winston	Fiona O'Neal	Eric Bowman	Danielle Lamont	Norman Hillquist	Unknown Assailant

One by one, she stared at the bits of brightly colored paper, seeing the faces, remembering their words and actions, wondering.

After only a few moments of consideration she moved Eric Bowman's stick-it to the far left, giving him the dubious honor of the number-one position. She was pretty sure he had smacked her over the head and stolen the ledgers and her notebook. That was reason enough, she figured, for his promotion.

Somehow he had gained access to the showroom without forcing a door or making a lot of noise. She had been certain to lock the doors behind her when she had entered the building that night. And the two patrolmen had found it unlocked the next morning.

If Bowman had been able to come and go easily the night he had attacked her, he could have done so just as effortlessly the evening that Jonathan had been killed.

Taking two more notes from the pad, she stuck them on the board under Bowman. On the first she wrote "Attack, Reid?" and on the other, "Easy Access to Showroom?"

In another row she had stick-its that read "Ledgers Stolen" and "Reid's Notebook Stolen." These she also moved beneath Bowman's name.

She stared at this arrangement with a puzzled quirk to one eyebrow. This one didn't ring quite right. Bowman just didn't strike her as someone who possessed a brain sophisticated enough to decipher a business ledger as complicated as that one. If he couldn't understand it, why steal it?

The answer wasn't long in coming. Bowman was acting on behalf of someone a lot smarter. He was just a paid punk doing someone else's bidding.

But whose?

Again she scanned the row of suspects. As with the majority of San Carmelita's populace, any and all of them fit the bill of being smarter than Eric Bowman.

Beneath each name she had affixed notes, signifying possible reasons they might have had for murdering Winston: revenge, jealousy, anger, and, in Beverly's case, all of the above, plus lots of money. His death had saved her from having to divide a sizable fortune down the middle in a messy divorce settlement.

Savannah's head began to throb again, making it difficult for her to concentrate or even focus on the tiny bits of paper any longer.

She glanced at her bedside clock: a few minutes after ten. This would be a very early taps for her, but every molecule of her body was telling her that she needed the extra sleep.

No sooner had she turned out the light than she heard the highly annoying, nerve-jangling racket that she was beginning to despise.

She fumbled for the phone and shoved it in the vicinity of her face, rapping her front tooth in the process.

"Hell-ooww!"

"Detective Reid?"

Savannah thought she recognized the voice, and her weary body received a jolt of adrenaline. "This is Savannah Reid," she replied, hedging the detective bit.

"I called you the other night, to tell you about the ball."

Yes, there it was—the Eastern Seaboard drawl. She could hear it in the "ca-w-lled" and the "ba-w-ll." Yep, East Coast, all right. More specifically, the New York City area.

"Yes; I'm glad you called back," she said, sitting up straight in the bed. Startled and offended, the two cats leaped off both sides, but Savannah never noticed. "I wanted to thank you for the tip, but, to be honest, it wasn't particularly conclusive. There were a lot of people at the Pavilion that night. And nobody was wearing a sign that said 'I done it.' "

"I'm sorry I can't tell you more. I wish I could, really."

The woman sounded sincere, as though she truly did want to help. In fact, she sounded like something was wrong. Something pretty badly wrong.

"Why can't you tell me?" Savannah asked. "Are you afraid for your own safety?"

"Not really . . . at least, not yet. But I'm not absolutely sure at this point. And I don't want to . . . you know, turn someone in . . . unless I'm positive."

Savannah thought that one over for a moment. "Okay. So, why are you calling me tonight?" she asked hopefully. Heck, hoping was still free, and it never hurt.

"Because I wanted to tell you that I think someone's life is in danger. I'm not sure, but if I didn't tell anyone, and she . . . well . . . I thought I should call you just in case."

"Have you heard someone threaten a person's life?"

"No, not directly. But I saw some papers and . . . it doesn't matter how I know. Maybe *you* can answer a question for *me*."

"I'll try. Shoot."

Savannah heard her hesitate, then take a deep breath. "Do you know anyone who was close to Mr. Winston who might be in possession of a lot of his money? Money he took from his business?"

With a quick glance at the board—and Fiona O'Neal's name—she replied, "Maybe. Why?"

"Because I think that somebody is after that money. And whoever has it . . . I think they're going to get killed if they don't hand it over."

"I see. Any hints about who we're talking about?"

A long, heavy pause. Then, "I think it might be Mr. Winston's first wife, Fiona."

Savannah thought it best not to confirm the suspicion, just in case the woman on the other end of the line was more interested in fishing for information than supplying it.

"I meant," Savannah said, "who the person is who's considering killing someone."

"I'm sorry; I just can't tell you that until I'm sure. I don't want to be responsible for destroying a person who's . . . never mind. Thank you for listening."

"Any time," Savannah said. "Any time at all. Please, do call back." But by then the woman had already hung up the phone.

For a little while Savannah sat there, holding the receiver in her hand, wondering what to do. She didn't want to go running across town, barging in on Fiona, and scaring the crap out of her for no reason. And yet . . . like the lady from New York . . . Savannah couldn't bear the thought of letting something horrible happen to Fiona if she could prevent it.

Crawling out of bed, she retrieved her address book from a dresser drawer and flipped it open to Fiona's name and number.

As she dialed, Savannah mentally rehearsed her apology. *I'm sorry for calling so late, but . . .* No, she couldn't tell her the truth. The singer had looked frazzled enough the last time she had seen her. No point in sending her over the edge.

. . . but I forgot to ask you one little question. Exactly where did you and Jonathan first meet?

It was a pretty lousy line, but she didn't have to use it. Fiona didn't answer the phone.

A man did, after about ten rings. "Hello?"

"Dirk?" She couldn't quite believe it. What the hell was he doing at . . .

"Van?"

"Yeah. What's going on?"

"You mean, you don't . . . oh, I thought you were calling because you knew."

The sinking feeling in the pit of her stomach plunged all the way down to her feet, leaving her knees weak and shaky as it passed. *No, God, please, not already. I just found out. I can't be too late.*

"Is she . . . ?"

Dirk hesitated a beat too long. It was true.

"Yeah."

"When?"

"Don't know for sure. But she's fresh. Dr. Liu is here, and she figures within the last couple of hours, more or less."

"How?"

"The doctor figures it was the shotgun blast that sent her on her way. But it's a little hard to tell for sure; there are quite a few . . . other injuries. Looks like somebody was trying to get something out of her."

Savannah thought back to those huge sums that had been withdrawn from Jonathan's business over the past year or so. People had killed for a hell of a lot less.

"Do you think the killer got what he was after?" she asked, her mouth suddenly dry.

"God, I hope so. A terrible waste of a beautiful woman. I'd hate to think it was all for nothing."

Neither of them said anything as Savannah regained her composure. Good ol' Dirk; he had always appreciated the value of a comfortable silence and didn't seem to need to sully it with worthless chitchat.

"Do you want to come down?" he finally asked.

"No. But I will anyway. See you in a few."

Hanging up the phone, she looked at the board, which she had dropped onto the bed, and the attached sticky note that named Fiona O'Neal as Murder Suspect Number Three.

With a sick ache that hurt all the way through, Savannah

reached for the note and moved it to the lower right-hand corner of the board. Next to Jonathan's.

For some reason, long ago, she had decided that was the proper corner . . . to stick the dead ones.

CHAPTER TWENTY

Fiona O'Neal's apartment might have seemed dreary before when Savannah had visited, but she found it far more depressing the second time around. The place had been torn to pieces by someone who was either extremely angry, extremely curious, or both. The vandal had left nothing intact, from the eviscerated sofa and recliner to the cardboard boxes, whose contents had been dumped on the floor.

But the destruction to the room was nothing compared to what had been done to Fiona O'Neal herself.

"Oh, God . . ." As always, Savannah had braced herself before entering a homicide scene, but no amount of preparation was enough when the victim was someone you knew.

"Pretty bad, huh, Van?" Dirk stood beside her, his hands shoved deep into the pockets of his old bomber jacket, looking more tired than she had seen him in a long time.

"Yeah, pretty wicked. Just like Jonathan Winston," she said as she watched Dr. Jennifer Liu kneel beside the body and make a small incision in the abdomen. A few seconds later the coroner thrust a long thermometer through the opening and into the liver.

"Really? Like her ex?" Dirk seemed surprised and acutely interested.

"Oh, that's right . . . you didn't see the Winston scene."

Savannah walked closer to the body, forcing herself to take a better look. Jennifer looked up and nodded briefly to her. Savannah returned the solemn acknowledgment.

"Exactly like her ex," Savannah told him.

"Unfortunately," Jennifer interjected, "I'm afraid that isn't totally true. I think the lady went through a lot more before she died than Mr. Winston did."

She pointed to the ropes that were still tied around Fiona's wrists and ankles, the laceration of both Achilles tendons, and the bruising and abrasions on her hands that looked as though someone had carefully and deliberately mangled each finger.

But, like Jonathan, it was the shotgun blast to the head that would have dispatched her into the next world.

Savannah realized sadly that the end must have been a relief.

"He was trying to get her to tell," Savannah whispered. "And she wouldn't. It was all she had left of Jonathan; she never would have told him if he hadn't . . ."

"To tell what?" Dirk asked.

"He wanted to know where the money was. The money that she was holding for Jonathan; the money he had embezzled from his own business."

"You can't embezzle from yourself." Dirk walked over to one

of the piles, dumped from a cardboard box, and knelt to examine the contents.

"You can if you're planning to run away with your ex-wife and you don't want to divide your worldly goods with your present wife. At least, that's what Fiona told me when I saw her last."

"Dr. Liu, have you taken all your pictures yet?" Dirk asked before he moved any of the items on the floor.

"All finished," she replied, reading the temperature on the thermometer.

He pointed to one of the many paperback books that lay open. "Look at this, Van."

As he held the book out to her, she instantly saw what he meant. Someone had cut a rectangular space out of the pages, leaving a convenient hole in which to hide something. Something that was gone now.

"What do you figure," he asked, "a drug stash?"

"Wouldn't be the first I've seen like that." Savannah lifted another box, revealing a heap of books that had been similarly mutilated. As she checked them one by one, she found they were all empty.

"If it was dope, there was a lot of it," she said as she searched the room, finding more and more of the same.

As she made her way through the living and dining areas, she spotted a couple more boxes in the kitchen, partially concealed behind a trash can. These appeared to still be intact, their contents undisturbed.

"Here we go," she mumbled under her breath. "Don't let it be pots and pans . . . please. . . ."

She eased open the lid and looked inside. Stephen King, Janet Dailey, Norman Mailer, Dean Koontz, even Charles Dickens. Fiona must have been a voracious reader with eclectic tastes.

She picked up a copy of *Little Women* and opened the cover.

"Ah . . . Dirk . . ."

"Yeah?"

"In here."

He appeared at the door. "What 'cha got?"

Holding the book open for his perusal, she said, "It wasn't drugs."

He whistled, long and low. "No shit. Are there more?"

One by one, she opened *Cujo*, *The Great Alone*, *White Fang*, and *The Firm*.

Every single book had been hollowed out, then filled with hundred dollar bills. So much for the mystery of Jonathan Winston's missing money.

"Whoever he was, he didn't get it all," Dirk commented.

Savannah walked slowly back into the living room, glanced down at the empty, gutted books, and then at what remained of the red-haired, Irish singer who had wanted to be Connie Francis when she grew up. "I'd say he got enough to make it worth his time. The bastard."

"Van, I suppose this isn't the time to lay something else on you, but . . ."

Savannah paused, her hand on the Camaro door handle. "What is it now?" she asked Dirk, who had followed her from Fiona's apartment.

"I had a feeling about your buddy, the Stone guy," he began. She could tell by the almost apologetic look on his face that she wasn't going to like what he was about to say.

"Spit it out," she said.

"I ran a little background check on him . . . specifically that stuff about having been a fed."

"Let me guess; you're going to tell me that he was never—"

"No, he was. But they didn't think as highly of him as you seem to."

Jealousy does not become you, my old friend, she thought. But her heart was thudding with anticipation mixed with dread, and she wanted to know. Now.

"I said, spit it out, Dirk! If you've got some nasty little news, let me have it."

"They kicked him out. Discharged. Dishonorably."

She said nothing but glared at him, hating what he had just said, nearly hating him. For a moment she related to what Atlanta must have felt when her idol had been yanked off his plastic pedestal.

"I just thought you should know," he added with a shrug. "Sorry."

"Sure, Dirk, I can tell you're just eaten up with remorse. Thanks so much for the enlightenment. I owe you one."

Dirk shook his head as she drove away, nearly peeling rubber. "One what?" he asked. "Lunch, a beer . . . a bullet between the eyes?"

Savannah didn't know whether to be relieved or not when she heard the heavy footsteps inside Ryan Stone's apartment, coming to answer her knock on the door. Normally she wasn't a woman who considered ignorance to be bliss. Usually she wanted to know the facts, pretty or ugly, so long as she knew what was real.

But, lately, she had had so damned many shocks, a few too many eye-opening experiences. Enough was enough.

Unconsciously she reached up to smooth her flyaway curls. Not that she cared what he thought of her anymore. He had lied to her, and his damned goose was cooked. Well, maybe he hadn't actually *lied*, but he hadn't told her—

The door opened and she found herself face to face with . . . John Gibson. He was wearing casual black slacks and slippers and an elegant smoking jacket made of dove gray satin brocade. The color complemented his silver hair, which was slicked back, every strand in place. In his hand he held a highly polished briarwood pipe. The perfect British gentleman.

"My dear!" he exclaimed, throwing the door open wide. "How de-e-light-ful to see you. Do come in."

"Actually, I was just dropping by to speak to Ryan. Ummmmmm . . . is he home?" she asked as she tried to peer over his shoulder.

"He is, he is, indeed. But I'm afraid you've caught him in the shower. Come inside, have a seat, and make yourself comfortable, love. I'm sure he'll be out straightaway."

She stepped into the apartment and felt as though she had entered the library of a Tudor mansion. The heavy leather furniture, the carved dark wood, the bookcases with their fine classic volumes of literature, even a painting of a hunt over the fireplace.

Nice, she thought. Just what she would have expected Ryan's home to be.

Gibson hurried to an ornately carved bar at one end of the room. "What may I get for you, Miss Reid? If you enjoy cognac, I have some Remy Martin that I would recommend."

"No, thank you, Mr. Gibson, I—"

"Please, please." He held up one hand, as though directing traffic in Piccadilly Circus. "Just Gibson, or John, whichever you prefer."

"Okay . . . Gibson," she replied, feeling a bit shy at calling a servant by his last name. It seemed so aristocratic, so deliciously snobbish.

"So, what is your position here with Mr. Stone?" she asked, feeling ignorant of such things as European social hierarchy.

"I beg your pardon?"

"I'm sorry, I mean . . . are you his chauffeur, his butler, or . . . ?"

He smiled. "Oh, yes. My position, as it were. Well, I consider myself more of a—"

"Savannah!" Ryan stood in the doorway leading to a hall, a towel wrapped around his waist. Water beaded on his bronzed skin and in the light dusting of hair across his chest that was . . . dear lord . . . even more muscular than she had dreamed. "I thought I heard the doorbell ring. I'm so glad to see you."

He hurried toward her and held out his hand. Mesmerized by his near-nakedness, she slipped her fingers into his and felt the contact all the way up to her shoulder.

When he sat on the sofa beside her, wearing nothing but that towel and a breathtaking smile, the warmth traveled into much more sensitive areas of her constitution.

"Why are you here?" he asked, his green eyes locked with hers, his dimples framing that sensuous mouth.

"Here . . ." She thought for a moment, but her mind was blank. Apparently, all of her blood had rushed south, leaving her brain dead. "Yes, here . . ." Then she remembered, and the sexual attraction dimmed.

She glanced over at Gibson, who was still standing at the bar, holding a snifter of cognac in one hand, looking like a magazine ad for the latest in smoking apparel.

"I'm sorry," she said, "but could we . . . could we speak privately . . . just for a moment? I apologize, Gibson, but this is . . . uh . . . private."

Why did she always lose half of her vocabulary when she was in the presence of someone with a British accent? The English were just so elegant, so sophisticated and urbane, so damned intimidating.

"Think nothing of it, my dear," he said, toasting her with his snifter. "My favorite BBC mystery series will be on the telly any minute now, and in the last episode my hero was in desperate straits."

When Gibson, his pipe, and the cognac had left the room Savannah said, "I didn't realize that Gibson was a 'live-in' servant. I suppose we Americans aren't used to that kind of thing."

He gave her a soft smile. "Gibson is a jewel. He's been with me for almost fifteen years now. I don't know what I'd do without him."

"Did you 'import' him from Britain?"

"No. Gibson has been a citizen of the U.S. for twenty years. Actually, we worked together at the bureau in Washington."

"The bureau." She hesitated a second, then plunged ahead. "Ryan, that's why I'm here. It's been brought to my attention that . . . well . . . frankly, I've been told that you were dishonorably discharged. I suppose it's not any of my business, but we have sort of been working together on this case, and if we work together, I need to know where you're coming from. We have to trust each other. Completely."

The smile on his face had disappeared, and a look of deep sadness had taken its place. "Does that mean you can't trust me if you know I was dismissed?"

She thought for a moment, wanting to answer him honestly.

"I'm not sure. But I wish you could trust *me* enough to tell me about it."

He sank back onto the sofa and closed his eyes. After a few seconds he opened them and breathed a sigh of resolution. "Okay. That's only fair." He reached over and covered her hand with his, giving it an affectionate squeeze. "I'll tell you anything you want to know, Savannah, but as your friend, not your fellow detective."

He seemed so sincere that she felt like a jerk for even questioning him. Damn that Dirk, anyway.

"What were the grounds for your dismissal?"

"The stated reason, or the real reason? Like you, I have one of each."

That stung. It hurt to think he had been in the same boat as she. "Both, if you don't mind."

"On the paper, it said, 'Gross Negligence of Duty.' "

"Were you grossly negligent?"

"I don't think so. But someone was killed, someone I was protecting from organized crime."

Savannah thought that one over. "I hate to say it, but that sort of thing happens all the time. No matter who you are, the mob has its connections, and sometimes there's only so much you can do."

"I agree. But, as I said, that was the *stated*, legal, written-on-the-papers reason."

"What was the real reason?"

He closed his eyes again, briefly, as though trying to blot out the pain. "You have to understand the turmoil of the times. There had recently been a lot of yellow, tabloid journalism about J. Edgar Hoover. Some pretty sensational stories that, true or false, were embarrassing to the bureau. Let's just say it wasn't a good time to be a fed if you were gay."

Gay.

Gay.

The word stuck in Savannah's brain like a scratch on an old 45. And, like the warped record, her mind just couldn't seem to be able to skip to the next groove.

"You're . . . you're . . . um . . . you're . . ."

"Gay; yes." He looked surprised at her reaction, though not as surprised as she was sure she must look. "I'm sorry, Savannah. I thought you knew. I mean, what did you think?"

"What did I think?" she blurted out. "I *thought* that you liked me."

Tears stung her eyes for the umpteenth time in the last few days. God, she was going to get dehydrated if this kept up.

He leaned closer to her and placed his hand under her chin, forcing her to look up at him. "But I *do* like you, Savannah. I like you very much. You're a wonderful person, and I enjoy every minute I'm with you." With the tip of his thumb, he wiped away one of her tears, then the other. "I like your sense of humor, and your wit and wisdom. I enjoy just looking at you; you're such a pretty woman."

"How can you say that?" she said, pushing away his hand.

"What? That you're pretty? But you are!"

"How the hell would you know? You're . . . gay!"

He laughed softly and shook his head. "I might be gay, but I'm not blind. I can still enjoy the sight of a beautiful woman, even if I'm devoted to someone else."

"Devoted . . . to . . .? You mean, you have a . . . a lover?"

Again he chuckled. "Of course I do. I told you before, Savannah, Gibson's been with me for nearly fifteen years. I—"

"Gibson! Gibson? You and Gibson are . . . Oh, my God!"

Savannah fell back onto the sofa and, although she had

never had much respect for overly delicate Southern belles, she could swear she was about to have a case of the vapors.

"Mercy," she said, sliding into her thickest Georgia accent, "I thought he was your *butler*, or your *chauffeur*. But he's your . . . Oh, dear, I just don't think I can take this."

Ryan disappeared for a moment, then hurried back from the kitchen with a glass of water. Handing it to her, he said, "I'm really sorry, Savannah. I didn't know you were feeling that way about me." He shook his head. "Men can be so dense sometimes."

"Oh, please . . . don't tell me you wish you were a woman."

He collapsed onto the sofa where he had been sitting, laughing so hard, he nearly dropped his towel.

Not that it mattered now, she thought.

"No, Savannah," he said, trying to catch his breath. "I don't wish I were a woman. I quite enjoy being male. Believe me."

"Shit. You're one of those 'well-adjusted' gays, aren't you?"

He gave her a quick peck on the cheek. "I don't think there's any such thing, Savannah, as a well-adjusted gay . . . or straight, for that matter. We're just all trying to get through the best we can, don't you think?"

Savannah didn't know what she thought. She was beyond cognitive thought . . . way beyond.

"Thank you for telling me," she said, returning his kiss on the cheek. "For trusting me. By the way, is this confidential?"

"No, not at all. Gibson and I have always been very open about our relationship. I honestly thought you knew. Are we still friends?"

"Sure. You bet."

She stood, picked up her purse, and headed for the door. All she wanted was a lavender bath . . . and maybe a stiff belt of Bailey's laced with a little hot chocolate. Naw, fuck the chocolate. She'd just take a bottle of Scotch into the tub with her.

"Well, there's one good thing about this," she grumbled to herself as she walked out the door. "Dirk will be tickled pink."

CHAPTER TWENTY-ONE

"Detective Reid, I've called you before . . ." the voice said as Savannah stood beside the answering machine, scooping Pacific Salmon Pâté into the cats' dishes. When she heard the distinctive *ca-wl-led* Savannah nearly dropped the spoon.

Hot damn! It was that New Yorker who had given her two lousy tips so far; the first too general, the second too late.

". . . and it didn't seem to help."

She was right about that.

"I'm sure now. I don't know who actually did it, but I know who set it up, who paid for it. And I think I know why. You need to . . ." There was a pause as she seemed to be searching for the words. ". . . to look into the fashion industry in more depth. I think Mr. Winston and Ms. O'Neal were killed more for business reasons, not personal."

Suddenly her voice dropped to a whisper. "Sorry, I have to go. I hope that helps."

Savannah listened as her machine told her the time. Four thirty P.M. Only ten minutes ago. And that had been the last message.

No one else had called since.

Aha! She almost cackled aloud. "I've got you now," she said as she yanked open a nearby drawer and pulled a slip of paper from inside the telephone book.

Carefully, she followed the instructions on the note, pressing the appropriate code numbers, then the star symbol.

She waited, breathless; then, sure enough, a phone began to ring.

One, two . . .

Pick up. "Elite, etc. This is Tammy speaking. May I help you?"

Elite, etc. Elite, etc. Where had she heard that before?

Suddenly she remembered, and the memory produced a shock of adrenaline that sparked every molecule of her body. Elite, etc. belonged to Paul Connors, the great-looking blond designer/manufacturer who had been escorting Beverly the night of the charity ball.

"May I help you?" the voice asked again. The New York voice.

"Hello, this is Elizabeth Worthington-Smythe," Savannah said, trying to disguise her own accent with something she hoped sounded as British as Gibson's. "Is this Tammy Reese?" she asked, staring at a bag of Reese's Pieces that lay on the kitchen counter.

"No," she said, "this is Tammy Hart."

"Oh, I'm sorry, dear. I believe I have the wrong number."

"That's quite all right. Have a nice day."

Savannah hung up the phone and did a little jig, nearly stepping in the cat food. "I got 'cha, I got 'cha, *I* got *you*, Miss Tammy Hart."

As Savannah flashed back to that night at the charity ball, to Paul Connors with his wavy blond hair and Armani suit, a very pleasant thought occurred to her: Tammy Hart might be a small fish in the pond, but Savannah had a feeling she had just gotten her hook into the mouth of something much bigger . . . maybe even a man-killing shark.

As the petite blonde hurried up the walkway toward the stairs that led to her second-story apartment, Savannah watched from the shadows of some nearby shrubbery. She didn't want to give the young woman a heart attack, but Savannah didn't know if it would be wise to present herself to Ms. Tammy Hart in public. Without more information she couldn't be sure that Tammy wasn't being watched; the last thing she wanted was to endanger the person who had tried to help her.

"Tammy . . ." she said softly, stepping into the light as the woman approached.

Suddenly she found herself staring down the nozzle of a small black spray canister.

"What the hell is that?" Savannah asked.

The young woman didn't bat an extremely long, nicely curled eyelash. "Pepper spray," she said in an ominous tone that left no doubt as to her intentions.

"You don't need that, darlin'," Savannah said in her laziest drawl.

"Savannah Reid?" she asked, comprehension dawning on her pretty little face.

"In the flesh," Savannah replied, then added with a sigh, "all of it." Thin women made her feel so . . . so . . . so *not* thin. "Why don't you just ask me in for a cup of tea and let's talk?" she said. "Woman to woman."

"I've invited you all here for a special reason," Savannah said as she looked around her dining-room table at some of her favorite people, several of whom had been added to the list quite recently.

The Tiffany reproduction dragonfly lamp cast its jewel-refracted light on John Gibson's silver hair, Tammy Hart's blond waves, Dirk's bald spot, and Ryan Stone's chestnut . . .

Dear lord, gay, straight, or celibate, he was still the most gorgeous man she had ever set eyes on. If she hadn't been so fond of John Gibson, she might have tried to redirect Ryan's sexual orientation. So what if the shrinks said it couldn't be done? Any man who said that it was an irreversible state simply hadn't enjoyed one of her hot oil massages.

But Savannah had known so few couples, of any gender combination, who had actually enjoyed their companion for fifteen years. No point in trying to break up something that solid.

"I'd like you all to meet Tammy Hart. A few hours ago Tammy gave me some information that I think we *all* should share. Everyone here is pretty sure about who actually did the murders: Eric Bowman. But we didn't know why, or for whom. Tammy has given me the other piece of that puzzle. And, with the combined talents of the individuals sitting at this table, I think we can wrap this up pretty quickly."

She turned to Tammy, who sat quietly, hands folded demurely in her lap, a notebook computer sitting on the table before her.

"Tammy, if you would just repeat to Dirk, Ryan, and John what you told me in your apartment a few hours ago . . ."

Tammy nodded, but Savannah could see the apprehension in her round hazel eyes. It was one thing for Savannah to trust her own personal safety to these individuals; they were her friends. But Tammy Hart was about to put her life in the hands of people she didn't even know, in the hopes of obtaining justice for two other murdered individuals whom she had never known.

"It's okay, Tammy," she said. "These are all good people. And they're pretty damned smart, too. Except for Dirk. He's a bit slow, but we keep him around for decoration."

Dirk flushed, but everyone else laughed, breaking the tension.

"Why don't you tell us a little about yourself," Ryan said.

Savannah could see Tammy melt under his green gaze . . . foolish girl. But he seemed to put her at ease.

"I work for Elite, etc., as the personal executive secretary to Paul Connors. Mr. Connors designs, manufactures, and distributes several lines of formal evening wear for women."

"Excuse me," Dirk said, holding up one hand. "How long have you been with Connors?"

"Five years."

"Then you must know him pretty well."

Tammy glanced down at her hands in her lap. "I thought I did. Until recently."

"Tell them what you found in the company's computer," Savannah prompted her.

"A month or so ago our system crashed. I was able to get us back on line." She grinned shyly. "I'm sort of a computer nerd. And in the process I discovered some hidden files."

"What type of files, dear?" Gibson asked.

"Mr. Connors's private files, which he had programmed with a password. Only he could access them. I stumbled into a couple of them and, to be honest, they were very suspicious. So I overrode his password and tapped into the others. That's when I first began to think that he wasn't the person I thought he was."

Ryan scribbled notes furiously on a leather-bound ledger. "Exactly what did you find, Tammy?"

"A different set of books than the ones we were operating from. Apparently, about two years ago, Mr. Connors invested heavily in Jonathan Winston's company. Elite, etc. was doing much better back then. But Mr. Winston didn't pay him back according to the schedule they had agreed upon secretly."

"Why was the loan a secret?" Gibson asked.

"I don't know. I didn't see anything in the files that explained that. But this past year Elite, etc., has been going under. We've had to cut back on production and lay off a quarter of our employees. Mr. Connors really needed to be repaid.

"I found a memo, something about Mr. Winston refusing to pay the loan at all. Somehow, my boss found out that Mr. Winston had been skimming money out of his own company and misleading Mr. Connors about his assets. From the tone of the memo I got the idea that Mr. Connors was furious."

"Can't say that I blame him," Dirk commented, taking a slurp from his coffee cup.

"Then I found all these letters to the creditors who were breathing down our neck. Mr. Connors was telling them that we had been approved for a major loan to help us over the hump, and they would be paid soon."

"Let me guess . . . no loan," Ryan said.

"That's right. He told us all that he had gotten a loan from a local bank. But in those files I found the letter, stating the reasons why they had turned us down."

"Did he pay his bills?"

"Yes, all of them in full—the day after Fiona O'Neal was murdered. He also paid some unnamed party ten thousand dollars."

"Eric Bowman?" Dirk asked, turning to Savannah.

"I don't know, but I've thought of a way to find out for sure."

Dirk returned his attention to Tammy. "This is all very interesting, Tammy. Is it documented somehow?"

She nodded and patted the notebook computer in front of her. "I copied all the files. They're right in here. And I reprogrammed the office computer so that I can override his password anytime I want. That's how I've been keeping up with him."

"What a brilliant young lady you are," Gibson said, giving her the full benefit of his warm smile.

"Obviously, this information is fascinating, but hardly conclusive evidence," Ryan said. "If Dirk is going to arrest Paul Connors for those two murders, he'll have to have solid evidence. What's your plan, Savannah?"

She grinned broadly and reached for one of the cream-filled pastry horns that were sitting on a silver plate in the middle of the table. "I thought you'd *never* ask."

The plans had been made, the pastry horns eaten, the coffee cups shoved into the dishwasher. And everyone had left . . . except Dirk.

Savannah walked into the living room and he followed, jingling his keys in his hand.

"Well, I'd better drag my weary ass home and stick it in bed," he said, "or I won't be any good to anybody tomorrow."

She felt a twinge of disappointment. A bit nervous about tomorrow's outcome, she wasn't ready to be alone just yet.

As she had sat at the table, making plans with the gang, she had done a quick inventory of Dirk and Ryan, comparing notes. All in all, she decided that she preferred Dirk anyway. He wasn't as pretty as Ryan, but then, Granny Reid had always told her never to trust a man who was prettier than she.

Excellent advice in retrospect.

Dirk was familiar, and therefore dear, as comfortable as a well-worn slipper.

Ryan had a gorgeous body, but would she have been too self-conscious of her own lumps and bumps to enjoy being with him?

Well, it didn't matter. It wasn't going to happen.

"Do you think it will work?" she asked, trying to keep her mind and her conversation on business.

"The plan for tomorrow?"

She nodded.

"Yeah. I think it's got a better-than-average chance."

He paused, his hand on the doorknob, and she took the opportunity to reach up and give him a kiss on the cheek.

"What was that for?"

She shrugged. "I just miss you, buddy. I miss working with you. I miss your smelly cigarette smoke."

He lifted one eyebrow suspiciously. "I doubt that."

"Okay, I don't miss the smoke. But it *is* good being on the same team with you again."

Tweaking one of her dark curls, he smiled and said, "Yeah, me, too."

Suddenly, more than anything else in the world, Savannah wanted to take his hand, lead him up the stairs, rip off his clothes, and throw him onto her bed.

The thought of being that close, that passionate, that connected to another person was sweet, indeed. She needed connection. She hadn't enjoyed nearly enough in the past few years.

Besides, her pride was still a bit wounded at finding that Ryan preferred Gibson to her. How could she have been so wrong about his feelings for her?

"What are you thinking, Van?" he asked.

She didn't reply.

"Come on," he said, "out with it."

"I was thinking how lucky I am to have you for a friend and, occasionally now, a partner," she lied. She was sullying her soul, to be sure. But better that than to hurt a friend with the truth.

He smiled and pulled the door open. "Me, too, kiddo," he said. Leaning down, he gave her a brief but sweet kiss on the lips. Just enough to make her really want more. But if she tried to seduce him tonight, she would never know if it had been because she needed *him*, as he had requested it be, or if she had been using him as a balm for the insults and a cure-all for her horniness.

Dirk deserved better.

Besides, Atlanta was upstairs, asleep in the guest room. Somehow, Savannah didn't feel inclined to share something as special as her first time with Dirk with her kid sister. Maybe it was just that old-fashioned ethic of being a good example and all that.

Another time. Another place. Well . . . definitely another time.

"Good night, Savannah," Dirk said. From the soft look in his eyes she wondered if he were reading her thoughts.

"Good night, Dirk. Sleep tight . . . and don't let the bedbugs bite," she said.

As she watched him walk down her sidewalk toward the street, that distinctly male, endearing lope to his step, she silently congratulated herself on her self-control.

Dirk deserved a *lot* better.

And she was looking forward to the day she could give it to him.

But for now Dirk's wasn't the only weary ass that needed to be dragged off to bed. She closed the door behind him, locked it, and trudged up the stairs.

Alone. Again.

CHAPTER TWENTY-TWO

Savannah climbed out of the Camaro and looked down the street to assure herself that her backup was in place. Good ol' Dirk . . . what would she ever do without him? No matter how tense the situation, she always took comfort in his presence.

Not that she suspected any real trouble from Eric Bowman. She had him pegged as the sort who was a lot braver with a shotgun in hand, coming against someone who wasn't expecting him or sneaking up on them from behind. Eric was a coward who did not want an opponent, only a victim.

But then, considering what she was about to tell him, he might not be cordial enough to whack her from the rear. In which case, Dirk would be a valuable asset.

"Well, here goes nothin'," she whispered into the microphone secreted in her jacket collar. "Time to rattle this polecat's cage and see what happens."

She rapped sharply on the front door, but there was no answer. His Studebaker was parked in the alley beside the complex, so she figured he was home.

Seeing a slight movement at the window, she called, "Open up, Bowman! I've got something to say to you, and believe me, you *do* want to hear it!"

A few seconds later the door creaked open and a pinched, ashen face thrust its nose through the crack.

"What do *you* want?" he asked, with all the charm and appeal of a warthog with acne. "I'm busy."

"Gilligan again?"

He looked at her, confused. It didn't seem to take much to confuse Eric Bowman.

"What?"

"Never mind. I just dropped by to tell you something interesting." She stepped closer to the door and lowered her voice. "I thought you should know that I slid a letter under the door at Elite, etc. You know, Paul Connors's place?"

He glanced quickly right and left, then cleared his throat. "So?"

"I typed it on this old typewriter I keep in my garage. I thought you might like to see a copy of it."

She held out a single piece of plain white paper with a few words clumsily typed with a faded ribbon.

He snatched it from her hand and read the short message.

Dear Mr. Connors,

I did a really important thing for you. Two important things. And I don't think you paid me enough. The cops have been coming around. I'm scared. I think you should pay me more, since it's this bad. I want you to have somebody bring ten thousand more to my house tonight. I'll be waiting.

E. B.

It took him a long time to read the letter, and for a moment she was afraid the whole plan would go down the pipes because he was illiterate. But, finally, she could tell by the horrified, then furious look on his face, that he understood what he was reading.

"You bitch!" he said, wadding up the paper and throwing it in the general vicinity of her chest. "What are you tryin' to do, get me killed?"

Savannah assumed her most naive, butter-wouldn't-melt-on-my-buttocks smile. "Now, how could this little ol' letter cause that much trouble? I mean, there's got to be hundreds of people with the initials E. B. If you haven't done anything wrong for him, you don't have to worry. Right? Of course, if you *have*, you may be in some big trouble. Paul Connors doesn't really strike me as a guy who would take extortion in stride. I'll bet he could be pretty nasty if he wanted to."

His eyes turned as cold and gray as slush on a New York City street. In that instant Savannah knew what Jonathan and Fiona had seen in the final moments of their lives. Judging from the intense hostility radiating from him, Savannah realized that if she wasn't careful, and Dirk alert, the same might happen to her.

"I'll get you for this," he said. "I swear to God I will."

Savannah knew better than to show fear, even though it was clear to her that he meant every word he was saying.

Looking him straight in the eyes, she said, "Any time. If you think you're man enough to take me down, give it your best shot."

As she turned on her heel and strode away, the thought occurred to her that if looks could kill, she would be lying there, chopped into tiny pieces all over the sidewalk.

Fortunately she wasn't, and she intended to keep it that way.

"Well, old man," she said softly to her collar, "we've rattled the bars and the specimen named 'Eric' has growled, nipped, and shown his teeth . . . both of them. It was *not* a pretty sight!"

The time had come to sit tight, keep her fingers crossed, and hope, hope, hope.

Hope that Eric Bowman was as stupid as she had predicted he was.

The equipment had been set up, the window left open just a tiny crack . . . but wide enough to mount a miniature camera lens and microphone on the sill.

"Lights, camera, if we only had some action," Ryan told Gibson as the two of them stared at the tiny black-and-white monitor that displayed a not-so-great image of the adjacent room—Paul Connors's office.

Earlier in the day Tammy had sneaked them into the building through a back door and stashed them in this large storage closet, which was perfect for electronic eavesdropping on the activities next door. Savannah, Dirk, and Tammy would join them shortly. Soon they would all know if the plan would work or not. They would know if this whole cat-and-mouse routine was going to be worth the effort.

For the better part of the past hour they had been watching, nearly going to sleep, as Paul Connors sat at his desk, scribbling on some papers. Nothing so far.

A knock sounded at Paul Connors's office door, and they peered at the screen, watching as Tammy Hart walked into his office and put some papers on his desk.

"Would you like something from the deli across the street, Mr. Connors?" she asked.

Ryan and Gibson snapped to attention. That was the signal. Savannah had called Tammy to let her know: Bowman was on his way.

Ryan turned to Gibson with a smile on his face. "That's it. He bought it! We're in business . . . again. . . ." he added, remembering the good old days, when they had worked together at the bureau.

"Jolly good show," Gibson said, fingering the briarwood pipe. "Our Savannah is as cunning as she is beautiful."

"Yes, Eric, what is so important that you felt you had to come here to my office?" Paul Connors asked the fidgety, scraggly punk who stood in front of his desk. "I told you not to ever, *ever* come by here again. That was part of our agreement."

"I know, I know. . . ." Sweat began to bead on Bowman's forehead. "But I had to tell you that I didn't send you that letter."

Paul Connors studied him for a long moment, saying nothing.

"I didn't, really," Bowman continued. "It's this cop, Savannah Reid, the one you asked me to keep an eye on for you; she sent it."

Paul raised one eyebrow slightly. "Oh? *She* sent it?"

"Yeah, really. . . . I wouldn't ask you for more money. I think you already paid me plenty. I mean, if you really *wanted* to give me more, I'd take it, but I'd never outright ask for it."

"She actually told you that she was the one who sent me the letter asking for more money?"

"Yeah, she did. Honest! I don't know why. I told her she

would get me killed doing shit like that." He laughed nervously, snorting through his nose.

"Why do you think she would lie to me like that?" His tone was even, his words nonthreatening. Bowman didn't seem to notice the fire of anger that had leapt into his eyes.

"I don't know! She figured out that I was the one who plunked her on the head that night, and she's all nuts about it. Go figure."

"I see." Connors stood and walked over to the window to look out.

In the other room five people held their collective breath. An extreme close-up of his pants' fly filled their tiny screen.

"Did she mention whether or not she thinks you might also have committed the murders?"

Bowman lifted his fingers to his mouth, chewed a hangnail for a moment, then cleared his throat. "Ah . . . no, she didn't say anything like that."

"Did anyone follow you here just now, Eric? Or did you even bother to check?" he asked, still staring out the window.

"No . . . I mean, nobody tried or I would have seen them. I'm good at spotting tails."

"Thank you for coming to tell me this," Paul said, turning abruptly from the window and walking toward the door.

"Then you're not pissed, about the letter or anything?"

"Of course not. As you said, you didn't write it. Why should I be upset?"

"Oh, okay . . . thanks a lot. I really appreciate this, Mr. Connors."

"Think nothing of it, Eric. You just run along home now, have a couple of six-packs, and relax. I hear they're running *Terminator* and *Predator* tonight on cable."

"Really? Neat! Thanks for the tip."

"No problem. Have a nice evening."

The moment the quintet saw Eric Bowman walk out the door they sighed.

"Damn," Savannah said, "Connors didn't say anything particularly incriminating."

"Perhaps not," Gibson replied, "but your young man was rather vocal about his activities."

"But she isn't worried about getting Bowman," Tammy said, her pretty face pained with guilt. "It's my boss she's after."

"Then she's going to get her wish," Ryan said thoughtfully as he stared at the silent figure on the screen. Paul Connors had returned to his desk and his paperwork.

"What do you mean?" Savannah asked.

"Look at him," he said, placing the tip of his finger over Connors's face. "He's got the look. He's going to try to kill Bowman." He turned to Savannah. "What do you say, Savannah? Would that be enough to satisfy your need for justice? If you can't get him on murder . . . how about attempted murder?"

Savannah stared at the screen, but not for long. "Sure," she said. "I could live with that."

CHAPTER TWENTY-THREE

"Do you ever feel like you've spent your life in closets?" Savannah shifted, trying to find room to breathe without stepping on Ryan's feet or mashing Tammy any farther back into the cubicle.

"Actually, I decided to come out a long time ago," Ryan said with a chuckle. "Closets are terribly stifling."

"Very funny."

"What?" Tammy could hardly be heard through the muffler of dirty, greasy-smelling clothes that were hung, stacked, and thrown into Eric Bowman's utility closet.

"Never mind," Savannah said. "It's a long . . . very sad story."

"Well, I think it's very exciting, trying to catch a killer." Tammy moved closer to Savannah, her voice low and menacing, like a bad vaudeville villain. "Even if he is my boss," she added sadly.

"You're doing the right thing," Ryan whispered. "I know it's difficult because you feel as if you're betraying a friend. But it has to be done."

"How did you get to be so wise about these things?" she asked.

Savannah could hear the gush in her voice. It made her want to barf, especially when she could recall sounding the same way a couple of days ago.

"Most guys I know are real bastards," Tammy continued, "but you're so . . . so sensitive."

"He's got an inside track," Savannah muttered.

She peered through the crack in the door and saw Eric, sitting exactly where they had placed him—in front of the television watching *Terminator*, a beer in his hand, a not-particularly-convincing casual look on his face.

"It wasn't so hard to talk him into it," she mused, remembering Eric's conversation with Dirk, who was now hidden behind the broken-down entertainment center. "Even a guy who's on his way to prison for the rest of his life needs a little 'protection' just to make sure he gets there in one piece."

"I think you're wrong about Mr. Connors," Tammy said wistfully. "I mean, I know he hired Eric to kill those people, but I don't believe he could actually do it himself."

"Well," Savannah said, "I guess we'll find out soon enough."

As if responding to her cue, a knock sounded at the door.

Eric jumped as though someone had shoved a cherry bomb up his butt.

She saw Dirk's hand, waving to him above the stereo, motioning him to go ahead and answer. Slowly, with a furtive look at the closet door, he did so.

"Who is it?" he asked, voice shaking.

"Paul Connors. I need to talk to you, just for a minute. There's something I forgot to tell you . . . about the letter, that is."

Cautiously, Eric eased the door open. Savannah reached for her Beretta. She could hear the soft, subtle sound of Ryan turning on his video camcorder.

"What is it?" Eric said as he stepped aside and allowed Connors to walk into the living room.

"I forgot to tell you that I never received any letter from anyone. Savannah Reid lied to you. She didn't send it, and you didn't either. There was no letter. Now does it make sense?"

The look of confusion that Eric gave Connors was genuine and profound. *God,* she thought, *he still doesn't get it!*

"I don't get it," Eric said.

Savannah shook her head in amazement. *Geez, I must be turning psychic!*

"I know you don't, Eric," Paul Connors said wearily. "And that's the problem. They've figured out it was you who committed the murders, but they suspect I put you up to it. Savannah Reid was just shaking you up a bit so you'd come running to me. And that's just what you did. You may have led her straight to me. If it didn't happen this round, it's only a matter of time."

Connors reached into his jacket and pulled out a small snub-nosed pistol. "I'm really sorry, Eric. This is all my fault. I should have hired someone a lot smarter than you for the job, but I couldn't exactly go shopping in the Yellow Pages."

Finally Eric *got* it. The color drained from his face as fast as it probably had from his victims'.

He glanced quickly at the entertainment center, a look that spoke volumes—and Connors heard every word.

"Damn you, you little—" He spun around toward the center, his gun held in both shaking hands. "Come out of there," he yelled, "or I'll fire one into the stereo."

Dirk made a slight sound, enough to unnerve Connors even further. Savannah knew that he was creating a diversion for her.

Silently, she slipped from the closet. The squirt of WD-40 beforehand had done its job well; there was no sound at all.

"I said, 'Come out of there!' Right now!"

His voice was so shaky, Savannah knew that the slightest miscalculation on her part might cost Dirk his life.

Fortunately, they had played this scenario many times, and she had the necessary high level of self-confidence—attained by past successes.

She continued to creep forward, placing her feet lightly on the wooden floor to keep the old boards from creaking. Her attention, her vision narrowed to only one object in the entire universe: the gun in Paul's hand.

Slowly, Dirk began to rise from behind the stereo. Again, drawing Connors's attention away from her and to himself.

"Don't shoot," Dirk said. "You don't want to do that. It isn't necessary, really.

Using the fact that he was preoccupied with Dirk, Savannah sneaked up beside him, swinging one leg forward and in a sweeping arc around the side of him.

As intended, her foot connected with the gun and sent it flying against a far wall.

In the same instant Dirk swooped down on Eric, who looked as though nothing would make him happier than being somewhere else. *Anywhere* else. Three seconds later both suspects were in cuffs.

Connors appeared to be deeply confused. "But no one tailed me here. I made double, triple sure of it. I *wasn't* followed."

"We didn't need to follow you," Dirk said, brushing the behind-the-furniture dust bunnies from his slacks. "We just knew you were coming. And, bless your little pea-pickin' heart, you didn't let us down."

Ryan and Tammy had emerged from the closet, Ryan attending his equipment, Tammy looking miserable.

"You?" Connors's eyes grew wide. "You helped them do this to me? Tammy, why?"

Tammy couldn't seem to say anything. Savannah's heart went out to her; she was obviously in a lot of pain.

"You were responsible for two people's deaths. And you were trying for a third," Savannah told him. "You didn't leave her much choice."

A few minutes later the entire troop filed out of the small apartment and down the walkway to the cars in the lot.

Once the prisoners had been neatly tucked into backseats, Savannah turned to Dirk. "By the way . . . 'your little pea-pickin' heart'? Where the hell did you hear that?"

"You."

"Mmm-mmm . . . I just might make a rebel of you yet, Yankee boy."

Savannah took a sip of the cognac and felt its warm vapor roll across her tongue and through her head before it burned a deliciously warm trail to her stomach. Then she nibbled just a bit from the tiny square of French dark chocolate, straight from Lyons. It was without a doubt the nicest she had ever tasted—and when it came to chocolate, she had thought she had tried them all.

"Like the combination?" Beverly asked from her seat on the chaise lounge nearby. Flames flickered orange and blue in the fireplace, bathing the library in a surreal amber glow.

Ah, Savannah thought, soaking in the ambience, *I could get used to this*. But common sense told her not to. After all, she was a retired cop who—

Get real, kid. You're an unemployed, fired cop. You'll be doing good to buy macaroni and cheese, let alone fine chocolate and cognac.

But as quickly as the disturbingly accurate thoughts appeared, she took another sip of the cognac and sent them on their way. There would be plenty of time to worry about the mundane concerns of life tomorrow. For tonight she was sitting in luxury's very comfortable lap, and she intended to enjoy it.

"You did a good job, Savannah," Beverly said. "I'm very grateful to you."

In spite of her words Savannah could hear the sadness behind them. "I wish the outcome had been less painful for you," she said.

Beverly shrugged. "I wish I had been wiser. I wish I had followed my better judgment and not fallen in love with someone other than my husband. I wish I had seen how much Paul loved me and what he was capable of doing. I wish I could have prevented him from harming Jonathan and Fiona. I wish . . ."

Savannah gave her what she hoped was a comforting smile. "You did your best, Beverly. In the end, that's all any of us can do. And as far as wishing goes . . . I save my wishes for things that can still come true. There's no point in wasting them on the past."

"You're right," she said with a sigh as she stood and brought over the crystal decanter and the golden foil box with its elegant delicacies nestled in white and black papers. She poured a dollop of the cognac into Savannah's snifter and offered her another chocolate.

Rather than hurt her hostess's feelings, she took two.

Beverly returned to the chaise and stretched out again; she looked tired, exhausted. The ordeal had taken so much out of her. Savannah hated to see the loss of such valuable life energy.

"I just can't believe I didn't see it," Beverly continued. "Paul lent Jonathan all that money just to bail him out of trouble—and help me—and then Jonathan intended to skip with it all. I thought he was a better man than that."

She paused and took a deep breath. Savannah knew that the tears were very near the surface. Even a strong woman like Beverly Winston had her limits.

"And Paul . . . even after he found out that I was seeing Norman, he was still loyal to me. Hiring Bowman to kill Jonathan and Fiona, having him follow you around and make sure that you found that videotape in Jonathan's apartment. Even having him attack you . . . in his own sick way, I think it was all done out of loyalty to me. He wanted to hurt those who were betraying me."

"True," Savannah said, "but don't forget, he wanted his money back, too."

Beverly nodded. "If it isn't sex, it's money. Why is it always one of the two?"

Savannah looked down at the check that Beverly had pressed into her hand along with the chocolates. With the generous tip there was enough here to pay several months of living expenses, and maybe buy a little something from Victoria's Secret.

"Hey, they make the world go 'round. I'd like to believe it's love, but it's money and sex."

"Why do you suppose that is?"

Savannah grinned. Maybe now that this mess was all over, she'd invite Dirk up to "see her sometime."

"Because they're both rather nice, don't you think?"

Beverly's face lit up with a youthful smile that dissolved some of the stress from her handsome features. "Yes, I suppose you're right. Oh, well, I've lost my life's work, but what the hell, I still have Norman. And I have all of this . . ." She waved her hand, indicating the opulence of the room. "Could be worse."

Savannah considered her own assets: Dirk's love and loyalty, new friendships with Ryan, Gibson, and Tammy, a fresh direction in a job that she loved . . . only this time she was her own boss.

"Yep," she said, thoughtfully. "Could be a lot worse."

Atlanta stood, suitcases in hand, a mournful look on her face. This time the pimps and perverts in LAX were keeping their distance. She didn't look like a fresh Georgia peach, ripe for the picking. She looked like a young woman who had grown up a lot in only a few weeks.

"I'll miss you," Savannah said, giving her and her assorted luggage a collective hug.

"Yeah, sure," she replied doubtfully. "You'll miss me like a briar in your butt."

"No, 'Lanta, I'll miss your pretty face, your singing around the house, the smiles you gave me when I came home . . . usually."

"Me, too."

Atlanta bit her lip and glanced over at the line of passengers who were disappearing through the gate.

"Gotta go, sweetie," Savannah told her.

"I know. But there's something I want you to know before I leave."

"Sure, what's that?"

"I didn't actually do anything with that Max guy. I just let him take a couple of pictures of me, but I didn't really show anything. And when he tried to . . . you know . . . I told him no."

"I'm proud," she replied with a smile. Then the smile faded. "Why did you let me think otherwise?"

"I just wanted to irk you."

"And a damned good job you did of it, too."

They both laughed and looked again at the line that was down to three.

"Go." Savannah gave her a gentle push. "Call me when you get there."

"Even if it's three in the morning?"

"All right, even if it's three. Take care of yourself, baby."

"You, too."

As Savannah turned to walk away, she was surprised at how much she missed the kid already.

Damn. Alone again.

But then again, maybe not.

Savannah stood in the moonlight in her front yard with Dirk, Ryan, Gibson, and Tammy, beneath the magnolia tree, which was in full bloom.

"Exactly what is it we're supposed to do?" Dirk asked with a bit of a growl in his voice.

"This is a very old and very sacred ritual," she whispered, looking up into the tree with its ivory blossoms glowing in the silver light of the full moon. "We take these wishes, which we've written on bits of paper, and tie them to the tree, like this. . . ." She demonstrated with her own. "We give our heart's desires to the tree, and later, when our wishes have all come true, we return and thank the tree."

Ryan, Gibson, and Tammy nodded reverently, thoroughly into the spirit of the event.

"We thank a tree?" Dirk asked, less spiritually inclined.

"Yes. Shut up and do it," she hissed at him.

Each carefully tied their own wishes to a branch, briefly closed their eyes, and sent their desires into the tree, into the night, into the light of the full moon.

"Does anybody else feel stupid?" Dirk asked.

"It doesn't matter," Savannah told him in a too-sweet, condescending tone. "It'll work, even if you're stupid. Granny Reid says so."

"What do you think we should call this new agency that we're forming here tonight?" Ryan asked, gazing up at the moon overhead.

"I've got it," Tammy said, inspired. "How about Moonlight Magnolias?"

Moonlight Magnolias.

Savannah looked at the circle of her new friends and one old, tried and true.

"Sounds good to me," she said. "Sounds very, very good."

Please turn the page for
an exciting sneak peek of
G. A. McKevett's
newest Savannah Reid mystery
SUGAR AND SPITE
on sale in January 2000
wherever hardcover mysteries are sold!

CHAPTER ONE

"I don't quite understand this," Tammy Hart said as she watched Savannah add three eggs to the skillet and several slices of bread to the toaster. "*You* help *him* nab the bad guy and *he* rewards *you* by letting you fix him breakfast?"

The "him" she was referring to was sitting at Savannah's kitchen table, a satisfied smile under his nose. Dirk was always happy when food was imminent. Especially if that food was free. And in keeping with her Southern heritage of hospitality, Savannah made sure that everyone in her presence was stuffed like her Granny Reid's Christmas turkey. Heaven forbid anyone should feel a pang of hunger. It wasn't to be tolerated.

"So I'm a sap for a pretty face," Savannah said.

"And what does that have to do with Dirk?" Tammy shot

a contemptuous look toward the table and its occupant, who was still dressed like a street bum.

Savannah chuckled and took a sip of the hot chocolate she had poured for herself . . . laced with Baileys . . . topped with whipped cream and chocolate shavings. Savannah suffered few hunger pangs herself, as was evidenced by her ample figure.

Tammy, on the other hand, was svelte, golden tanned, golden blond, the quintessential California surfer beach beauty.

Savannah loved her. Anyway.

So the kid was scrawny and ate mostly mineral water, rice cakes, and celery sticks; everyone had their faults.

Savannah retrieved several jars of homemade jams and preserves from the refrigerator and shoved them into Tammy's hands. "Put these on the table," she told her.

The younger woman took the jars and looked at the labels disapprovingly. "Gran's blackberry jam . . . probably full of sugar."

"I'm fresh out of sea-kelp spread," Savannah muttered under her breath, and swigged the hot chocolate.

Tammy sashayed over to the table and plunked the jars in front of Dirk, who gave her a cocky smirk. "Now I have to cook for him, too?" she complained. "It's bad enough that you're his slave, but now I have to—"

"Oh, stop . . . enough already." Savannah snapped her on her teeny-weeny, blue jean-covered rear with a dish towel. "I'm not Dirk's slave, but you *are* my assistant, so assist. Butter that toast."

"With real butter?"

Savannah sighed. "Yes. Cholesterol-ridden, fat-riddled butter. I'm fresh out of tofu."

"I'll go shopping for you."

"No thanks."

"Why are you having breakfast at four o'clock in the afternoon, anyway?" Tammy dipped only the tip of the knife into the butter and made a production of spreading the one-eighth of a teaspoon over the slice of bread.

"Because we didn't eat this morning," Dirk replied, watching the meal's progression with the acute attention of a practiced glutton. "We were working, remember?"

"Spraying the genitalia of youthful offenders," Tammy said with a giggle. "That's work?"

"Savannah did that all by herself. Thank God, or I'd be up on charges. You shoulda heard that guy screeching when they were scrubbing him down in the emergency room."

He and Savannah snickered. Tammy shook her head, pretending to be appalled.

"There are advantages to going freelance," Savannah said as she dished the eggs, some link sausages, and thick-sliced bacon onto the plate, then ladled a generous portion of cream gravy beside a scoop of grits. Where she came from, grits might be optional but gravy was considered a beverage.

Dirk's eyes glistened with the light of hedonism as he picked up his fork. "Van, you've outdone yourself. This looks great."

"Yeah," Tammy said as she sat down to a bowl of long-grain rice across the table from him. "She's good at CPR, too. And if that doesn't work, I'm pretty good at angioplasty." She hefted her knife and punctuated her statement with a skewering motion.

Savannah was reaching into the cupboard for a box of marzipan Danish rolls for herself, when she heard a buzzing, coming from Dirk's leather coat, which was draped across one of her dining chairs.

"I see you've got it set on VIBRATE again," she said, digging through his pockets and handing him the phone. "Your love life in a slump?"

"Eh . . . bite me." He flipped it open and punched a button. "Coulter here."

"He's sure grumpy when somebody gets between him and his dog dish," Tammy whispered to Savannah. "Reminds me of a pit bull I knew."

Savannah didn't reply. She was watching the play of emotions over Dirk's craggy face: irritation, fading to surprise, softening to . . . she wasn't sure what, but she was fairly certain the party on the other end was female.

"Ah, yeah . . . hi," he was saying. He turned in his chair, his side to her and Tammy. His voice volume dropped a couple of notches. "I'm . . . ah . . . here at Savannah's. No, not like that. We were working together this morning. No, really."

Savannah didn't like the sound of that. Why, she wasn't sure. She and Dirk weren't anything "like that," but she didn't like to hear him saying so . . . so clearly . . . to another woman.

Another woman? *Where did that thought come from*, she wondered. *To hell with that*, she quickly added to her mental argument. *Who is he talking to?*

"Yeah, I was going back home right after . . ." He looked wistfully down at the plate of goodies on the table in front of him. ". . . actually, I was leaving right now if you want to. . . . Yeah, that's good. Sure. See ya."

He flipped the phone closed and rose from his chair. The look on his face reminded Savannah of a sheep after an embarrassingly bad shearing. "I . . . ah . . . gotta go," he said.

"Sorry about the"—he pointed to the food—"ah, breakfast. But I really should—"

"No problem," Savannah said as she snatched the plate out from under him and carried it over to the cabinet. "If you gotta go, you gotta go. Obviously it's an important meeting."

"Ah, yeah, it is . . . kinda." He slipped on his jacket and fished for his keys. "I'll see ya later, okay?"

Savannah nodded curtly.

He grunted a good-bye in Tammy's direction, then headed toward the front of the house.

"Don't let the door slap your backside on your way out," Savannah called after him.

Another grunt. The sound of the door slamming.

"Well," Tammy said, recovering from her shock. "I never thought I'd see the day that Dirk Coulter would walk away from a free meal . . . especially one *you* cooked," she told Savannah.

From the kitchen window, Savannah watched his battered old Buick Skylark as it pulled out of her driveway. He was practically spinning gravel.

"Hmm," she said thoughtfully as she took his heavily laden plate from the cabinet and carried it back to the table. She sat down, picked up his fork, and dug in.

"That's all you've got to say?" Tammy asked her. "Hmmm. That's it?"

"I'm thinking."

"And eating." Tammy watched disapprovingly as Savannah shoveled in a mouthful of grits, dripping with butter.

"I think best when I eat."

"That explains your mental prowess," Tammy mumbled.

"Shut up. I've almost got it."

"Got what?"

"The plan of action."

"You've gotta know, huh?"

Savannah snorted. "Only if I intend to sleep tonight."

She downed a few more bites, then jumped up from her chair. "Be back later," she said as she snatched her cell phone off its charger base.

"What's the story?"

"He forgot his phone."

"That's *your* phone."

She shrugged. "We bought them at the same time. They look so much alike. It's an honest mistake."

"Going out there is a mistake," Tammy grumbled as she followed her to the front door. "There's nothing honest about it."

"I don't recall asking for your editorial comments. Go on the Internet while I'm gone. See if you can drum up some business for me so that I can continue to pay you that high, minimum-wage salary you've grown accustomed to."

Tammy sputtered, stood between her and the door, then moved aside with a sigh of resignation. "That's it? The phone story? It's a bit thin."

Savannah grinned and tossed her purse strap over her shoulder. "Yeah, well . . . Dirk's a bit thick. It'll work."

CHAPTER TWO

As Savannah pulled her 1965 Camaro into Dirk's trailer park, she grimaced at the cloud of dust that was settling on her new red paint. There was a nice mobile-home park down by the beach, but Dirk was far too tight to spring for that. He had parked his ten-foot-wide in the Shady Vale Trailer Park fifteen years ago, and once Dirk was parked anywhere, he tended to stay until he rusted.

Shady Vale was inappropriately named. Flat as a flitter, without a tree in sight, the property's picturesque description must have been a figment of some developer's imagination.

Dirk's neighbors were mostly transient, and more than once he had been forced to arrest one of his Shady Vale-ites for everything from armed bank robbery to blowing up half the park while cooking up a nice batch of methamphetamines in one of the trailer's kitchens.

The only residents who had been at Shady Vale longer than Dirk were the Biddles. They were a cantankerous, nosy old couple who watched the comings and goings of everyone in the park, as though they owned the dusty, gravel road themselves. From their #1 spot at the entrance, they saw every arrival and had an opinion as to whether that person had legitimate business in Shady Vale.

Their trailer was right next to Dirk's, which was parked in spot #2, and Savannah was hoping she could avoid her usual argument with Mr. Biddle or an interrogation from Mrs. Biddle. If luck were on her side, she might be able to recognize Dirk's mystery visitor's vehicle and find out who his guest was without having to use that ridiculous cell-phone ruse.

But the new silver Lexus parked beside his Buick didn't ring any bells. Since when did Dirk have a girlfriend . . . let alone one that could afford to drive a new Lexus?

Looks plumb out of place in this neck of the woods, Savannah thought as she slowed down to see if the car had vanity plates. But the series of random letters and numbers told her nothing.

She saw Harry Biddle sitting in his broken-down lawn chair, swigging a beer, scratching the roll of hairy belly that was protruding from beneath his gray undershirt. As she drove by he watched her with a lascivious gleam in his eye that made her want to crawl out of the car and slap him goofy. Half a slap would probably do the job.

Feeling like an adolescent whose curiosity was about to land her in trouble, Savannah parked her Camaro behind the Lexus and got out. Harry perked up when he saw her walking in his direction, until she turned toward Dirk's trailer.

"Wouldn't go in there right now," he said, his ugly, snaggled grin widening.

"Yeah, why not?" she asked, knowing she wasn't going to like the answer.

"Let's just say, he's already got hisself some company." He waggled one bushy gray eyebrow suggestively. "I think three'd make a crowd, if you catch my drift."

"Well, catch mine, you old coot. Mind your own business."

"Or then . . . maybe you three are into that kinky stuff. . . ."

"And maybe you're a dork with a dirty mind and a grubby undershirt."

Leaving Mr. Biddle behind to mutter obscenities into his beer can, Savannah strode to the door of Dirk's trailer and rapped a shave-and-a-hair-cut greeting. Might as well be friendly. Might as well be casual. Might as well pretend she wasn't there to snoop.

Dirk might even believe it.

He didn't. She could tell right away by the irritated look on his face when he opened the door. Considering his less than cordial mood, she pushed past him before he could ask her to enter . . . or to leave, which was far more likely.

"Gee, I hate to drop in on you unannounced like this but . . ."

Savannah's voice trailed away when she saw who was sitting on Dirk's 1973 vintage, beige-and-gold-plaid sofa. It was the last person she expected to see.

The former Mrs. Dirk.

The hated and often maligned—though not often enough in Savannah's book—ex-wife who had run away with a shaggy-haired, twentysomething rock-and-roll drummer several years ago.

"Polly!" Savannah replaced her look of shock with a carefully constructed facade of nonchalance. The act probably would have been more convincing if she hadn't been choking on her own spit. "What are you doing . . . I mean . . . what a surprise. I didn't expect to ever see you again."

"You mean, you *hoped* you'd never see me again."

"Yeah, that too."

Polly leaned back and propped her arm along the top of the sofa. She looked as casual as Savannah was pretending to be. Her long legs were stretched out before her, every inch of them bared by her short-short shorts. Savannah noted with just a bit of catty satisfaction that her knees were starting to sag a little.

So was her heavily made-up face. Foundation applied with a trowel, spider eyelashes, red lips that had been painted too far outside the natural lipline to fool anyone . . . except some fool like Dirk. He had admitted to Savannah that he had actually thought Polly was a real blonde for the first year of their relationship. Savannah could spot Golden Sun Frost a mile away . . . especially when it was on a swarthy-skinned woman who, undoubtedly, had been born with dark brown hair.

Like most of the men who had crossed Polly's path, Dirk had been taken in . . . in more ways than one . . . by a used-to-be-pretty face and a not-too-bad body, and lots of skillfully worded female flattery. Those had always been Polly's greatest weapons when hunting.

"Hope I'm not interrupting anything," Savannah said smoothly. She was pretty sure by the frustration on Dirk's face and the way he was pacing the ten foot span of trailer floor that she had. If she hung around long enough, she might just put a stop to this nonsense all together.

Some might call it interference; she called it charity. The guy needed to be saved from himself. On a nearby TV tray lay a single red rose. Probably a pre-Valentine gift from her to him or from him to her. The thought completely irked Savannah . . . either way.

"No problem," Polly said smoothly. "I'm sure you'll be leaving soon. Right? I mean, now that you see Dirk has company . . ."

"And now that you've seen who that company is," Dirk growled as he nodded, not so subtly toward the door.

In her peripheral vision, Savannah could see Dirk's cell phone sitting on top of the television set in the corner. She sauntered across the room in that direction.

"Actually, I had a good reason for dropping by, old pal," she told Dirk. "I brought you something. It's in my car."

She craned her neck to look out the window at her

Camaro. As she had hoped, they did the same and she took the opportunity to sweep the cell phone into her jacket pocket.

"What is it?" Dirk said. She could hear the suspicion in his voice. She didn't really expect him to buy this pitch. The best she could hope for was that he would be a gentleman and not call her "liar, liar, pants on fire" to her face.

"Your cell phone," she replied. "You left it at my house. I figured you'd need it."

Dirk shot her a "yeah, right" look and glanced around the room. He didn't see his phone. But that wasn't unusual for Dirk. The guy would lose his rear end if it weren't stapled to his tailbone.

"So where is it?"

"In my car."

"Why didn't you bring it in with you, Savannah?" Polly asked, flipping her lush, golden mane of split ends back behind one shoulder.

"Forgot." Savannah held out her car keys to Dirk. "Why don't you go get it. I think I left it on the passenger's seat."

He grumbled under his breath and headed for the door. "Aren't you coming with me?" he said, not bothering to hide his anger.

"In a minute, darlin'," she said, much too sweetly. "You go ahead. I'll be along shortly."

He looked from her to Polly and back, then shook his head. "I don't think it's a good idea to leave you two broads alone."

"Go on, Dirk," Polly said, stroking one of her legs as though checking for razor stubble. "I'm not afraid of Savannah. We're old friends, right?"

"You may be old," Savannah replied. "I'm barely middle-aged. And just for the record, you and I have never been friends." She tossed the keys to Dirk. "Go get your phone. I'll be right out."

Reluctantly, he exited the trailer, leaving the door ajar. Savannah waited until he was out of earshot. Then she took a few steps closer to Polly.

In spite of what Polly had said, she did look a bit worried, just enough to satisfy Savannah's perverse streak.

"I don't know what you're doing here," Savannah said. "After the number you did on Dirk, I can't imagine why you would come back into his life, or why he would allow you to. But if you use him and hurt him again, like you did before, I swear, I'll beat the tar outta you. And if you think I mean that figuratively, you're wrong."

A flicker of fear crossed Polly's eyes; then she reached for the pack of cigarettes on a nearby TV tray and lit up. She blew a long puff of smoke in Savannah's direction before answering. "Now what is this I hear? Do I detect a note of jealousy? Was I right all those years ago . . . you really do have a thing for Dirk?"

"Yeah, I have a thing for Dirk. It's called friendship. Loyalty. Concern for his well-being . . . all things you wouldn't know about."

"I think you want him all to yourself." Polly released more smoke through her nose. *How perfectly lovely*, Savannah thought. *Quintessential femininity. I'd like to snatch her bald.*

Savannah reached over and, before Polly knew what was happening, grabbed the cigarette out of her hand. She crumbled it between her fingers and dropped the remains into a glass of white wine that was sitting next to the ashtray and a bottle of half-drunk beer on the TV tray. Dirk's beer, no doubt. Polly's wine.

"If you hurt Dirk again," Savannah said, using a voice she usually reserved for suspected murderers and child molesters, "I'll hurt you. My interest is not romantic; it's self-preservation. I'm not going to listen to him bellyache for two long, miserable years like he did when you left him before. If I have to pick up the pieces of Dirk, Miss Priss Pot, somebody's going to have to pick up pieces of you. You got that?"

Polly didn't answer. But Savannah could tell by the wideness of her spider eyes and the way her too-lipsticked mouth was hanging open that she had heard and believed . . . at least a little.

Savannah left the trailer, slamming the door behind her, and nearly ran, chest first, into Dirk.

"My cell phone isn't in your car," he said, his nose inches from hers, his voice as low and ominous as hers had been a moment before. "But then, neither one of us really expected it to be, right, Van?"

Savannah reached into her left jacket pocket and took out his phone; hers was still in her right. "Oh, silly me," she said. "Here it is. I guess I remembered to bring it in with me after all."

When she handed it to him, he looked puzzled and apologetic enough to make her feel a little guilty. "Oh, you really . . . oh, thanks, Van."

"No problem. Watch yourself, buddy, with that gal." She nodded toward the trailer. "Remember last time?"

"Yeah, I remember. But it ain't like that this time. She just wants me to help her, to take care of somethin' for her."

"That's all she's ever wanted, Dirk, from anyone. She's a leech. That's the problem."

"Naw. I can take care of it. Don't worry."

Don't worry, yeah sure, she thought as she left him, got in her Camaro, and drove away. Dirk wasn't stupid—not by a long shot. But he had a blind spot where women were concerned . . . especially women he loved.

Why else would he buy a stupid story about a cell phone?

Savannah had no idea what line of bull Polly was going to try to sell him, but she was pretty sure he'd buy it, too.

Savannah had just dropped off to sleep when the telephone rang, exploding in her right ear and sending her pulse racing like a scared rabbit's. She grabbed the receiver, dropped it on the floor, picked it up, and smacked herself on the teeth with the mouthpiece. She could swear she tasted blood.

"What?" she shouted, ready to kill whoever was calling her at—she squinted at the red, glowing numbers on the bedside clock—1:22 A.M.

"Van . . ."

Savannah didn't need Gran's extrasensitive radar to detect the distress in that one word. She sat straight up and flipped on the bedside lamp. "Yeah, Dirk, what's going on?"

"It's Polly."

Savannah had a half a second to utter a quick, silent prayer, one that she instinctively knew was pointless. *God, let her be okay. They just had a fight, right? She's alive, but they just argued and—*

"She's dead."

Let it be natural causes, or . . . "A car accident?"

"Murdered."

ABOUT THE AUTHOR

G. A. McKevett is the author of five Savannah Reid mysteries: *Just Desserts*, *Bitter Sweets*, *Killer Calories*, *Cooked Goose* and the forthcoming *Sugar and Spite*. She loves to hear from readers and you may write to her c/o Zebra Books. Please include a self-addressed stamped envelope if you wish a response.